# Books by Matthew J. Metzger

*Single Titles*

Sharing Secrets

Sharing Secrets

ISBN # 978-1-78686-316-4

©Copyright Matthew J. Metzger 2017

Cover Art by Posh Gosh ©Copyright 2017

Interior text design by Claire Siemaszkiewicz

Finch Books

# SHARING SECRETS

MATTHEW J. METZGER

# Chapter One

Adam's morning was routine. Breakfast—seven o'clock. Shower and get dressed—seven-thirty. Ignore Mum's warning about being late for school—anywhere between seven and eight.

Right before that last warning, at eight-thirty every morning, knock back a pill and stare into the bathroom mirror.

"Adam! Hurry up, you're going to be late!"

"Nobody knows," Adam whispered to his reflection, just like every other morning. School mornings or weekends, home or holidays—every morning Adam looked himself in the eye and said, "Nobody knows."

"Get a move on, love!"

Of course people did. Some people. But nobody outside the family. Nobody in this new life, new place, new school. *Especially* the new school.

"Coming!" he yelled and frowned at himself in the mirror again. "Nobody knows."

Nobody outside this family knew. Or ever would.

"Adam!"

He grabbed his bag from the landing and hurtled down the stairs at full pelt. His mother flung his blazer at him in the hall and shouted a goodbye before he slammed the door and sprinted down the front path to the only other person in the village who attended Sir Henry Grey's Academy.

"Hi, Adam."

"Hey, Phoebe," he said, unchaining his bike from the gate. "Sorry. Let's go."

Nobody knew.

Adam was the new kid. Sort of. Okay, he'd started in September and it was now April, but he was still the new kid. Sir Henry Grey's was in the middle of a lonely clutch of villages in Gloucestershire and people didn't really come and go very often. He'd be the new kid around here for the next decade or something.

It wasn't all bad, though. Country kids were generally nicer than city kids – and Adam had been shuttled through enough inner-city schools to know. Leaving Manchester had been the best thing ever. And okay, the village he lived in was about two hundred people strong and boring, but... the school was better. The kids were all right.

"Guess who's fucking *leeeeegal!*"

...but kind of crazy.

Turning up to see a girl standing on a chair and bellowing at the top of her lungs had been normal in Manchester. It usually involved knives and the word "slag" a lot. Here it involved –

"Ollie! Happy birthday!" Phoebe shrieked, bouncing once on the balls of her feet before sprinting across the canteen toward her. Phoebe, like Adam, was very fair. Ollie wasn't, with dark eyes, dark curls and dark skin. The hug that Phoebe bestowed on the birthday girl looked...kind of like a squashed yin-yang symbol.

Or a squashed Liquorice Allsort.

"Look!" Ollie said when Adam got acceptably close enough. She climbed up onto the table and lifted her skirt right up to her waist. Half the canteen gawped. The other half were too used to her and kept chattering. "Check it out!" she crowed.

"Is that a *tattoo?*" Phoebe gasped. An ornate black symbol of a butterfly decorated Ollie's bare thigh. Adam wrinkled his nose. *Lady legs.*

"Gorgeous, in't it?" Ollie grinned. "Mum let me!"

"Oh, my God, is that *real?*"

"Nah, but it will be, only two more years!" Ollie beamed.

"Miss MacFarlane, get down!"

6

Ollie rolled her eyes and slid off the table as the chubby headmaster, Mr. Weeks, stalked through the canteen. Adam had seen more intimidating chickens, but then he was used to schools where the kids tried to stab one another—or him—rather than ones where a girl could stand on a table, flash her knickers and not get so much as a wolf whistle.

Or maybe that was Ollie. Nobody would dare wolf whistle Ollie.

"So!" Ollie thumped her folded arms on the table and grinned. She had an enormous smile with Hollywood teeth—perfect, pearly-white and kind of plastic. Ollie was all sports, wild ideas and parties. Phoebe was pale, delicate and refined. Adam hadn't yet worked out what they had in common, but apparently they were friends. "You guys are coming tonight, right?"

"*Duh!*" Phoebe said, beaming in turn. "It's your sweet sixteen—of course we're coming! And we got you the perfect present—*but!*" she added when Ollie's face lit up. "But you don't get it until tonight. It's not safe for school."

"Awesome," Ollie breathed, and turned those dark eyes on Adam. Her smile was wild and Adam squirmed under the scrutiny. "Did you have a hand in this, new kid?"

Adam flushed as Phoebe smirked. "Oh, he chose it," she said.

"Didn't."

"You so did," Phoebe insisted, shaking her head. Her fair hair slithered around her shoulders, already falling out of its messy ponytail.

"Hidden depths, you have," Ollie sniggered, then slid her gaze past Adam and shrieked, "Charlie! Charlie, you *dick*, where you been?"

Adam's heart stopped.

"Move it, you lazy twat—you're late!"

Adam's heart restarted as Ollie jumped up and pounced on the newcomer—a lanky kid in a crumpled school uniform who managed to look startled every time she hugged him, although Ollie spent more time hugging Charlie than not.

But it wasn't the hug that threw Adam.

It was Charlie himself. The sight of him knocked the wind out right out of Adam and threw off his equilibrium, and just like every other time, Adam couldn't—

"Shut your face, and what's this about you getting your knickers out, you tart?"

—breathe.

Charlie Fielding was, in Adam's opinion, beautiful. He shouldn't have been—he was the exact opposite of Adam's type. He ought to have been uninteresting...only he wasn't. He was *gorgeous.* Who cared if it sounded girly? He *was.* And he wasn't at the same time, which only made him more beautiful—and shut up, it made sense. Charlie was...

Charlie was all lanky build and wide, thin mouth. He had dark hair that was never tidy or properly cut, caught somewhere between curly and wavy, and bright blue eyes that were the exact color of summer skies and mania. Yes, mania had a color and it was the color of Charlie Fielding's eyes, so *shut up already.* He had long limbs, long fingers, long feet and...he was just long in general. He was this huge smile and talking-with-his-hands and he'd sort of grin and duck his head when embarrassed in a way that made Adam's stomach twist, and...

And he was completely, totally, absolutely off-limits. Forever. There was no way it would, could or should ever happen.

But it didn't stop Adam's gut from clenching at the sight of him or his heart simmering in jealousy when Ollie had bounded across the linoleum and jumped on Charlie in a hug. Sometimes, Adam hated Ollie a little bit. She could touch Charlie. She could be all over him in public and in private. She didn't have to be afraid.

But then when she touched him, Charlie would laugh and that pale face would light up like the bonus round on a pinball machine, and Adam *loved* her for that look.

Phoebe nudged his foot under the table and Adam swallowed and looked down. It was hard to tear his gaze away from Charlie's magnetism and when it fell on Phoebe, she cocked her head. She was smiling and Adam shook his head.

"You should tell him," she whispered and he shook his head again. "You *should*. You could, you know—he'll be there tonight, too, and you'll be able to separate him from Ollie long enough…"

He kicked her under the table and she rolled her eyes. Phoebe thought him shy. Adam was happy to let her think it—anything was better than the truth.

"Even if he doesn't—"

"Gossip!" Ollie cheered, pouncing on Adam from behind in a hug. "Even if who doesn't what?"

Adam shrugged her off awkwardly, flushing, and she wriggled in next to Phoebe to hug her instead. Ollie was incredibly huggy and Adam hadn't worked out yet whether she'd taught Charlie or Charlie had taught her.

Probably a bit of both, he decided, as Charlie crowded into Phoebe's other side and she got squashed between them, her blondeness framed by black.

"Nothing," he said.

"Lies!" Ollie said. "C'mon, it's my birthday, it's my *sixteenth*, you have to tell me."

"We were saying," Phoebe said and Adam's throat tightened in fear for a moment. "At this party—Charlie, you keep your hands out of those pockets," she interrupted herself to scold, and Charlie pouted at her in an exaggerated fashion.

"But I can feel lumpy things!"

"Chocolate, you perv, and it's mine," she said. Ollie cackled. "Anyway. We were saying that Nate in my drama group totally fancies you, Ollie, but if he's not brave enough, we'll lock you two in a cupboard together tonight."

"Ew!" Ollie shrieked. "Ew, *no*, no-no-no—my birthday, not allowed!"

Charlie's eyes gleamed and a wicked grin spread across that narrow face. Adam's heart rattled like an engine on the brink of stalling.

"Nate has a crush on you?"

Phoebe was released as Charlie launched at Ollie instead to begin a merciless campaign of teasing and she stood up and pulled on Adam's arm. "Come carry books for me," she said and Adam let himself be towed. Phoebe had practically adopted him when he'd arrived and even though he was almost a clear eight inches taller than her, he appreciated her easy acceptance and the free ticket into not being a sad loner and a prime target for other kids to pick on. So much so that he just let her drag him along. Anyway, Phoebe was nice. Proper nice, not evil-nice like Ollie.

"You know," she said, halfway to her locker, "you should tell him."

"Tell who what?"

"Tell Charlie," she said patiently, "that you like him."

She'd caught him out around Christmas. He'd been staring just a little too much. Adam was just quietly grateful Charlie hadn't noticed yet. Because the answer was—

"No."

"He won't freak out."

"He might," Adam said. He probably wouldn't, actually, Charlie was really relaxed about that sort of thing. He'd be dead nice about it, but it was out of the question, anyway.

"No, he wouldn't," Phoebe insisted. "Tell him tonight! Then if he turns you down, you've got all weekend to deal with it, right?"

Adam swallowed and curled his toes in his shoes at the fleeting fantasy that—in some other universe, where it would be okay—Charlie would actually kiss him at this party and he'd have all weekend to worry about whether it was too soon to text him.

Then he crushed the fantasy. Brutally, under the heel of his shoe. Until it squealed.

"I can't, Feebs," he said eventually, holding out his hands for her books as she unloaded her locker. "I just...I can't, okay?"

Her face softened and she squeezed his wrist. "You should," she insisted but then let it go and asked if they really should lock Ollie and Nerdy Nate in a cupboard together.

Adam voted yes and tried to forget about Charlie at a party without Ollie on his arm.

* * * *

Ollie's parents were cool.

Ollie bitched, but Mr. and Mrs. MacFarlane were the coolest parents ever. They'd gone off to visit Ollie's nana for the evening and left them the whole house for the party, under the 'supervision' of Ollie's older brother, Jamie.

And judging by the fact Ollie was always being supervised by Jamie and Adam had never even *seen* Jamie, he was beginning to suspect that Jamie wasn't actually *real*.

Still, the house bulging with people was a bit intimidating and Adam inched through the front door feeling a little tense and a lot nervous. He'd never been to a house party before and felt faintly surprised every time he bumped into someone and they didn't recoil. Felt calmer every time someone greeted him by name and not…not some jeer, some sneer, some slur.

Then he learned to breathe again when Phoebe materialized out of thin air and hugged him.

"There you are! Here," she added, pressing a bottle into his hand. An orange-flavored alcopop. "I snagged it for you before Ollie could break into the cabinet. She's got her dad's liquor out—he's gonna *kill* her."

Adam seriously doubted that. Mr. MacFarlane had books called *Open Dialogue With Your Teenage Daughter* and *Expression and Creativity—Rebellion in Young Adults*. He'd probably praise her lock-breaking skills or something.

"She hasn't got round to presents yet," Phoebe confided and Adam pulled a face.

"Good?"

11

"It was your idea!"

'It' was a—well, a dildo, actually, that they'd bought online last week using Adam's sister's credit card. Phoebe had even added some condoms to the box, with a note saying *'now you're legal and all.'* Adam wished he'd never used Nat's Amazon account to do it—he'd learned *way* too much about his sister's browsing history.

"Wasn't," he said weakly and Phoebe giggled.

"Totally was," she said then stepped back and did a little twirl. "What do you think?"

She was...actually dressed up for once. Phoebe was very pretty but very natural—as far as Adam could tell, not being into girls. Lady legs and stuff. She always just threw on her uniform and wore her hair messy and haphazard and her socks never matched, but tonight—

"Are you wearing makeup?"

She blushed.

"You *are*."

It looked...good but kind of weird, too. Adam decided he preferred the freckles. But the weird basket-weaving thing she'd done with her hair was kind of nice. Kinda sci-fi with the sparkly silver dress, too.

"Josh Denbar's here," she whispered and blushed harder.

"Oh." Josh Denbar of the way-too-long fringe and old-enough-to-smoke gorgeousness. Apparently. Adam thought his eyes were too close together. And that he wore weird shoes.

"And he broke up with his girlfriend this morning. So." Phoebe spread her hands and smiled shyly. "What do you think?"

Adam blinked. "Um. You might want to ask a girl. Or a straight guy."

Phoebe laughed and hit him on the shoulder. "Look out," she confided. "Hannah Barfoot has her eye on you."

"Um, what?"

"Yeah. And—"

"Hey!"

Ollie's voice boomed over the chatter. She was standing on her mum's prized coffee table, thankfully not so alien as Phoebe—because if Ollie had voluntarily put on a skirt, Adam would have to go home and call a doctor or something because what the *hell*—and holding a couple of vodka bottles aloft.

"Let's play Seven Minutes in Heaven!"

Across the room, Adam locked eyes with Hannah Barfoot—a giggly ginger girl in their year who reminded Adam a little bit of an overexcited puppy.

"Oh, hell no," he whispered.

"Run!" Phoebe whispered in his ear and Adam ducked backward through the clusters of people. He didn't know much about house parties, but the movies always said the same thing, right? *When in doubt, make for the kitchen.*

He made for it—hard—and snapped the door shut on the cackles and cheers behind him. No Hannah Barfoots and cupboards. No *anybody* and cupboards. He couldn't. He couldn't, he'd—he'd have to give himself away and—

"Hiding?"

Adam spun around and flushed hotly at the sight of Charlie sitting on the kitchen counter, hand in a packet of sweets. Starbursts. He had ripped jeans on and Adam could see one bare kneecap.

"Oh," Adam said. "Um. Sorry. I'll just…"

"Not a party fan?"

Adam's flush deepened. "No," he said flatly. "I didn't get invited to many back…at my old school."

Charlie 'aah'ed and rolled his eyes, sliding down from the counter as someone banged on the door. "C'mon," he said, seizing Adam's wrist in one of those long-fingered, bony hands. *Strange hands.* "Ollie's dad has this cool shed. Let's hide there."

Adam let himself be towed into the darkness of the back garden—because anything was better than Seven Minutes in Hell with Hannah Barfoot—and soon they were swallowed by the night and the only thing he knew was the iron grip of Charlie's thin fingers around his arm.

"In here," Charlie whispered and Adam's trainers went from the soft squish of damp ground to hard wooden boards, and a door closed.

"It's dark," he complained.

"Hang on—ow! Motherfucker!"

Adam sniggered then a light came on—a lamp, in fact, on an upturned bucket. The shed was full of odd bits and bobs and Charlie shoved what looked like an old chest of drawers sawn in half in front of the door.

"There," he said. "Nobody'll see the light. Pull up a bucket and get comfy. They'll have all forgotten about us in half an hour and we can sneak back in."

"Ollie throws a lot of parties?" Adam guessed.

"Nah, not Ollie, but Megan—you know, ginger Megan in Mrs. Thompson's group—she does. Ever fancy a snog, get on her—she's right easy."

Adam grimaced. "Not...really my type."

"What, easy girls aren't your type?"

"No," he said and Charlie laughed.

"Good on you, mate," he said and raised his hand. "Five me."

Adam clapped his hand and curled his toes in his shoes at even the brief contact. Dear God, he was fucked. He was *that* hopeless to find a high-five amazing and he was shut in a shed—alone—with the giver of the five.

"Starburst?" Charlie asked, offering the packet. Adam picked out an orange one. "So what's your type, if not ginger Megan?"

Adam shrugged. "Um. Dunno really. Nice...girls. Nice girls. You know. With, um. Personality."

"Like Feebles?" Charlie asked.

"Well...not Phoebe, no, but...*like* Phoebe, I guess."

"Don't blame you," Charlie said, unwrapping a Starburst. His hands were oversized, the knuckles huge, and his fingers twitched and shivered as he worked. Adam stared, fascinated. He had never had the nerve to properly look before, but—Charlie's hands weren't just weird, they were actually deformed. "She's sweet, Phoebe. Knows how to keep a secret, too. She's not totally gossipy like Ollie."

Adam laughed. "Thought you and Ollie were joined at the hip?"

"Yeah, means I know how gossipy she is!"

Adam relaxed and perched on a wooden box. "What about you? What kind of girls do you like? Apart from Ollie."

"I don't fancy Ollie."

Oh. "No?"

"Nah, she's like my sister. That'd be weird. I've known her since we were like…four? Five? Little, anyway," Charlie said. "Actually, she's not my type, either, so even if I'd met her yesterday, I wouldn't fancy her."

"What's your type, then?" Adam pressed. He felt kind of safe, a little bit. He usually dreaded having to talk about girls, but Charlie was just…funny and casual and gorgeous and he seemed so—so not-probing-even-though-he-was-asking-questions that Adam just eased into it and lied and…didn't feel bad about it.

Because, really, in a shed on their own was a bad time, Adam figured, to tell his straight crush he was exactly Adam's type.

Charlie pulled a face. "You don't get a lot of time to meet girls with Ollie scaring off the competition. I mean, don't get me wrong, she's 'mazing and I love her to bits, but she'd scare the shit out of them Islamic State bomber nutters, man."

Adam laughed. "Yeah, maybe."

"So where'd you move from?"

"Um."

Charlie squinted at him in the low light of the lamp. "You know, I don't know nothing about you."

"Anything."

Charlie snorted. "Feebles, like, adopted you, but I don't think you and me ever had a conversation." They hadn't.

"Or been alone together." They hadn't. "Fact, this might be the first time I've heard you say more than like ten words." It probably was. "So c'mon, new kid, where you from?"

Adam drew his foot away from the prod. "Manchester," he said. "Mum got a new job so we moved."

"What's she do?"

"Lawyer."

"Ew," Charlie said, wrinkling his nose. He had a long, straight nose, but it crumpled in the middle when he did that and creased up all his freckles. It was weirdly...kissable. Adam bit his lip. "My mum's a farmer. Stoker Farm. My granddad left it to her because my uncles are wasters. His words," Charlie added with one of those huge, manic grins. "Granddad was *awesome*. He used to take me shooting up in the top field because he said I was the only one in the family who could hit a barn door from ten feet away so I might as well have it."

Charlie's wide mouth and huge eyes were excitable and crazy and Adam just laughed. "Really?"

"Yup!"

"That's brilliant. You gonna be a farmer, then?"

"*Naaaah*," Charlie drawled. "S'boring. Dunno what I'm gonna do yet, though, m'no good at English and stuff."

Adam privately thought he had to be good at something. Farmers were usually poor, right? And Sir Henry Grey's was a private school. Charlie had to have gotten in there somehow.

Then Adam realized he was leaning too close and staring. *Shit.*

"Reckon we can go back inside?"

"Probably," Charlie said, jumping up off the sawn-off chest of drawers and hefting it aside to peer out of the door. "Yeah, maybe. You wanna risk it? Hannah might catch you again. She right fancies you."

Adam flushed. "No, she doesn't."

"She does." Charlie grinned. "She's been making eyes at you since you got here, Ads. You're her type, even if she's not yours."

"You never said your type," Adam said, trying to distract him. He didn't want to get set up or anything. And girls didn't usually like him anyway, so Charlie was obviously wrong.

"Mine?" Charlie's eyes were glittering and almost white in the light of the lamp. "Me, I prefer blonds. No 'e.' If you know what I mean."

"No 'e'?" Adam echoed, bemused, then—

Then Charlie leaned forward and kissed him. There were...there were lips on his, lips that tasted like lime Starbursts and felt chapped and rough and vaguely sticky from the sweets. A mouth a little wide and a lot warm and Adam's heart was trying to punch its way out of his ribs. Charlie was kissing him. Charlie *Fielding,* the gorgeous and funny and brilliant and amazing Charlie bloody Fielding— was *kissing* him. His...those hands, those weird pale hands were on Adam's sides and he was tilting his head and Adam could feel his tongue, and—

And Adam could feel his tongue.

Adam was being kissed.

Instinct kicked in and he planted both palms on Charlie's chest and shoved. Hard.

"Fuck!" Charlie yelped, tumbling into the mess inside the shed, and startled blue eyes stared up at Adam. Adam felt panic rising in his chest like a tsunami and put both hands over his mouth to stop himself blurting something out. "What the hell, Adam?" Charlie demanded. "I just—"

Adam bolted.

# Chapter Two

The car headlights were like beacons in the dark and Adam slid off the wall and opened the door before it had completely stopped.

"This is a bit early, isn't it?" Mum asked.

Adam shrugged, putting his seatbelt on without a word. His mouth was tingling. Charlie had *kissed* him.

"Why are you waiting around the corner, anyway?" Mum asked as the car rolled away from the street. Adam said nothing. "Adam…"

"I don't want to talk about it," he mumbled.

"Something happened." It wasn't a question.

"I said I'm not talking about it."

She sighed. "Adam. Is it about—"

"No," he interrupted. "It was just…just one of the other kids. That's all."

"Are you sure?"

"It was something else, Mum." Charlie didn't know about that. So—it was, because if not for *that* Adam wouldn't have shoved him, but…but Charlie didn't know about it, so he couldn't tell anybody about it. It was still secret. "Promise."

"All right," she said quietly. "You know where to find me if you want to talk about it."

He shrugged again. He couldn't talk to Mum about this sort of stuff because she totally disagreed with him. She would say he should have kissed Charlie back and told him about it. Which would be social suicide—maybe even *real* suicide—because then Ollie would find out, then the whole school would find out and it would be like Manchester all over again. It would be the end of these fragile friendships and the beginning of another spiral into bullying, hatred, fear and being cast out by the entire student body as one.

And Adam knew he couldn't do that again.

It wasn't a long journey back from Ollie's — ten minutes in the car, max — but Adam wanted it to go on forever. The quiet radio was soothing and the soft *plut-clink-plut* of rain on the roof calming. Everything was okay when it was just him and his family. Nobody in the family cared. Everyone knew and nobody cared and the secret wasn't a secret. There was no risk of anyone finding — or freaking — out.

It was just everyone and everything *outside* the family that was the problem. Sometimes, Adam figured that hermits had the right idea.

He switched his phone off as the headlights homed in on the front of Dad's little old Rover and decided to just… leave it off for the weekend. Ollie wouldn't notice. Charlie… Charlie wouldn't be trying to call him. And Phoebe would just think he'd chickened out early. Hopefully.

Unless Charlie said anything.

Oh, God, what if Charlie said something?

"M'going to bed," Adam mumbled to his mother, shedding his shoes and jacket in the hall and jogging up the stairs before she could catch his arm or stop him, his mind already preoccupied with the possibility. What if Charlie *told* people? What if he —

Adam groaned and buried both hands in his hair, staring at the ceiling. If Charlie told…*okay. Okay, get it together.* Why *would* Charlie tell? Tell everyone he'd kissed *Adam*. Adam was okay. He'd pushed Charlie away. He could…he could pretend he was disgusted, or —

Unless Phoebe had told Charlie Adam liked him? Then Charlie would out him, maybe, or —

Charlie wasn't like that, though, was he? He wouldn't just out him, right? He'd know about outing and that kind of thing. Why would he want to out somebody? But then, maybe Adam being out didn't even compare to Charlie being out, so —

Adam took a deep breath and tried to calm himself down. Charlie *probably* wouldn't tell anybody. Except maybe Ollie, but Ollie loved Charlie to bits and outing Adam might reflect badly on Charlie. So she wouldn't. So…so he didn't *really* have to worry about Charlie saying anything, not really.

He just had to worry about what *he* was going to say to *Charlie.*

He'd panicked. Plain and simple, he'd panicked. He didn't exactly walk around beating people away from him with a giant stick. People didn't just kiss him, and it was *risky* for people to kiss him, and he'd just…panicked. He wasn't supposed to be kissing people. People weren't supposed to be kissing *him.* It wasn't allowed!

Even if…

He traced his fingers over his lips. They still felt strange. Almost tingly, like…like Charlie had electrocuted him. He licked them and could faintly taste the Starbursts. He bit them and they felt smoother than before.

Adam had never been kissed before.

\* \* \* \*

For Adam, family was an escape.

"*Aaaaaaads,* honey!"

*Sort of.*

"Hi, Auntie Ruth," he mumbled as best he could through the bone-crushing hug. His Aunt Ruth — Mum's sister — was a professional boxer, and what she called an affectionate cuddle everybody else called manslaughter.

"You're looking wonderful, darling. All ready to get spruced up?"

He liked Aunt Ruth. She seemed to think he was about eight, but she was fun. And getting married, which made her even more fun because she was prone to just spending money wherever. He'd scored a lot of free clothes out of it so far because he was 'growing'. He hadn't grown an inch in two years, and if he found any more inches, even just the one, he'd hit six feet tall and be even more out of place than he already was.

His brain chose that exact second to point out that Charlie was about five eight and had stretched to kiss him, and the smile slipped a fraction.

Thankfully, Aunt Ruth had already whirled away to greet Mum, so only her fiancée saw. "Everything all right?" Lily asked.

Aunt Lily had been Aunt Ruth's girlfriend since Adam could remember, and she was the total opposite of her, too. Aunt Lily was tall and willowy, all long blonde hair and delicate features. She could have been a supermodel, in Adam's opinion. As it was, she sold jewelry in a High Street chain, so he supposed she kind of semi-modelled the jewelry for them, being so pretty and all. He'd never quite worked out why she fancied Aunt Ruth, but liked Aunt Ruth not breaking his legs, so had never asked.

"Yeah," he mumbled.

"Uh-huh."

He flushed. "It's just stupid stuff."

"Usually is the stupid stuff that gets us anxious," Aunt Lily agreed. "How about we go pretend to pick out a good color for your tie and you tell me about your stupid stuff?"

"Yeah, okay." Aunt Lily was kind of cool, too. She didn't tell people things. She wasn't gossipy like Mum and Aunt Ruth. So he followed her to the back of the wedding shop and let her hold up suit ties against him. "What's the frown for?"

"Don't tell Mum."

"Okay."

"Promise?"

She raised an eyebrow. "Oh, it's *that* kind of stuff."

"Maybe."

"Well?"

"Promise?"

"Sure." She shrugged. "Not like Kathy won't find out

anyway." Adam grimaced at the mention of his mother. "So?"

"So…I went to a party last night."

"Oh, well done, you finally acting like a teenager?"

"*Lily.*" Lily could be funny like that. Aunt Ruth was forty-eight. Aunt Lily was thirty. It was kind of weird. She was the same age as his sisters. Which meant, you know. Aunt Lily was the same age as her nearly-by-marriage nieces. *Weeeird.*

"Sorry, sorry. Carry on. Urgh," she added, tossing a purple tie back with disgust.

"So there's this boy."

"*Oh,*" she said, and a smile crept across her pale face. "So a boy you like?"

"Yeah."

"And what happened at this party?"

"He kissed me," Adam blurted out.

"And this is a problem *because?*"

Adam scowled and gestured at himself. "Because of *me.* I can't start—start kissing people, and…"

"Oh, right, yeah, you'll turn into a pumpkin," Lily said and snorted. "Time you got over yourself, Adam, honey. You're sixteen—you're *supposed* to be kissing random boys at parties. He's not going to magically turn into a frog if you kiss him."

Adam reddened and picked at one of the ties. "I'd…I'd have to…you know. If…"

She tilted her head. "You'd have to tell him if you wanted to actually go out with him?"

"Yeah," Adam whispered. "Then it'd be all over the school in like ten minutes and it'd…it'd be like Manchester all over again." *Manchester.* Where he'd got through four schools before Dad had just started home-schooling him. Where he hadn't been able to go into the city center without kids jeering at him and spitting at him in the street.

She sighed and squeezed his upper arm. "Adam. I'm not going to lie to you and pretend it'll all be okay, because

we both know it won't be. But the kids in Manchester...
they're not like every other kid in the world. Not everyone
is going to be afraid of you or hate you for what you are. If
you really like this boy, try just weighing him up a bit first."

Adam winced.

"Or is it a bit late for that?" Lily asked slowly.

"Yeah," he mumbled. "I kind of...shoved him."

"Ouch."

"Into a shed."

Lily burst out laughing and Adam reddened.

"Lils!"

"Sorry, sorry, but—you pushed him into a *shed*!" Lily
cackled. "Oh, *Adam*! Oh, you're priceless. Sorry. No, I will
stop—okay, in a minute." She descended into another fit of
giggles and Adam rolled his eyes, the somber mood most
definitely broken. He picked out one of her approved ties
and wandered back to his mother with it. Green. Whatever.
A suit was a suit. He just had to hold still long enough for
the photos, anyway, then he could take it off.

"What's wrong with Lily?" Mum asked when he presented
the tie and said he was ready to be measured for his suit.

"Dunno," Adam lied and tried to forget about it all for the
day, with the one group of people who'd never cared at all.

\* \* \* \*

Adam gulped back the pill and drained his water. His
fingers shook on the glass. "Nobody knows," he told his
reflection in the bathroom mirror.

"Adam!"

"Nobody knows," he repeated, but he felt sick. They'd
know something. If Charlie had said anything at all, they'd
know something was up. *Please —*

"Adam, come on, you'll be late for school!"

*— let Charlie have not said anything.*

"Coming!" he yelled hoarsely and shuffled out of the
bathroom. He grabbed his bag from his room, stared at

himself once more in the mirror and kind of wished his parents were religious like Phoebe's so he had someone to pray to. He could use a prayer right about now.

Then he headed downstairs, let himself out the front door and Phoebe waved.

"Hi, Feebs," he mumbled.

"Hey," she said brightly. He eyed her, but she simply blinked. "What?"

"Nothing," Adam said. "Um. How was the rest of Ollie's party?"

Phoebe made a so-so gesture with her hand. "It was okay. Right up until Josh snogged Melissa. Then I went home. Did you go early, I didn't see you or Charlie for ages?" Then her face lit up. "Did you tell him?"

"Um, no," Adam said quickly. "No, I just...I don't really like parties. I hung around for a bit then I went home."

"Aw, Ads..."

"I just felt out of place, that's all," he half-lied.

"Well." She pushed off and he mounted his own bike hastily to catch up. "I can't blame you," she continued when he pulled level with her. "I don't really like parties, either, but you can't *not* go, right? And Ollie's a riot."

"Shame you didn't get Josh."

"Shame you didn't get Charlie," she parried in a high, singsong voice that told Adam that Charlie at least hadn't said anything to Phoebe.

But then maybe he was waiting to confront Adam at school. That was what other kids had done in the past when they'd found out about Adam. Confronted him loudly and in front of loads of people. Entire assemblies and school canteens, proper crowds, *that* kind of confrontation. And Charlie could be a loud bastard, Adam knew that—he and Ollie weren't above bellowing at each other in front of hundreds of people. It had been how Adam had *met* Charlie, Ollie screaming at him clear across a canteen about some dirty picture he'd sent her on Facebook.

A sweat broke out under Adam's arms and it was nothing

to do with the bike ride. Charlie would have told Ollie, right? Charlie told Ollie everything. He'd have told her he was going to try kissing Adam, then he'd have told her Adam had shoved him and now Adam was going to have Ollie blowing her lid at him in front of the entire canteen...

Wildly, he thought about turning around and going home. He couldn't deal with another school going mental at him. And they would, because if Phoebe learned Adam had shoved Charlie, she'd want to know why and tell everyone Adam *liked* Charlie. And them Adam would have to explain why he couldn't kiss Charlie even if he did want to, and —

And he might as well go back to being home-schooled, because they'd tear him apart. He wasn't *wanted.* People didn't want to be anywhere near him when they found out.

"Heard from Ollie or Charlie at all?" he mumbled as they hit the crest of the hill and started to coast down the other side. It was sunny, because the weather never lined up to Adam's life, and the school was a glittering mass of glass below.

"Nah," Phoebe said. "Ollie just said on Facebook she has loads of party pics, so be super nice to her today in case she has any of you."

Adam sourly thought that if she had any of him and Charlie, he'd have been torn a new one by now.

"Speak of the devil and she'll appear in her brand-new Vans," Phoebe added as they turned into the back entrance of the school. Ollie's violently purple bicycle was easily visible in the bike sheds and the girl herself was wrestling with the chain. "Hey, Ollie! No lift today?"

Ollie straightened and blew her hair out of her eyes. Her face was creased into a scowl.

"No," she said, folding her arms over her chest. "Guess who's pulling a sickie? I can't believe he's conned his mum into it. Says he has a cold."

Phoebe giggled. Adam suddenly felt very, very ill.

"He's so faking," Ollie said, and snapped her fingers

at Adam. "You're in maths with Charlie, right? Grab the homework for him? He's being a wuss so I'm going to punish him and take his homework round after school."

Phoebe punched Ollie in the arm. "That's cruel!"

"So deserves it," Ollie snorted. "Man-flu—it's totally man-flu."

Adam wondered for a heart-stopping second if he could have caused it but then decided Ollie must be right. It was just one kiss and not even a really long or intense one. Charlie was...Charlie was faking. Nobody else had a cold he could have caught, and—and he couldn't have caught anything off Adam, not with one kiss.

But if Charlie was pulling a con to get the day off and avoid Adam...

Oh, God, he was mad. And if he was mad, he'd tell people. And Adam was so totally screwed.

"What's with you?" Ollie asked.

"Just...feeling a bit sick," he mumbled and Ollie groaned.

"Oh, piss off," she said. "It better *not* be a real cold. Charlie stayed over Saturday night and stayed in my bed with me. If he's given me something, I'll kill him."

"You sleep in the same *bed?*" Phoebe asked incredulously. Adam stopped dead in his tracks.

"Well, yeah, he's like super warm and he's a good cuddle," Ollie said. "We've shared the bed on sleepovers since we were like five, and I'm not stopping now he's finally learned how to spoon properly."

Phoebe went into fits of giggles and Adam wanted to be jealous of Ollie for knowing how Charlie could spoon, but—he felt too sick. Charlie was angry. Charlie was playing truant, which meant Charlie was angry, and when Charlie came back to school...

Adam hugged his books to his chest and steeled himself. When Charlie came back to school, Adam would have to leave it. And that would be it. No more persuading from Mum, no more talking-tos from Dad. If he had to leave this school, he wasn't going back to *any* school, not ever again.

He was totally done with schools and being bullied and everyone skirting around him like he was a bomb about to go off. This school had been the last chance, the last attempt.

And Charlie Fielding was about to destroy it all.

# Chapter Three

Charlie reappeared on Tuesday morning like he'd never been away. Adam walked into second period English and there was Charlie, sprawled out in his chair and tossing what looked like a rubber ball back and forth between his hands. His stare was wide-eyed and vacant and Adam averted his eyes and hurried to his seat at the back of the room, feeling the hot wash of a blush creeping up his face. Jesus Christ, what was he supposed to *say*? Beg Charlie not to tell? Threaten him? Ignore it all and hope it would go away? Hope Charlie was just as embarrassed as him and wasn't going to push the issue?

Charlie would tell Ollie, though, and —

"Quiet, the lot of you." Miss Moody was very much her namesake — a grumpy blob of a woman who, in her pasty complexion and wobbly figure, always reminded Adam of an undercooked dumpling. She dropped her books on her desk with an ominous clap of paper on wood and put her hands on her hips to glower at them. "Right. Last week's essays were a disappointment. Not one of you would have gotten a decent grade in a GCSE paper for that. So —"

Adam propped his chin on his hand and tuned her out. What was he going to do now Charlie was back? He was — Okay, so Adam didn't really know Charlie very well, because he'd always felt too tongue-tied and too confused by the attraction to talk to him, but he knew agitation when he saw it. Charlie was twitchy and, in Adam's experience, other kids being twitchy spelled danger. Would he attack Adam? This was a nice school, but not *that* nice, and Adam had seen Charlie get into a couple of fights before. What if—

"Mr. Wood, focus." Miss Moody's voice was a shrill snap. "Miss Dunstable, put your phone away. And, Mr. Fielding, stop fidgeting and put that ball down."

Charlie kept tossing it. It hit his palm with a dull clap, in a sharper rhythm. *Clack-clack-clack.*

"Mr. Fielding. *Now.*"

Adam frowned. Charlie didn't so much as pause, nor did he look up. Adam had spent more or less every English and maths lesson since joining the school staring at the back of Charlie's head, and it was obviously mental to say the back of a head could look pissed, but...

But Charlie kinda did.

Miss Moody stalked around her desk, puffed up like a chunky bullfrog and snatched the ball from between his hands. For a split second, Charlie kept moving like he was throwing it, then dropped his hands to the desk and finally stilled.

"*Thank* you," the teacher snapped. "And look at me when I'm speaking to you, Mr. Fielding."

Nothing.

"You are trying my patience," she warned, and still nothing. "Charlotte Fielding, I suggest you either start paying a modicum of attention, or you leave my classroom."

The class cringed as one. A full name was a humiliation— and for Charlie, a source of rage. It was one of the only things that Adam had seen that would *really* hack him off. And yet Charlie didn't move. Adam felt a little bit sick at the mute belligerence. Charlie *was* going to hit him. Adam had upset enough people to know when a guy was mad.

"Headmaster's office, Mr. Fielding."

The order was delivered coldly and crisply and Charlie finally moved, pushing himself up from his chair with sharp, jerky motions. The fingers on his left hand were twitching erratically and he pushed back from the table so hard that the chair fell over onto the carpet behind him.

"Pick it up," Miss Moody snapped. "And you can check

your attitude at the door, Mr. Fielding. I've had quite enough of your tantrums in my class."

There was a pause in the classroom like an intake of breath. Adam felt simultaneously afraid and angry and when Charlie finally turned his head to look the teacher in the eye, there was a mutinous fury in the hard set of his jaw.

"I've had quite enough of your fucking waxing lyrical over bloody *Hamlet* but nobody fucking asked me, either," he snarled.

The entire class winced. "Headmaster," Miss Moody shouted. "Now!"

Charlie slammed out of the classroom, banging the door so hard behind him that the catch pinged noisily and the handle sagged, broken. Miss Moody inhaled through her nose, her bulletproof cleavage threatening to burst the buttons on her blouse, then pursed her lips and stalked back to her desk.

"Anybody else feel like following Mr. Fielding's fine example?"

Silence.

"Good. Now. Your essays."

Adam slid down in his seat a little. Charlie was going to kill him.

* * * *

Phoebe was waiting outside the classroom when third period French disbanded.

"C'mon," she said, slipping her arm through Adam's. "Lunch out on the playing fields."

"Why?"

"Ollie texted me." Phoebe shrugged. "Apparently, Charlie's in a funny mood so we're out there—I don't know."

Adam swallowed. "He, uh. He got kicked out of English."

Phoebe groaned. "Oh, one of *those* funny moods."

"Those?"

"He has mood swings worse than a girl's," Phoebe grumbled. "Worse than *Ollie,* if you can believe it." Adam smirked. "We'll find out, I guess."

Adam felt sick again, his stomach rolling unpleasantly. "Yeah," he mumbled.

"You okay?"

"Mm," Adam said as they left the English block and headed out over the grass. It was still damp from the morning and the air was really too cold to be eating outside, but he said nothing.

"Oh, hell, he really is in a mood."

"What?"

Phoebe pointed. Ollie was visible on the bleachers by the athletics track, her curly hair escaping from its ties, and a lone figure was doing laps, head down, shoulders up. Adam felt nauseous all over again at the tense, angry picture Charlie made, even at this distance.

"What's going on?" Phoebe called as they reached the bottom of the bleachers and Ollie's snort was derisive.

"Fuck knows," she said. "He's in a right snit and won't talk to me." Her brown eyes were watchful as she tracked Charlie's movements. "Something's right up. I'm giving him another lap before I rein him in."

Adam perched gingerly on the step beside her and hugged his knees. Charlie was out-and-out sprinting, and in his school uniform, too. He'd shed the blazer somewhere, but otherwise —

"Should he be running in school shoes?" he asked feebly.

"He's not wearing that binder, is he?" Phoebe demanded. "He can't run in that!"

Ollie snorted again. "He shouldn't be running at all," she said cryptically, then cupped her hands around her mouth and bellowed, "Oi! *Charlie!*"

The figure on the grass slowed and, when she repeated his name at the top of her lungs, peeled away from the sprayed white lines and loped back toward the bleachers. His hair was windswept and tangled and the angry expression when he'd slammed out of English had been replaced with something...

Something painful. The little lines around his mouth and eyes were tight. His lips were twisted down at the left corner, like a grimace right before tears, and the shocking blue of his irises were rimmed in bloodshot pink.

Adam's gut clenched. Hard.

"I...I left my lunch in my locker," he blurted out and leaped up. Charlie paused, not five feet shy of the bleachers, and Adam wanted to hurl when that lean face twitched. "I-I have to..."

"Adam!" Phoebe called.

"What'd you do, Charlie?" Ollie yelled and Adam bolted. He'd tell her. Charlie would tell her everything, because they were like frigging married or something, so then he'd have Ollie and Charlie after him, and—

And Charlie had looked so upset.

"Adam!"

He dropped out of the run as he reached the English block and hefted his bag higher on his shoulder. He could hear footsteps, but just one pair, and kept walking.

"Adam, wait!"

Phoebe caught his arm as he rounded the corner into the drama block and Adam ducked hastily into the boys' toilets. To his discomfort, she huffed and just followed him, shoving some poor Year Seven kid out into the corridor before locking the door behind him.

"Okay," she said, folding her arms. "Spill. What's up with you and Charlie?"

Adam flushed and dropped his bag. He leaned against one of the sinks and ran both hands through his hair, exhaling heavily. "I don't know," he tried and she raised her eyebrows. Phoebe usually did sweet and giggly, not folded arms and raised eyebrows and stuff. "I don't!" Adam insisted.

"Right, okay. He's in a snit and you just practically ran away from him."

Adam winced.

"*Adam.*" Her voice was low and sympathetic. "Did—?"

"Hey!" One of the cubicle doors banged. "You can't be in here!"

Phoebe rolled her eyes, unlocked the door and ejected that boy, too. Definitely not a sweet and giggly day, then. Adam was so fucked.

"Charlie's gonna kill me," he blurted out. "Or Ollie will. Which will hurt less?"

"Charlie," Phoebe said automatically then frowned. "Why is he going to kill you?"

Adam shook his head. "I...I screwed up."

"I got that," she said. "But how? I mean, no offense, but you're always too shy to actually talk to him and I love Charlie to bits, you know I do, but he's not exactly the sharpest crayon in the box. He wouldn't get it if you insulted him, anyway. You'd have to really spell it out for him, and even then, you know, he thinks you're neat, he wouldn't usually be so upset..."

Maybe not, but Charlie wasn't so stupid or so blind that he'd miss being shoved over. Adam checked the response on his tongue and shook his head.

"C'mon, Adam, what was so bad? You could just apologize for whatever it is. Or I could talk to him for you?"

Adam swallowed and hunched his shoulders. "You... you can't tell anyone."

"Okay?"

"I'm serious, Feebs."

"Okay," she said. "I won't tell anyone."

"At...at Ollie's party...you know, when everyone wanted to play Seven Minutes in Heaven and you were off chasing down Josh Denbar, and—"

"Uh-huh."

"*Charliekissedme.*"

Phoebe blinked. "Huh?"

"Charlie...Charlie kissed me."

"Charlie—he—Charlie *kissed* you? But that's—that's

great!" she enthused, her entire face lighting up. She clapped her hands, bounced on her toes, then Adam was being hugged. "That's *great*, Adam, why are you so panicky! That's good! I don't think Charlie's ever —"

"I pushed him," Adam whispered.

"You — what?"

"I pushed him away," Adam repeated and went scarlet. "I…I shoved him into the shed. I shoved him so hard he fell over then I…then I ran off and went home and…and now he's…"

"Oh, Adam," she said. "Oh, Adam, you need to talk to him. You know what he'll think!"

"W-what?"

"He'll think you reacted that way because he's — you know. *Charlotte.*"

Adam colored. "I didn't!"

"That's what he'll think, though. You need to tell him and take it back. If you just tell him you were surprised, or…"

"No, I can't," Adam said miserably and hunched his shoulders. "I can't take it back, Feebs. And he's…he's really angry with me."

"Oh," Phoebe said again. "I thought you liked him?"

"I *do.*"

"So why — ?"

"Don't ask me to explain, Feebs, I can't," Adam begged. "I just…I do like him, but I can't go out with him or kiss him or anything, not Charlie. And — and it's not because of *that,* either. But I can't." *Not anyone, but especially Charlie. The thought of Charlie getting — no. No.*

"Okay," she said in a quiet voice and this was why Adam loved her. She just said okay and squeezed his arm. The little anxious frown shifted into a little pensive one and she sighed. "Okay," she repeated. "Well…Charlie can't be mad forever, you know? He obviously likes you, but…he bounces, you know. He'll be okay. Just tell him you're not interested and…and ask if you can both just forget about it. Yeah?"

Adam swallowed. "Yeah," he whispered.

Only he didn't want to. He *wanted* to say screw it and kiss Charlie back and find out what those crazy hands were actually like. But he couldn't—not ever—and it made him want to cry. There was no explaining that.

"Adam?"

"Can you...can you go and tell him I'm sorry and I didn't mean to shove him so hard?" Adam mumbled.

"You should tell him yourself."

Adam snorted. "Before or after he decks me?"

Phoebe giggled. "Oh, please. Charlie's a lousy fighter. Ollie's bullied it out of him. That's why he's so gobby. You do know he hasn't won a brawl since they were in primary school?"

Adam managed a laugh before it cracked in the middle and to his horror, his vision blurred.

"Oh, *Adam.*"

Phoebe was how Adam knew he wasn't bisexual, because her hugs were perfect and she smelled like fruit and hairspray and she'd murmur in his ear like comfort personified. Or something. He hugged back, maybe a little too tight, and the hair that was escaping her ponytail tickled his face.

"It's okay," she whispered. "He'll calm down and you'll both get over it. I promise. Charlie's too soft to be mad for long. But you need to tell him it's not about him."

Adam tightened his grip a fraction before he let go.

"How about I tell him he needs to talk to you and not hit you, huh?" Phoebe coaxed. "Then you can tell him and you can both get over it, yeah?"

"Yeah," Adam croaked, even though he seriously doubted it would happen. Charlie would punch him first. And that would be okay, because being punched was way better than Charlie finding out *why* he shouldn't have kissed Adam. If Charlie found out why...

Phoebe let herself out of the toilets and Adam splashed water on his face and stared at himself in the grimy mirror.

"Nobody knows," he told himself fervently and closed his eyes. If Phoebe talked to Charlie for him, he might be able to get away with this. Charlie would avoid him forever and Adam would have to get over this attraction at a serious distance, but...but maybe that was the best way of getting over it. Maybe this was all for the best.

Except...except for the bit where Charlie had, for a brief moment in Ollie's back garden, liked Adam, too.

"You've ruined that now," Adam whispered and opened his eyes again. He hated his reflection for a minute and curled his fingers into the edge of the sink until his knuckles hurt. He hated his stupid hair — a wavy, dark blond, nothing like Mum and Dad or the twins — and his stupid eyes — dark blue, see previous — and his stupid, freakishly tall body. Especially the stupid body. Everything about it. *Everything.*

Taking a deep breath to compose himself, Adam fished his phone out of his pocket and texted his mother.

*Can we have spag bol for tea tonight?*

Her reply — as it always when she wasn't in court — was instantaneous.

*If you want — tell your father. I won't be home until six. Everything all right?*

*Crappy day,* he said, non-committal, and slid the phone into his bag. He could check it later. Call Dad after school, maybe get a lift home instead of cycling back with Phoebe, if Charlie was *that* mad...

He sighed, rubbing his hands over his face, and gave himself a stern look in the mirror. "Get it together," he said. "Nobody *knows*. It could be worse."

Nobody knew.

As long as nobody knew, Adam was safe. As long as nobody found out, there could be no sneering in the halls, no shoving in the toilets or the changing rooms, no jeering in the street. No...no being beaten up for daring to use the same bathroom as the other boys, or thinking he could go swimming in the school pool. No having to stay home because there'd been death threats on Facebook — no shutting down Facebook again, just to get away.

As long as nobody knew, none of it would happen again. And if Phoebe was going to talk to Charlie for him, then nobody had to find out. It would remain a secret. He was safe.

So Adam squared his shoulders, picked up his bag and opened the toilet door.

And walked smack into Olivia MacFarlane. Who was scowling.

"Oh."

"Hello," she said and shoved him right back into the toilets. "You and me need a word. Piss off!" she added at a boy who attempted to follow them.

"But—"

Ollie slammed the door behind them and locked it. The boy yelled and thumped the door once, but Ollie was already turning on Adam with a face like thunder.

"Ollie, lunch break's nearly over..."

"What you got next?"

"Maths."

"It'll hold," she said fiercely. "I need to talk to you."

"But—"

"No," she said. Ollie was athletic and dark and — scary. Fucking scary. She had a sharp, hard face and eyes like lasers.

"Ollie, I..."

"You upset Charlie."

"I didn't mean to—"

"Didn't *mean* to? How else was he supposed to take it!"

"Take...?"

"Charlie *kissed* you!"

# Chapter Four

"Charlie *kissed* you!"

Ollie's voice echoed in the bathroom and Adam folded his arms over his chest, feeling sick again.

"He told you." Oh, God, he'd told her. He'd told her and now it was going to get all over the school that they'd kissed and Ollie was so sharp she'd figure there was something else going on, then there'd be rumors, and eventually —

"Of course he told me," she snapped. "When Charlie gets set off, it's my business to know. And after the last time —"

Adam swallowed.

"Look," she said finally. "I thought you liked him. Phoebe hinted you did and I caught you staring a few times and even Charlie thought you might — so where the hell did shoving him into Dad's shed come from?"

"I didn't mean to push him that *hard*…"

She snorted and waved a hand, as if physically brushing it aside. "He bounces. Not the point. The point is he kissed you and you like him, but you decided you didn't want to kiss him, after all?"

"It's not that simple, Ols…"

"What, you think you were going to catch it?"

The irony was bitter.

"No! It wasn't about that!"

"So explain it to me," she snapped.

"I can't."

"Why the fuck not?" she raged. "You've really upset him, Adam! He's completely swung. He was fine on Friday and now he's bloody running again and being aggressive and shit. He's not been this bad for months and —"

"What's running got to do with it?" Adam asked, confused, and Ollie snorted.

"There's a reason he got kicked off the football team," she said cryptically. "But because he's fucking precious about it, I can't tell you that, either. But he shouldn't be doing laps—he's not allowed, and *you've* put him back in that headspace!"

"What are you talking about?" Adam demanded, bewildered. He didn't even know Charlie had ever been on the football team.

"Never mind. Do you like him?"

Adam reddened. "Yes." He couldn't lie about that, couldn't let Charlie think he'd gotten it wrong. And anyway, it was obvious, wasn't it? Phoebe had guessed before Adam had even been there a month.

"So did you want to kiss him? Like, ever?"

*Ever?* "Yes." But— "Want to doesn't mean I—"

"So you wanted to kiss him and you like him, but he kisses you and—what, it was that bad you felt shoving him into a shed was okay?"

"It's not to do with Charlie!" Adam blurted out. His voice cracked. "It's me. It's nothing to do with him!"

"What're you to do with it, then?" she asked ruthlessly.

"I can't get involved with Charlie," he said and hunched in on himself. Her brows-furrowed-mouth-downturned expression wasn't easing in the slightest and it made him shaky. "I just can't, okay? I can't explain it, but it's not Charlie, it's *me*. I can't have…I can't kiss him and I can't go out with him."

"And what, some other boy would do? Some other girl?"

"No. Nobody! No boys—or girls! I just can't."

"Why?"

Adam shook his head, his throat swollen and useless. *Please, God—*

"You been abused or something? You ill? You turn into a crazy psycho? Your therapist say you can't?"

*—don't let her try to guess.*

"I'm not talking about it, Ollie," he said through gritted teeth. "It's my fucking life and I'm sorry I've upset Charlie and I'll apologize for shoving him, but it can't happen and there's no way around it so he'll—"

He hated himself before the words even left his mouth.

"—just have to deal with it."

She stepped back. She looked downright feral. A cold sweat broke out on the back of Adam's neck and he was genuinely afraid for a split second.

"I thought better of you," she ground out. "I thought you'd be good for him, get that shitty self-esteem issue of his to fuck off. But you're not, are you? You've got no fucking idea what he's about."

"You don't know the first thing about me, either," Adam retorted.

"So tell me."

"Tell me about Charlie."

She curled her lip. "He's not made of fucking stone, that's what I'll tell you about Charlie. You really upset him and if he backslides because of this, I'll make you fucking *pay*, new kid."

Adam opened his mouth—to say what, he wasn't sure—but Ollie was already unlocking the door and slamming out of the toilets, leaving him alone against the sink with a thousand questions about Charlie and absolutely no way of getting any answers.

And the distinct impression that he needed to do some serious damage control...without giving himself away.

\* \* \* \*

When Adam got home, there was a shiny new Audi on the driveway instead of Dad's car and a dirty old motorbike on the road behind Mum's car. The twins were home.

Adam was adopted. Mum had had a shitty pregnancy with the twins and been left unable to have any more and, as they'd wanted a boy, too, they'd adopted Adam once the twins had been old enough to be left to their own devices. Which meant Adam was the youngest by about fifteen years.

Not that thirty-year-old Nat gave that away. She was lounging on the stairs vaping when Adam let himself in.

"Dad'll kill you," Adam said.

"Dad'll kill me anyway," Nat said and blew the smoke out between her teeth in a Cheshire-cat grin. "Got new ink, didn't I? C'mere, Splodge, gimme a hug."

Adam wriggled down on the stairs beside her for the obligatory hug. He didn't mind too much. Mum was all about hugs and it was hard to hug Danni lately because of the huge baby bump. And anyway, Nat gave pretty sweet hugs. They always smelled of biking leather and petrol and she'd squirm when giving them so he kind of got rocked a bit. It was nice.

"How's my Splodge?"

"Shut up, Nat."

"Ooh, moody Splodge," she teased and ruffled his hair before letting him go. "Want a fag?"

He gave her a look.

"Pft, Daddy's little boy, aintcha," she drawled. "I'll get you one day, Ads. How's school?"

Adam snorted.

"Bump me," Nat said, beaming again and bumping her knuckles against Adam's. "Any news? They're in there talking baby names," she added, waving her e-cigarette at the closed living room door. "You might want to give it twenty, Danni's into the pickles-and-ice-cream-and-crying-into-the-spoon mode."

"I don't want to know," Adam said and toed off his shoes to settle in. He liked Nat. She was cool. Danni was all romance novels and slushy films and she was okay, but she was a bit like Mum, really. Good when he needed a hug, but he couldn't tell her about embarrassing stuff. "I fucked up at school."

"What kind of fucked up?"

41

"There's a boy."

"Ooh-er," Nat said and smirked. "You sure I'm mature enough to have this conversation with you?"

Adam snorted. "Never."

"Okay, so what. You fuck him up, or fuck him *up,* if you know what I mean?"

"Ew, Nat!"

She cackled and he shoved her.

"That's gross!"

"It's your game, gayboy," she sniggered. "Okay, okay. What happened?"

"He kissed me at a party."

"Wahey, go Splodge!"

"I, um…overreacted."

"You wanked him off and didn't get his first name?"

"Nat!"

"What? You're a total player, Ads, I know your type. All blond-eyed blue-haired innocence and you just bat your eyelashes at some poor bloke and *bang,* he gets a wank and you get his wallet. You *did* get his wallet, right?"

"Nat," he whined, and tried to push her off the stairs. She fought back and he ended up being hugged against the wall again. "You suck."

"I'm your favorite."

"I hate you."

"You *lurrrrv* me, Splodgy-Kins."

"Shut up!"

"Okay, okay. What happened with this boy? You kissed him?"

"He kissed me."

"Same diff."

"He kissed me, and I—you know, I can't let the kids at school know, not after…"

"Uh-huh. So, you played the straight card? 'Cause unless them private school kids are thick as pigshit—"

"No, I…pushed him."

"Pushed him?"

"Into a shed."

"You pushed him into a shed?"

Adam went scarlet. "And he fell over."

There was a sharp pause then Nat crushed him in a hug and shrieked with laughter. "Oh, my God, Ads, that's *class!*"

"Naaaaat…"

"That's *beautiful,* Ads! Holy shit, that's amazing. You win. You totes win the embarrassing first kiss award. You beat Danni. Hands down that's better. I am so buying you a pressie for that. You want to trip down to the chippie on the bike with me and avoid Her Up-The-Duff Majesty's health regime? 'Cause you *so* earned it."

Adam scowled. "I hate you," he said, very seriously.

"Yeah, yeah," Nat said and grinned. "So? Bike and chippie, just you and me? I need a bit of sister-Splodge time, man. Mum's all broody for grandbabies and Dad went purple when I showed them my new ink."

"Where is it?"

"On my arse."

"Well, that's why."

"It's cool! Look!"

"No!" Adam leaped up and jogged up the stairs. He had *no* intention of seeing his sister's arse, thanks very much. "I'll get changed."

"Heavy jeans and helmet, Splodge!" she yelled up the stairs after him. "I'm not taking the rap like last time you went joyriding on my bike without the right gear!"

Adam slammed his bedroom door and rummaged for clothes. He loved it when Natalie came to visit, 'cause she was awesome and he could forget about school and shit when she was around. She was just crazy and it took all his brain to keep up with her.

By the time he ran back downstairs, she'd migrated back into the living room. His other sister, Danni, looked like a beached whale. She was nine months pregnant with twins and showed it. He hesitated then leaned over the back of the sofa to hug her from behind.

"Hey, honey," she said, squeezing his elbow. "Don't listen to anything Nat tells you." It was an auto-hello in their family. "How's things?"

"Fine," he said.

Danni and Nat had been identical twins, but Nat had gone for hair dye, tattoos and piercings and Danni had gone for fluffy jumpers, ponytails and pregnancy. They were totally different now and Adam kind of liked it. Nat's bright blue hair made it less obvious he was different and he also earned automatic brownie points for not letting her lead him too far astray. Being a younger brother was kind of awesome sometimes.

"Splodge snogged a boy!"

Then again, sometimes it royally blew.

"Nat!"

"You've got a boyfriend?" Danni asked.

"No!"

"Adam's got a crush!" Nat declared gleefully and Adam threw a cushion at her.

"Adam! Natalie, leave him alone," Mum chided.

"First comes love, then comes marriage, after all the wanking in the back of Dad's garage!" Nat sang.

"NatIhateyougodie!"

"Adam!" Mum scolded.

"Make her shut up!" he whined and Nat grinned.

"Come on, bitch." She cuffed him around the head, ruffled his hair again and grabbed him in a hug. "We're going to the chippie."

"Not fair!" Danni protested.

"No greasy food for expectant mums!" Nat cackled. "Anyone *not* pregnant want anything? Dad? The usual?"

"Mark," Mum said in a clear matrimonial warning.

"Oh, one round won't kill me," Dad sighed. "Go on, then." He didn't lower his paper an inch and Nat loudly blew him a kiss.

"Love you too, Daddy! Come on, Splodge, move your arse."

The air outside was cold and night was beginning to draw in. Adam turned his face into the wind and rolled his shoulders as though shrugging off Charlie and Ollie and all the shit that was about to go down at school. It could wait, right? He only had to be at school a couple more years, then he didn't have to see a single person outside his immediate family if he didn't need to.

"Nat?"

"Uh-huh."

"You ever like someone you can't have?"

Her face was sympathetic in the yellow glow of the porch light. "Course I have. Everybody does."

"Yeah, but…someone you really, really can't *ever* have?"

"Sure," she said. "But, you know, if you really want them bad enough, there's not many genuine *can't* situations."

"What about mine?" he whispered.

"Not even yours," she said and slid onto the bike. "Now get on board, you little ponce. I'm hungry."

* * * *

*I'm sorry for shoving you. It's not you, it's me. I can't do relationships and stuff and you really surprised me. Can we just forget about it? I didn't mean to push so hard or piss you off.*

It was the fifteenth draft and Adam scowled at it. It was still shit, but…but there was only twenty minutes of the lesson left and he just didn't have the guts to tell Charlie to his face yet.

He added another *I'm really sorry* and folded up the paper. It was as good as it was going to get.

It was first period maths. Nat had given him a lift to school on the bike that morning, so he hadn't seen any of the others and Charlie hadn't even looked at him when they'd arrived for Mr. Bagshaw's tortu—er, maths instruction. Usually Charlie would at least pull faces at Adam or mime slitting his throat before they had to sit down. Today? Nothing.

So Adam steeled himself, tweaked the end of the little

paper aeroplane and flicked it. It sailed gaily over the space between them, got caught in a stray curl and tumbled to its doom onto Charlie's textbook.

Charlie's hand paused and the scratch of his pen was silenced. And a second later, his other hand — the one with the missing fingers — curled over the paper. Adam watched, heart in his throat, as Charlie tugged at the plane, pulled it apart and —

"Mr. Fielding, is there something you and Mr. Wood would like to share with the rest of the class?"

Charlie jumped as though he'd been electrocuted and Adam scowled. He hated this school for that 'Mr. Wood' bollocks. He had a fucking name. This wasn't the Victorian era, Jesus.

"No, Mr. Bagshaw."

Mr. Bagshaw was a great corpulent walrus of a man. He didn't walk, he *morphed*. He wore a shirt and braces and every month one of the braces snapped under the pressure of his enormous rolling gut. He had a mustache that would have put Joseph Stalin's to shame and it quivered and twitched when he talked. And when he did, it created sound-wave-ripples through the flabby jowls and fifty chins that surrounded his neck.

In short, he was a right ugly git.

"Then perhaps you would like to explain Mr. Wood's letter, Mr. Fielding."

The class tittered. Adam went scarlet as a couple of the other kids smirked at him.

"Not really, Mr. Bagshaw."

"Read it out, Mr. Fielding."

Adam's stomach plummeted. *No!* Charlie sighed.

"And stand up."

Charlie slid to his feet. He sort of curled up, standing before straightening his spine and head and smoothing out the note between his hands. Adam's hands shook. If Charlie read it, everyone would work it out. He wanted to panic or shout or cry. He felt as if he was going to hurl.

Charlie opened his mouth.

Adam opened his own—ready to scream, interrupt, stop him, *something*!

"There once was a man from Nantucket..."

The class collapsed. Adam felt like doing it, too. Mr. Bagshaw sighed gustily, the curtains of his moustache vibrating as though he was blowing a noisy raspberry.

"Very funny, Mr. Fielding," he drawled. "Give it here."

Charlie handed it over.

"Extra homework for the both of you. Control yourself, Mr. Johnson. It isn't that funny," he added waspishly. "Mr. Fielding, you can remain standing. Mr. Wood, please keep your lyrical compositions to music class. This is mathematics."

"Yes, sir," Charlie said. Adam mumbled an echo, hiding his red face in his textbook. What a bastard. Bastard Bagshaw, that was him.

"Mr. Johnson, you can wipe that smirk off your face or join Mr. Fielding. It's your decision." When Ady Johnson didn't stop sniggering, Mr. Bagshaw sighed again and ordered him to stand up.

Adam huddled in his chair, forgotten, and fervently prayed Mr. Bagshaw wouldn't read the note—aloud or otherwise. Stupid. So fucking *stupid* to try passing in Bagshaw's class. The old fart had eyes like a fucking hawk between the flab folds.

"Back to work."

Adam bent over his trigonometry and tried to stop his hands shaking. It was okay. Okay, so Charlie hadn't managed to read the note—probably—but Mr. Bagshaw hadn't read it out and the secret was safe and...

And Adam could always write another note.

"Mr. Johnson, Mr. Fielding, *out.*"

Adam snapped his head up in time to see Charlie snigger and drop his hands. They had been—dancing? Seriously?

"Mr. Fielding, stand outside the door. Mr. Johnson, the window. It's a nice enough day, you can top up your tan."

Charlie's chair scraped on the floor as he left his desk, everything abandoned where it was. Adam watched him go, swallowing against some unidentifiable emotion in his throat, before Charlie paused at the door and glanced over his shoulder.

And smirked at Adam, drawing a line across his throat as though he was slitting it.

Adam smiled — shaky and unsure, but he *did*.

"Out, boys!"

They went. Adam turned back to his work and figured... figured maybe he wouldn't need that other note. Ollie had been exaggerating. Charlie was fine and they'd be fine and everything could go back to the way it was and ought to be. They could forget about the whole sorry episode and put it behind them.

Right?

# Chapter Five

Mum picked him up outside the school gates. She was still in her court gear—the sharp blue suit and the pearl earrings—and as the car turned right instead of left and started heading for the supermarket, he decided to angle for some snacks.

"Your hair looks nice." It was the same old black bun, but snack food was calling him and Mum preened as he knew she would.

"Thank you, darling. Good day?"

"Was okay." It was, sort of. Charlie had landed himself a lunchtime detention with Bagshaw and Ollie had been giving him dirty looks, but Phoebe had been chatty and bubbly, enthused by some project she'd got in her art lessons. So yeah. Could have been worse, all things considered.

"Your father's decided on chili tonight."

"Four bean?"

"Three. You know how the butterbeans give him gas."

Adam wrinkled his nose. "Cheers, Mum."

"Thirty-two years of marriage, you learn a man's bowel movements."

"Mum!"

"It's perfectly natural."

"And you wonder where Nat gets it from," Adam complained and Mum chuckled.

"Give over. The two of you are as bad as each other. No news on Danielle yet, by the way. They're due tomorrow."

Adam tuned her out. He wasn't really interested in being an uncle and let Mum chatter on about impending grandma-hood—or whatever—while he stared out of the window and let his brain wander off to Charlie's smirk and throat-slitting gesture, and —

And the kiss in Ollie's back garden.

That was the shitty part. Adam wanted to kiss him again. For a split second it had been as though his entire world had imploded, but in a good way. He'd never even really entertained the thought of kissing Charlie because it had always seemed so impossible, but now…

He bit his lip, right where Charlie's mouth had been, and wished things were different. Wished he could kiss him again and find out just how Charlie kissed properly, not awkward lunges in the dark. Find out what Charlie tasted like, if he liked having his hair played with, what those insane hands felt like, what *he* felt like…

"Earth to Adam."

He jumped and Mum laughed.

"Come on, dear," she said. She was holding the passenger door open for him. They were already at Waitrose. "If you carry the basket and do the packing, I'll let you get a packet of those laces."

*Score!* "Okay."

She frowned at him. "Are you all right?"

"Yeah."

"Adam —"

"I am," he interrupted. "Just thinking."

"About?"

"Nothing."

She paused. "Was Natalie just teasing you, or was she being truthful?"

"About what?"

"About you kissing someone."

Adam flushed. "Wasn't anything."

"Uh-huh."

"Was just…just a boy at school. And just one kiss." But it had gone on for a little while and it had been amazing. "And I pushed him away. And he's not spoken to me since."

Mum was quiet for a moment and Adam took his time

getting the basket. He didn't want to discuss it. It wasn't going to happen again, anyway. Even if Charlie wasn't angry with him anymore, Adam wasn't stupid enough to really believe they could just forget about it. It would be the elephant in the room forever and after school ended they'd have to stop being friends to forget about it. That was how this stuff worked, right?

"Did you push him away because you didn't want to kiss him," Mum asked quietly, "or because you don't think you're allowed to kiss him?"

Adam swallowed.

"Adam."

"I can't."

"Darling, we've talked about this."

"And I can't!" Adam snapped. Mum pursed her lips. "I won't, Mum. I'm not running the risk."

"And I've told you and Dad's told you—the risk can be minimized—"

"It's still a risk," Adam retorted and hefted the empty basket higher. "Can we go? Phoebe's coming round to do our history essays after dinner."

Mum exhaled heavily through her nose and folded her arms. "Adam, you are going to make yourself very miserable if you cut people out because you won't trust them. And I know you have plenty reason not to trust other boys your age, but it won't always be like that. I don't want you to end up sad and alone because you think you're not permitted to have relationships like everybody else."

"I'm not," Adam snapped and dropped his gaze to the floor. "Can we hurry up? Phoebe's coming over."

"Ad—"

"Phoebe's coming over," he repeated and scowled when Mum groaned. He hated arguing with her about it—or worse, arguing with *Dad* about it. They didn't understand. They didn't get what it was like, this fear that if he kissed Charlie—or anyone—he'd—

"Don't shut this boy out just for the crime of liking you,

sweetheart," Mum said then turned and started walking toward the canned vegetables aisle.

Adam followed. And his vision *wasn't* blurring. Absolutely, definitely not.

* * * *

Dinner was a quiet affair and Adam retreated upstairs the minute he'd cleaned his plate, ignoring his mother's attempts at conversation and his father's…well, okay, Dad was always nose-down in some tome about gardening, so ignoring Dad was easy.

He turned on some heavy metal and put his pillow over his face until Phoebe came over, because it was his *go away I'm brooding* signal and meant Mum wouldn't try and come up to talk to him again. And really, Adam didn't want to talk about it. Talking about it did no good. Talking about it wouldn't change anything — least of all him and Charlie.

And all the time he could feel that phantom kiss on his mouth and he both hated it and loved it.

He didn't hear the doorbell — or the voices, or the footsteps — over the music and removed the pillow when the music clicked off to see Phoebe by his desk.

"Fuck!" he said, startled.

"Hi." She'd undone her hair for once and it trailed down her back in a shimmering wave of messy color. Like a platinum ring in the sun. "You okay?"

"Yeah," he said. "I think Charlie's not mad at me anymore."

"Oh?" she asked.

"Yeah, he got chucked out of Mr. Bagshaw's class…" Phoebe winced. "But he grinned at me before he went. I think maybe he's over it."

She hummed. "Well. Maybe. I hope so. So, um. Essay?"

"Which one?"

"The Stuart one," she said. "I hate history, seriously. I'm dropping it the minute we're done with our exams. The

Stuarts are so *boring*."

Adam privately agreed as they cleared a space on the floor — because the floor was way more comfortable than working at a table, obviously — and spread out their things.

"Just give Charlie some time," Phoebe said as they opened their textbooks. "He's generally okay with crushes and that kind of thing, but I think maybe he took it a bit personally this time. But he won't hate you or anything."

Adam bit his lip. "Yeah."

"Adam?"

"Mm?"

"Why can't you go out with him?"

"I can't, Feebs," he said brokenly and she squeezed his wrist.

"Okay," she said. "Tell me one day, maybe?"

"Maybe," he hedged. *Like fucking never.* "I just didn't mean to piss him off so much."

"Yeah, well, he did kind of take a big risk, snogging the new boy," she said and they both giggled guiltily.

"Well, what am I gonna do, out him?"

"You never know."

"Wait, people don't know he's gay?"

"Nobody knows what Charlie is," she said dismissively. "I don't think anyone would be surprised, but — I don't know. I think people just figure he's sexual and that's it. You know. Boys and girls and anything else."

"Ew, Feebs!"

She giggled then shook her head. "No, he's not that bad. He just flirts a lot. The flirty-jokey thing. It's nice. *I* used to have a crush on him."

"Seriously?"

"Uh-huh. He used to flirt with me and call me Rapunzel. Back in Year Seven, *way* back, when he was still just that weird kid in Mrs. Potter's class and I didn't know his name. It was kind of nice." She'd gone very pink.

"Er," Adam said. *"Used* to — right?"

She hit him. "Yes!"

"Okay, okay, just checking!"

She snorted then pulled a face. "Did you hear?"

"Hear what?"

"Oh, good, you didn't. Charlie's got detention again," Phoebe said as she rummaged for her pen. "From Mr. Langford again, too. His mum's gonna kill him."

"Really?" Adam said. "It can't be that bad."

"Yeah, but Mr. Langford always makes it out like you killed something." Phoebe spread out her history papers. "He's such a pest."

"A pest?" Adam echoed incredulously and she laughed.

"Sorry, been helping Dad clean out the garage. Mr. Langford's a prick," she amended. "Anyway, it means keep your phone off because it means Charlie can't go to the cinema with Ollie tomorrow and she's going mental."

"Oh," Adam said and switched his phone off. Ollie going crazy on him — again — was the last thing he wanted. "Isn't she used to it?"

Phoebe shrugged.

"But Charlie's always getting detention."

"He..." Phoebe pulled a face and waved a hand. "When he's not feeling great, he acts up. Plays the clown, you know, or just plays the prick. He's at his stupidest when he's trying to make someone feel better, including himself. So, you know, when you said you'd shoved him I wasn't exactly surprised he kept being weird."

Adam winced, Ollie's accusation knocking at the back of his head.

"And Ollie's been hovering more than usual," Phoebe added. "You know how she gets with him. I think something's up but I don't want to ask. Charlie's not..."

"Charlie's not what?"

Phoebe hesitated. "He's...he's not...normal."

"Normal? Feebs—"

"Not like that! I mean, he's not how you'd think. Oh my God, I'm making it worse. In his—personality. Not the other stuff."

"How d'you mean?"

"Like…like I always thought he was just this manic idiot, you know? He's always up for a good time. He's always getting in trouble and laughing it off. I thought he was just this dumb kid. I didn't even really like him at first, besides the crush and all. I never actually wanted to go out with him."

"But you changed your mind. About the liking him bit?"

"Mm." Phoebe shook her head. "He's…you can't take Charlie at face value. He just plays this daft berk, like he's an actor. He's actually…he's really different underneath. He takes things to heart. Way too much, actually. He's not what he seems and I was… Okay, look, you *can't* tell him I told you. Or Ollie. Promise. They'll both kill me."

"I promise," Adam replied obediently, mind racing. Charlie had *secrets*? It didn't make sense, because everyone knew what Charlie was—but then, it kind of did, because Adam knew loads of stuff about the girls but nothing about Charlie. He didn't even know his sisters' names. And the way Ollie had raged at him, the things she'd said about Charlie in the bathroom…

"In Year Nine, he kind of went off the rails a bit," Phoebe whispered, leaning forward as though the room was bugged or something. "I don't really know the details, him and Ollie never really said much, but he used to be—like in Year Eight, ages ago—but, anyway, he was pretty…not, you know, not *fat* but he was…kind of…"

"Fat," Adam said flatly and she wrinkled her nose.

"Okay, fine, yeah, he was a bit fat," she said. "Then he just—wasn't anymore. It was like all the weight just fell off and he got really thin and lanky and he'd do laps of the playing fields at lunchtime and he was in all the sports teams, and he could go from really mad and funny to dead quiet and depressed just like *that*." She snapped her fingers and Adam flinched.

"He was like…bipolar or something?"

"I dunno," Phoebe said. "I didn't really want to ask and I

didn't know him very well. Ollie was in my tutor group so he was always hanging around but we just used to tease her about Charlie being her boyfriend, or her being a — well, a lesbian. It wasn't nice. We were like fourteen or something. We didn't get it. And he'd be so funny and charming one minute, then the next he'd be having screaming arguments with teachers or smashing locker doors. I mean, proper crazy. He'd just flip his shit and get kicked out of class all the time. He even got suspended once — but then usually if someone just starts trashing crap they get expelled, so obviously there was something else going on already..."

Adam winced. "Jesus. Really? Ollie kept saying stuff like he was backsliding and shit..."

"Yeah," Phoebe said meaningfully. "Then in the middle of Year Nine, he just disappeared. He spent nearly half a term in the hospital and nobody heard from him at all. Nobody would say anything. All the teachers acted like he'd never existed and he refused to see anyone except Ollie — and he just reappeared with this huge smile on his face like nothing had ever happened, right before the year ended. I was still hanging out with the girls then. I didn't really talk to Charlie much, but everyone knew he'd been in hospital for something."

"For what?" Adam pushed, his curiosity more than a little stirred up. He couldn't quite match up the guy she was talking about with *Charlie*. Being in hospital wasn't a Charlie thing to do, stupid as it sounded.

"I don't know."

"Yeah, but...you've guessed some stuff, right?"

She chewed on her lip before saying, "I dunno," again. "Look," she continued, "he just reappeared and he was different. Or the same, I don't know — but it was like he was back to being happy old Charlie the fat kid, only not fat anymore. And he was dropped from the football team and the teachers used to get really 'is everything okay, Charlie?' if he went a bit funny in class, so..."

"So?" Adam prompted.

"I figured it was up here." She tapped her forehead and Adam stared.

"Seriously?" Seriously? Charlie had mental health issues and had needed to go to a hospital? He'd been bipolar? Or was it the skinny thing? He'd had, what, an eating disorder or something? Did boys even *get* eating disorders and shit? But then, Charlie wasn't exactly a regular boy, so maybe he did?

"Uh-huh," Phoebe said and shrugged. "And you know me. I started trying to be super nice to him when he came back to school and I realized he wasn't an idiot and he's actually pretty sweet under all the...*boy*, and I started hanging out with him and Ollie proper."

Adam fiddled with his pen, turning it over and over in his hand. "I'm not trying to be mean, but—how'd Charlie get into that school, anyway? His family can't be affording the fees."

"They're not. He's on scholarship," Phoebe said and pushed her hair over her shoulder. "He's—"

"Charlie got a scholarship?"

Phoebe blinked. "Well, yeah."

"I just...I'm only in English and maths with him, and..."

"Okay, yeah, he sucks at English," she admitted. "But he's crazy with numbers, Charlie is. Really scary good. That's what he got it for. He can just...he can do stuff in his head in minutes I'd need like four hours, paper and a calculator for. It's really freaky. Test him next class, get him to show you."

Adam frowned at his notepad and the barely started essay, his brain churning. It didn't want to line up Charlie—loud, manic, wild Charlie—with the guy Phoebe was describing. Someone who was a maths genius and had mental health issues and had been hospitalized.

But then the memory of the way Charlie had looked at him on the playing fields and on the floor of Mr. MacFarlane's shed—wide-eyed and hurt—rose, and the things Ollie had shouted at him in the toilets...and what Phoebe was saying didn't sound so strange.

Jesus, had Ollie *not* been exaggerating? Had he really hurt Charlie's feelings over the whole kiss thing? Adam had been so sure Charlie would just wave it off, but maybe... maybe Ollie wasn't just being mega-protective of her gay boyfriend.

"Ollie said he's not allowed to do laps of the field," he said quietly.

Phoebe shrugged. "I don't know," she admitted. "They never told me much — you know how they are. It's Charlie-and-Ollie like they're one person sometimes. I know Ollie knows *everything,* but she always does and Charlie hates talking about it. He either laughs it off and says he went loopy and they scooped his brain out and he's fine now, or he goes quiet and walks away from you."

So, Charlie had been in hospital and he was probably bipolar and maybe had an eating disorder or something, and — and what? Adam couldn't go out with him, anyway, so there was no way this wouldn't have happened, right? There was nothing he could have done about it anyway, right?

"Is he okay now?"

"I don't know," Phoebe said. "I mean, he must be a bit better — he's not in hospital."

"Yeah, but that's hardly better, is it?"

"I don't know," she repeated. "I mean...I know he's still pretty...down on himself."

"What?"

"You'll never get Charlie tell you he's good at maths," she said and rolled her eyes. "He proper thinks he's weird and spastic and stuff. Even when he hugs you, he closes up his hands into fists so you don't feel his fingers."

"Really?" Adam hadn't noticed — but then, Charlie didn't hug him very often. If at all.

"Yeah. Seriously, try taking his hand — he'll jerk it away like you tried to rip the leftover ones off."

"Uh, how about no?"

"Oh, yeah, maybe not."

"So he's…wait, got self-esteem issues?"

"Trust me," Phoebe said wearily. "He'll have told himself off for being stupid and crazy to think you'd ever like someone like him when you pushed him away." Adam grimaced. "Don't tell him I said any of this."

"I just—this fucking sucks," Adam complained. "I can't go out with him and that's not going to change but…but I *would* have done, you know? I wanted to kiss him back."

"So, why not?"

"No, Phoebe."

"Is it something you're not allowed to talk about?"

"I *can't* talk about it," he hedged.

"But, Adam—"

"No."

"Adam, it won't make us turn our backs on you," Phoebe said, because she was mega fucking scary sometimes, like clairvoyant or telekinetic or something. He told her so and she laughed. "Telepathic, idiot."

"Whatever. But I can't."

"Why not?"

He shook his head.

"Did…did the kids in your last school know?"

"Yeah," he said. "And that's why I can't tell you because it'll happen all over again and I *can't*, Phoebe. I can't go out with Charlie—ever, or anyone else—so…so he'll just have to get over it. I know that sounds horrible, but…"

She squeezed his wrist again. "Look," she said. "Anytime you want to tell me, I promise I won't tell anybody else. Not Charlie, not Ollie—nobody. Okay? So anytime you want to tell me, I'll listen."

Adam swallowed—hard—and squeezed back.

"Thanks, Feebs," he mumbled. But it still wasn't happening.

Because if she found out, she'd be gone—just like everyone else.

# Chapter Six

*Come over today? :) Otherwise dads going to make me help at church!!!! :(*

Saturday morning, not even ten o'clock, and the cry for help had materialized. Adam had been expecting it.

"Mum, I'm going over to Phoebe's in a bit," he dutifully reported, thumbing out a quick reply and pushing his mostly eaten breakfast away.

"All right, dear. Will you be staying for tea?"

"Probably not," he hedged. Reverend Cooper made him uncomfortable. He was pretty sure the reverend wouldn't want Adam in his house if he knew about it all.

"Back by seven, then."

"Sure, Mum." He hesitated in the doorway then stepped back into the kitchen. "Mum?"

"Mm?"

"Can boys get eating disorders?"

"Yes, dear." Her reply was distracted — and why wouldn't it be? Dad was a retired GP. Adam used to love opening his medical textbooks as a kid and asking questions about all the gory pictures.

"And...and can you go to hospital for being bipolar?"

She raised her head from the court papers she was working on. "Well — yes, I suppose you can, dear, if you're putting yourself at risk. Why?"

Adam bit his lip then shook his head. "Just curious. Telly last night."

"Ah," she said. "Storyline on one of the soaps, is it?"

"Yeah." Mum never watched the soaps — she'd never find

out. "Thanks." So maybe Charlie *had* had an eating disorder. But didn't people die from those? "How long does it take to get over an eating disorder?"

"Recover, dear, not get over. And it depends on the patient, darling. You'd best ask your father, I don't know too much about it."

"'Kay," Adam said. "Thanks."

\* \* \* \*

Phoebe lived — unsurprisingly — at the rectory behind the seventeenth-century Anglican church, St. John's. It was a ten-minute walk from Adam's house — mostly because the two fields that separated them were given over to a really aggressive bull at the minute — and he ambled, meandering along the narrow country lanes and over the village green, which the recent rain had turned into a marsh. It was half past ten, the church clock informed him, as he cut through the graveyard and around Anne Meeks' sagged, cracked gravestone. Over the wall, along the dirt track and toward the red front door. Adam liked the house and Phoebe but not so much the aloof Persian cat that eyed him from the flowerbed, or the doorbell that sounded like a funeral march.

But then Phoebe opened it with a sunny smile and wearing a floury apron. "C'mon," she said enthusiastically. "I made brownies!"

"Are they edible?" Adam asked dubiously.

"Yep!"

They kind of looked okay when she presented him with the still-hot tray before plonking it on the side and rummaging for a knife.

"Let's take some and go up to my room. Mum's picking up Melissa from ballet so we can hide before they get home."

Adam stared.

"Mum's been nagging me about spending too much time with you," Phoebe admitted and Adam sniggered. She giggled. "I know! I even told her—is that okay? That I told her you're gay?"

"Well, yeah, but…doesn't your dad mind?"

"I didn't tell *Dad*," she said. "She didn't believe me, anyway. But you have a name now, you're not 'that boy' anymore, so—hey! Progress!"

Adam accepted a brownie. Warily. Phoebe wasn't exactly the best baker in the universe. She'd poisoned half the class at Christmas with her flapjacks. But— "Huh. This is kind of good."

"I know!" Phoebe beamed. "Okay, so I had my nana on the phone the whole time helping me. And I didn't mix up salt and sugar this time."

"Um. Good?"

"C'mon, upstairs, before Mum gets back."

The rectory was enormous and Phoebe had the attic room. The friendly cat was on the first flight of stairs and Adam picked her up on their way. She was a brown Ragdoll, the fluffiest and floppiest cat in the universe, and sagged into his arms purring happily. Adam felt like purring when he came to the rectory, despite Phoebe's awkward parents and her annoying little sister. It was just so far away from everything else. It didn't exist here. He was normal here.

"I wanted to talk to you, actually."

The normal feeling popped with the snap of Phoebe's bedroom door.

"About what?" Adam asked cautiously, sinking onto the bed. It dipped heavily under his weight and he let the cat go to adjust himself. She stretched and rumbled a deep purr before jumping down and padding back out to the sunlit landing to find whatever warm spot she could.

"Well." Phoebe dropped to sit cross-legged on the other end of the bed and started fidgeting with her hair, pulling it out of its ponytail. "About you, actually."

Adam swallowed. "Um. About me?"

"Yeah," she said and exhaled. "Look, um, I just…I don't mean to be nosy or anything, but I just—everything lately…"

Adam drew his knees up to his chest. His heart was suddenly pounding and he felt vaguely sick again.

"I didn't want to ask. I mean, you know, it's your business and your…issue…"

*Oh, fuck.*

"But, I mean, I'm worried about you, Adam, and so would Charlie and Ollie be if they weren't having to already deal with Charlie going completely nuts last week, and I…" She was fidgeting, hair down all around her shoulders, carding her fingers through it. "I really like you, you know. It's nice to have someone to take shopping and watch girly films with who isn't going to compete with me for Josh Denbar."

"Well, I would, you know, but…straight," Adam mumbled awkwardly.

Phoebe giggled, the sound high and nervous. "Good," she said and squeezed his knee. "Adam, I just — I'm worried. Okay? There's something wrong. I know there is, but — tell me?"

Adam shook his head.

"Why not?" she whispered. "It can't be that bad?"

"You have no idea, Feebs —"

"So *tell* me."

"I can't!"

"Why not?" she pressed. "I promised not to tell anyone, didn't I? And maybe I could help?"

The idea was laughable and Adam snorted. "Nobody can help me with this, Phoebe," he said miserably. "It's not something you can help with."

"I can help with a bit of it, can't I?" she pleaded. Her eyes were huge and earnest and Adam's chest creaked with pain at telling her no. "Have you told anyone? Does anyone know?"

"At school?"

"Anywhere."

Adam shrugged. "My family knows." *Obviously.* "Some people found out once." *Several times.* "Nobody at school."

"Adam, you need to tell someone," Phoebe whispered. "It hurts—I can see it hurts. You're always so quiet, but every now and then you forget and you're so *different* and—and Charlie saw it, too. Charlie saw that and he liked you for it and—what's wrong, Adam?"

"I can't," he begged. "I can't, Feebs. I can't. You don't understand. When people found out last time—they always find out…"

"Nobody's going to find out from me, I promise," she said. She was squeezing both his hands and Adam didn't know how she'd got them. "Adam, please—look, can I—can I just ask? Can I just ask, just…just so I know I asked, and you don't have to tell me."

"Feebs—"

"Have you been—you know…?"

"What?"

"Were you abused?"

Adam's brain hiccupped and, around the burning in his eyes and the razors in his throat, a stray rational thought materialized in his head. "I—what? What?"

"I mean, you freaked out when Charlie kissed you but you don't mind me or Ollie touching you and you said you like him and I know you're gay and you refuse to talk about it, so I—were you ever abused, you know, like—"

"No!" Adam blurted out. "No! Oh, my God, *no!*"

Her grip on his hands eased.

"No!" he repeated. "Fucking hell, Phoebe, *no*, I'm—" And he checked it. At the very last second, he checked it and Phoebe chewed on her lip.

"What, Adam?"

His ribs were too small. His lungs couldn't catch enough air. His palms were sweaty on her fingers and his arms were shaking. He felt cold and hot all at once, claustrophobic as though the room was too small and yet in desperate need of a hug, all at the same time. And his tongue unstuck from the roof of his mouth and his jaw sagged and out poured the secret he'd fought so fucking hard to keep a bloody *secret*.

"I have HIV."

Phoebe's jaw dropped—and Adam burst into tears. He dragged his hands away from hers and covered his face, mortified. Oh, God, he'd said it. He'd said it—he'd let it out and now she'd—

Hug him.

*Wait, no.* He jerked and Phoebe's grip tightened, her wiry arms around his chest and shoulders and her hair tickling his face. "Don't do that," she murmured. "Don't cry. It's okay—well, no, it's not. It sucks and I'm so sorry, but it's okay—you know, by me, it's okay. I'm not—oh don't cry."

She was hugging him. She was—she was hugging him, she wasn't afraid to touch him, she hadn't recoiled, she—

"Oh, Adam, don't cry," Phoebe pleaded. "Don't! Don't— I'm not going to tell anybody and I—"

"You're fucking touching me," Adam croaked.

"Um. Well…do you not want me—?"

"Nobody wants to touch me when they find out," Adam whispered.

"Well…I can't get it from hugging you, right?"

"No."

"Then," Phoebe squeezed her arms tight, "you look like you need a hug right now."

Adam choked on a sob and ground the heels of his hands into his eyes. She started to talk, murmuring low promises not to tell anybody and that it was all fine and Adam wanted to shake her and make her react like normal people, or—or hug her back and just cry for a minute. Nobody had ever—nobody had—

"I'm going to kill you, you know," Phoebe whispered. "You had me so scared there was some big horrible evil secret, like…like some creepy pervert uncle had touched you up or something!"

Adam snorted with wet laughter and she started giggling.

"Or, or—or maybe a Santa in a Christmas grotto. They're always weird. Or a Scout leader—did you do Scouts?"

"No." Adam coughed then started scrubbing away the

tears. "Feebs?"

"Mm?"

"Marry me."

Phoebe giggled. "Aw, Ads. I'm flattered, but I might get a bit pissed off when you keep bringing boys home."

Adam sniffed and shook his head. "Can't."

"Can't what?" Phoebe asked, steadily pulling him sideways until they were resting on her pillows together in a tangle.

"Can't bring boys home," Adam whispered.

"Oh, Adam. Is that why you pushed Charlie?"

"I could give this to him, Phoebe," Adam croaked. "I could pass this on."

"Oh, Adam..."

"And you can't tell him."

"I won't!" she said. "I promised, didn't I? Are you okay?"

"Mm." Adam untangled himself to rub at his face. The mattress shifted and a minute later Phoebe was pressing a wad of tissues into his hands. He tried to mop himself up and she rubbed his arm soothingly.

"I'm glad you told me."

"Thanks for not...being disgusted," he mumbled.

"It's not like you can just magically give it out, is it?" she said gently. "Can I...do you mind if I ask..."

"How I got it?"

"Well...yeah."

"My mum."

"Your mum has it?"

"Yeah. Not Mum. Not proper Mum. My—I'm adopted. *That* mum."

"Oh," Phoebe said. "Okay. So...no touching up?"

Adam snorted and finally smiled. *"No,* Phoebe."

"Just checking," she said and gripped his wrist. "Hey. It's okay. It *is.* I mean, it's not, but it is. I'm not going to freak out or ditch you. Is that what happened at your last schools? You told people and they freaked out?"

"Last time I told someone, I was eight years old," Adam

mumbled. "And I wasn't allowed to go round their house to play anymore. Their mum didn't want me there."

"*Ads…*"

"Other times…other times people found my medication in my bag, because I used to take it at lunchtime, way back from nursery school and so the teachers in primary school could give it to me with my lunch. The first secondary school…someone stole them and they must have googled them or something because the next day everyone knew."

She wriggled around him in a hug again and Adam swallowed against the new lump in his throat.

"The next school, a friend found out and he told everyone. I got…I tried to stay there. I figured I couldn't run away every time, but…"

"But?"

"I couldn't do it," Adam whispered. "They'd steal my clothes and burn them behind the bike sheds. They'd trash my locker. They'd try and shove me under cars outside the school gate. They put death threats through the letterbox…"

"What *scumbags!*"

"I left after a couple of boys beat me up in the toilets. They put…they put latex gloves on first. I ended up in the hospital with two cracked ribs and a concussion."

She was hugging him impossibly tightly now and Adam wanted to just be…fucking *buried* in hug, if it was possible.

"Dad homeschooled me for a bit after that," he whispered. "I just…they tried to enroll me in another school but I got panic attacks just putting on the uniform… then Mum got a job offer from another law firm and we had to move all the way out here."

"So, how did you come to our school?" Phoebe asked. "If you couldn't put the uniform on…"

"It's gonna sound stupid."

"Okay."

"No tie."

"What?"

Adam went red. "No tie. I'd panic trying to do the tie up.

They used to pull me around by the tie."

Phoebe started giggling. "No way!"

"That's not funny!"

"It is," Phoebe said. "They got rid of the ties at our school because this kid in Year Eleven got in a fight with Charlie and yanked his tie. Only 'cause the tie broke, they both fell off the bleachers and the other kid broke his leg."

Adam blinked. "Why—no. Never mind. I don't want to know. But the ties are banned, cool, yeah, that's why I didn't freak out and I could come to school."

"Then I adopted you!" Phoebe sang cheerily. Her hair had spread out around both their faces and it itched. "Adam? You should tell Charlie."

"No."

The response was fast, automatic and permanent.

"He wouldn't—"

"He would."

"I didn't."

"You've never kissed me," Adam pointed out and Phoebe sighed. "I can't. I didn't even mean to tell you. If one person finds out, everyone finds out, that's how this shit works—and I *can't* go through that again. I can't do it again."

"Okay, but—just listen for a sec? Charlie isn't going to freak out. No, *listen.* He's not, okay? Charlie's...Charlie's sweet. I know he seems like a bit of a berk and he's been a bit pissy lately, but he's not horrible. You know? He's not horrible. He wouldn't freak out and he wouldn't tell anybody. I mean, come on—he has crazy hands and a crazier brain and he knows all about being something, being some*one,* that other people don't like."

"And this is different, Phoebe," Adam breathed. "I never thought Jamie would tell, but he told the whole fucking school. I can't tell him—and neither can you."

Phoebe's face was sympathetic and wide-eyed, pretty in a way Adam wished he could appreciate. He wanted her to be right, but he knew she wasn't.

"You thought I'd freak, too."

"You've not kissed me," he repeated dully.

"Guess so," she mumbled, then her face brightened. "Tell you what."

"What?"

"Let's take the brownies up into the belfry and make up ghost stories again. We need to get in some practice before Ollie and Charlie come up next week."

Adam laughed and packed away some of the hurt. Just... None of the gratitude.

* * * *

Then Charlie snapped and forced his hand.

# Chapter Seven

Adam usually spent his maths lessons…not doing maths. Maths lessons were the tiny three-hours-a-week he got to safely stare at Charlie and not get caught. In maths, he sat directly behind Charlie — Fielding and Wood were only a row apart in top set maths, thanks to the class being about fifteen people in total — and directly behind meant he could just stare. He'd lost advanced trigonometry to the back of Charlie's head.

Today, though…today Adam hunched his shoulders and bent over his textbook as though his life depended on it. He focused so hard on sine and cosine — and not, definitely not — the hurt look on Charlie's face when he'd run away from the bleachers or the angry tirade from Ollie or Phoebe's open, pleading face asking him to just spill his secret.

He didn't think about that stuff. He focused on sine waves and making sure his graphs were perfect, so much that Mr. Bagshaw had to repeat himself and said, "Dismissed includes you, Mr. Wood," after what seemed like a lifetime of…of maths Adam couldn't remember.

"Oh," he said and fumbled to gather his things. The rest of the class was already bustling, ready to go home. He looked up, caught Charlie's freakishly blue eyes and looked away again.

"Mr. Fielding," Mr. Bagshaw drawled in that low, idle voice of his. Mr. Baghsaw had a voice like a…like a *smirk*. He always sounded so bored and condescending and Adam scowled on reflex at Charlie's surname being dragged out like that. *Fieeelding*. Like it was something disgusting. "A word."

"Yes, sir," Charlie said, then there was a hand on Adam's arm and he jumped as if he'd been shot, jerking away from those pale, spidery hands. Charlie's face flickered, his mouth twisting, then he said, "Hang about? I need to talk to you."

Adam flushed. He didn't like that little pinch at the corner of Charlie's mouth, but at the same time he kind of did, because the faintest edge of one of Charlie's dimples was showing and Adam always wanted to kiss that dimple. Worse, since Charlie had —

He pulled away. "'Kay," he mumbled, dropping his gaze to the floor, and hefted his bag over his shoulder. He closed the door on Mr. Bagshaw's arrogant sneer and kicked the trophy cabinet outside the staff room. He didn't want to talk, but the twist at the corner of Charlie's mouth made his stomach hurt. He didn't want Charlie to be upset. He wanted…he wanted to say it wasn't Charlie's fault and it wasn't about him, but if he did —

Charlie was like Ollie. He pushed and pushed and pushed and sometimes it made Adam want to smack him, because Charlie didn't *want* to know about this. *Adam* didn't want him to know. Anyone, but least of all Charlie.

So he kicked the cabinet and peered through the glass window in the door. Mr. Bagshaw was droning as Charlie stuffed what looked like extra homework into his bag. Bastard Baghsaw. Like anyone needed more trigonometry, Adam thought. Charlie didn't like school. He was always complaining about the workload and Adam swore Mr. Bagshaw singled him out after every lesson to —

Adam jerked back when Mr. Bagshaw reached out and clapped Charlie's shoulder, and went back to kicking the cabinet just in time for the door to creak open.

"C'mon," Charlie said.

"What'd Bastard Bagshaw want?" Adam asked, falling into step as Charlie headed for the stairs. He seemed… quiet. Head down, stride long. Adam had to hurry to keep up even though Charlie wasn't any taller than him, and his stomach clenched. *Upset.* Charlie was upset and Adam had a horrible feeling it was more to do with him than Mr. Bagshaw.

"Extra homework," Charlie mumbled and took a left so sharp Adam had to back up to follow him into the drama block neither of them ever visited. That was Phoebe's homeland, not theirs, and he struggled to keep pace.

"Charlie—"

Charlie slammed through the fire exit like it wasn't even there, the heavy glass door almost bouncing on its hinges, then they were out on the open playing fields at the back of the school. It was cold and windy and Charlie's hair was torn up into a messy dark halo as he turned very sharply on his heel and said, "I get it," in Adam's face.

"What?"

"I *get* it," Charlie repeated. His hands were twitching at his sides and he licked his lips. "I get it, okay, you're not interested. I'm sorry, all right. Is that what I have to say?"

Adam blinked and backed up. "I—what? I don't—sorry for what?"

"For Ollie's party," Charlie said flatly and Adam's stomach twisted.

"Oh."

"Yeah, *oh.* Stop it."

"Stop—?"

"Stop fucking twitching away from me!" Charlie shouted. He kept swallowing and biting his lip and Adam was torn between horror and fascination. He'd seen Charlie mad and manic, right? But not agitated, not like this.

"Charlie, I—"

"I'm not going to jump you again, not after you nearly threw me into a rusty lawnmower. I'm not a masochist or a fucking perv, Adam! I get it, you're not interested—you don't have to act like I'm going to fucking attack you or something! You don't have to avoid me or chuck me shitty apology notes or talk to the girls about me!"

Adam felt sick. Proper sick, like he was gonna chuck on

the grass. Ollie had said he'd upset Charlie, but he'd done more than that and he felt ill at the idea.

"If you want me to leave you alone or not talk to you or whatever, then fine," Charlie snapped bitterly and Adam's heart lurched.

"No!"

"But you don't have to act like I'm catching or something," Charlie continued hotly and Adam wanted to laugh—or cry—at the irony of his words.

"You're—I don't mean to. I just—it's—"

"A simple 'no' would've done, you didn't have to—"

"*Charlie!*" Adam raised his voice. "I'm sorry if—if I've made you think— Look, it's just...I didn't see it coming!"

"How"—Charlie's voice was cold as ice, brittle and thin—"could you *not* have seen it coming? What, you think it's a thing at parties, boys sneaking off to the garden shed together? Fuck's sake, Adam, I was hanging out in the kitchen because I figured you'd show up there! You're not into parties and shit! I figured it'd be a good way to sneak us off out the way for a bit!"

"I didn't know you liked me!" Adam insisted. Even saying it seemed wrong, because Charlie couldn't be attracted to Adam. It just wasn't possible—and even if Charlie *was,* it couldn't go anywhere. Adam couldn't—wouldn't—let it. "I had no idea, nobody even told me you were gay!"

Charlie snorted. "Yeah, well, nobody told me either, mate."

The *mate* seemed drawled and sarcastic and Adam flinched. Charlie's face twisted again.

"It's not about the *shed,*" he snarled. "It's about you shoving me over and legging it and every time I've seen you since you get this look on your face like I've got fucking HIV—"

Adam flinched.

"And a big gaping chest wound and blood all over the place and you're going to have to mop it up. You can't get away from me fast enough anymore and I—"

"I'm sorry, okay, but it's just—it's *awkward*. You kissed me and I overreacted, and—"

"And I thought you would at least let me down gently!" Charlie shouted. His hands were practically fluttering, almost dancing in the frigid air. "I thought you of all people wouldn't act like I could give you the queer!"

"I'm not transphobic!" Adam blurted out, shocked. "I'm *gay*, Charlie, I—"

"Oh, what, am I too much of a girl for you, then?" Charlie snapped.

"That's not it!"

Charlie snorted and started to pace and Adam hunched his shoulders, folding his arms against the cold that wasn't entirely to do with the weather. He felt shaky and sick and—and part of him wanted to prove Charlie wrong and derail him and just kiss him back and the rest of him knew that he just *couldn't*.

"Charlie…" he whispered.

"Just stop it," Charlie said. His voice cracked. Adam's heart wrenched and his throat closed up as Charlie's voice shifted from fury to…to begging. "Just *stop* it, Adam, please. I can't—I get it, okay, I get it. I've got the message. You don't want someone like me anywhere near you. I get it, but it fucking hurts when you look at me like I'm some kind of fucked-up freak or a weird perv and you make excuses to not be in the same room as me and—just stop it, yeah? *Please*. I get enough of that already. I get enough of people crossing the fucking canteen to avoid me. I get enough weird looks off the other kids. Don't add to it for one fucking lousy stupid mistake?"

Adam opened his mouth and nothing happened. His throat was too large and silenced him and Charlie looked so …

He looked fragile, in a way he never had before. He was suddenly thin rather than lanky and his face was pinched rather than angular. Adam itched to reach out and hug him, touch him, kiss him—and Adam blinked and mentally shook himself. He *couldn't*. That was the whole problem, and—

Wait.

His brain caught up. "What do you mean weird looks?"

Charlie snorted. "Like you haven't heard."

"No, I-I really don't—what?"

"Whatever, Adam." Charlie's shoulders and voice dropped as one. "I get it. Got the idea. You don't want me and my stupid hands and weird mouth and my girly bits and whatever else near you. You didn't have to be a dick about it."

"Wait, I—what? You don't have a weird mouth," Adam blurted out, because it seemed to be the only thing he could say. What the hell was Charlie talking about? "It's not—it's nothing to do with you, it's—"

"Oh, right, yeah. Not you, it's me, sure."

"It is!" Adam insisted. "It's—look, I—if...if I was anybody else, if...if things were different, I wouldn't have shoved you away!"

"Right," Charlie said, the same way Mum did when Adam said he'd cleaned his room.

"Listen to me!" Adam snapped, a tiny bit of anger worming its way out from under the heap of hurt. "Just listen, okay? I-I do like you."

Charlie snorted.

"I do!" Adam insisted, even as his face flooded with heat. "It's just—I can't. I can't...I can't like you and I can't...do anything about it, and I—"

"Right," Charlie said again and folded his arms. He looked small and thin in his uniform, the wind pulling at his blazer and hair. His eyes were bluer than the sky. "You would have kissed me if you were someone else and if I were someone else and—"

"It's not that easy."

"Do you like me?"

"Yes," Adam croaked.

"Well, I think we've established I'm fucking mental

enough to keep liking you even when you seem to think I'm contagious, so what exactly is the problem here?" Charlie snapped.

"It's — I can't."

"Why not." There it was. The ruthless tone, the still stare, the one Ollie did, the one that showed just how they had grown up together. But where Ollie looked so staid and determined, so dogged and patiently cruel with it, Charlie looked manic, the way he froze in place and only his mouth moved, like —

Like someone on an edge. Things were starting to slot together unpleasantly, between Charlie's words and Phoebe's whispered theories and Adam wasn't liking the picture he was getting.

"I know it sounds stupid," he pleaded, "but it's not you. It's nothing to do with you. It's *me*. I can't — I can't have... have boyfriends and...and kissing and stuff. I can't do it."

"What are you, a nun?"

Adam swept right past the incredulous disbelief. "I can't explain it, Charlie. It's really intense nasty personal stuff and..."

"Like we haven't crossed that line. Why can't you?"

"It's not that simple."

"But why!" Charlie shouted, throwing up those strange hands. "Why not? You're either making it up and — you know what, fuck it. I don't blame you not wanting to get with some nutter who looks like he belongs in the fucking circus, and — "

"Stop it!" Adam shouted. "You don't! It's nothing to do with — "

Charlie started forward and Adam backed up. And Charlie stopped, that pale face twisting into a sneer. "Right," he said. "Nothing to do with me."

Adam wanted to cry. It had gone so wrong. Charlie was — Charlie wasn't supposed to like him. Charlie was meant to just shrug it off and bounce to the next boy, just come out laughing like he always did. He wasn't meant to like

Adam enough to get upset. He wasn't meant to be able to get upset! And he certainly wasn't meant to think it meant Adam was disgusted by him or —

"I get it, you know. I'm not exactly the hottest guy in school and I'm mental and fucked-up and I have enough baggage that I shouldn't be allowed on aeroplanes," Charlie said bitterly. "But I figured, you know. I figured the way you'd look at me sometimes when you thought I couldn't see, and the way Phoebe teased you…"

Adam swallowed. Hard. "She was right."

"What?"

"I've…I've liked you since I moved here," Adam whispered. "It's not—you're not weird or fucked-up or any of it and I've liked you for ages, but—I *can't*. There's… there's stuff you don't know about me and I can't tell you, but…but it means I can't." He felt sick at the look of open skepticism on Charlie's face. "I can't do relationships and stuff. With anyone. And I want to, but I can't and I'm sorry. I'm sorry I've been stupid and I-I don't mean to make you feel like—"

"Like you're trying to convince yourself, not me," Charlie interrupted flatly, then his head dropped and he was eyeing the damp grass around their shoes. "Whatever, Adam."

"Charlie—"

"I said whatever," Charlie snapped. "You keep telling yourself it's not me, it's you, and you know, maybe you'll believe it, but I don't. And I don't blame you, you know. I wouldn't want to date me, either. But you don't have to make out like being in the same room as me is bad for your health, you know?"

"I…" Adam croaked.

"You don't know everything about me, either, and there's some shit there that makes me kissing you a really stupid idea, but I did it anyway and you know what? I wish I hadn't because then I could keep my little fantasy that you might actually kiss me back and not try and gut me with a chainsaw or something."

"You're not being fair," Adam said. "I've told you—"

"You've trotted out some line that you can't do relationships, and what*ever*, Ads. You were pretty skittish about mates, too, and you gave that a chance," Charlie said ruthlessly then shook his head. "Look, if you actually want to tell me what this mythical reason is that touching me is going to make you explode, you know where to find me. Until then, can you just stop fucking acting like I'm some kind of sicko with a contagious disease or something? 'Cause it really hurts, actually."

And with that, he was—gone. Where Ollie had stormed and shouted and strutted out, Charlie had just…bled away, just turned on his heel and vanished over the playing fields to the brook at the bottom and the bridle path that headed back out toward the ridge and the villages and Stoker Farm.

And Adam wanted to be sick, or chase him and kiss him, or blurt it all out and tell him the truth, because—because he wanted to be mad and insist Charlie just accept it wasn't going to happen, but Adam could…kind of see his point. Adam wouldn't believe him, either, some fluffy 'can't' and no reason behind it at all. Not even a halfway decent lie.

Adam stood on the playing fields and hugged himself for a little while, turning the idea over and over in his head and feeling by turns nauseous at the idea of spilling the secret and sick at the memory of Charlie's hurt fury. He'd never meant to let Charlie get hurt by it, but then Adam was getting the idea that Charlie wasn't anything like what he'd assumed.

He had to tell him *something,* but…

But what?

# Chapter Eight

Tuesday — *tell him tell him tell him!*
Wednesday — *tell him! :)*
Today — *tell him, Ads!!*
Adam was starting to feel…

The thing with secrets was once *one* person was told, it was like the brain said, "Now tell the next one." It was like playing minesweeper. That habit of thinking the more shots taken without losing, the closer winning became — only, in reality, that was when shit got real. At least, that was how Adam saw it. And with Phoebe texting him every day telling him to tell Charlie…

"Mum."

"Mm?"

Adam turned over a forkful of beef and ale pie. "I told Phoebe."

"That's nice, dear."

"*Mum.* I told Phoebe about…you know."

She looked up from scrubbing the casserole dish. "About what, dear?"

"Me."

"Adam…"

He poked the pie. "About my HIV."

Mum turned from the sink. "You told her?"

"Mhmm."

"Oh, sweetheart." Her voice was a croon and heat flooded his face. Mum abandoned the dish and stooped to hug him, pressing her mouth to the top of his head.

"Mum!"

"Oh, shush," she scolded. "Adam, darling, that's

*wonderful*. I am—stop pulling faces, young man!—I am so proud of you right now."

Adam flushed and contemplated burying his face in his food.

"And I'm guessing from the lack of tears and drama it went well?"

"Mum!"

"Did it?"

"Yes—I don't have drama!"

Mum snorted and sank into the seat opposite. "Eat your dinner," she said. "So, Phoebe knows and the world didn't end?"

"No, but…"

"But?"

Adam squirmed. "She, um."

"Um?"

"She wants me to tell Charlie."

"All right," Mum said and ducked her head to give Adam that scrutinizing expression of hers. "And are you going to?"

Adam prodded the pie and squashed a glob of thick gravy out from under the pastry. "Dunno," he mumbled.

"Adam…"

"He kissed me, Mum."

"So Nat wasn't just teasing you?"

"No," he mumbled. "He kissed me at Ollie's party and I…I kind of overreacted and, um, shoved him."

"Ah."

"And he's been weird with me ever since." Well, except for the row on the playing fields. "Ollie says I upset him and he's been acting funny. Like…he's avoiding me." Or Adam was avoiding Charlie, because…it was just *hard*. It was hard being in the same room when they'd kissed and Charlie thought he hated him and he *didn't* but he couldn't explain, and—

"And you think by telling him, he might understand?"

Adam shrugged. "Phoebe says he will." He tapped the

crust again and gave it up as a lost cause. "I mean…she didn't freak out, and…I want him to understand it's not *him*."

Mum hummed. "It's not you, either, Adam."

"It is."

"Well, yes," she said. "But not for the reason you think. You've always been so stubborn, sweetheart, and don't get me wrong—you will *always* need to be careful. But maybe it's time you learned that careful doesn't mean celibate."

"Mum!"

"Don't you 'mum' me," she scolded. "Cautious is good but you're being overcautious, Adam. I think if you and this Charlie like each other, then maybe you need to talk to him."

Adam swallowed. "What if…"

What if Charlie didn't want to…go out or anything? Afterward? Wouldn't that mean it was just down to the HIV and not…not anything else? Or maybe it *would* be down to something else—he'd been so mad on the fields that Adam was suddenly struck with the fear that it was too late to fix it and—

"There might not be any point."

"Why not?"

"I…Ollie said I really upset him, and…I think I did," Adam admitted.

"Well," Mum said. "Maybe it's time to remedy that. If he doesn't know why you rejected him, then he might get the wrong idea and think you don't like him." Adam twitched. "Maybe you can take the chance to correct him?"

"And if he freaks out because he kissed a positive—"

"Then he isn't the kind of boy you need in your life," Mum said. "But it might be prudent to have Phoebe with you when you do tell him."

"Mum…"

"Just in case, eh?"

Adam bit his lip, staring at the forgotten pie. "D'you reckon I really should?"

"It's up to you, dear," Mum said. "But if you do tell him and he is all right with it, then you also ought to really think about the possibility of going out with him."

"*Muuuum.*"

"You only limit yourself," Mum said, standing up and brushing off her skirt as though it could possibly have gotten dirty sitting at the table. "You've got the opportunity to make him understand, sweetheart. And if he's half the boy you seem to think he is, then you also have the opportunity to push your boundaries a little with someone who isn't going to be putting either of you at unnecessary risk."

Adam bit his lip.

"Can I…?"

Mum cocked her head.

"Can I do it here?" Adam blurted out. Then if it went wrong…if it went wrong he could make Charlie leave and he and Phoebe could have a sleepover and he'd be home. And it wouldn't feel so…so…

The storm erupted in his stomach. *Scary.* The word supplied itself and he suddenly swallowed against a dry throat.

"Of course you can."

\* \* \* \*

His heart was beating far too fast when he walked through the doors to the school canteen and it seized when Charlie — standing behind Ollie and pointing at the open pages of her maths textbook — straightened up and backed away from the table.

"I should probably go," Adam heard, clear as a bell, and he shook his head, quickening his pace.

"Wait," he called and Charlie paused, hand on his backpack. "Don't."

"Don't what?" Phoebe asked.

"Charlie, sit down," Ollie said, tugging on Charlie's elbow. "You can't go. I don't *get* it."

Charlie's face was tight and thin, the angles seeming sharper somehow, and Adam's stomach wrenched. It was the wrench that spurred him to talk without getting tongue-tied and so it just poured out.

"I need to tell you all something."

Phoebe's eyes went wide and she reached up to squeeze Adam's wrist. He swallowed. Charlie's expression didn't change and Ollie seemed to miss the entire thing, still scowling at her textbook.

"Not here," Adam amended. "Um. Come to my house tonight? Mum said I could have a sleepover."

"Oh, cool, okay," Ollie said. "Charlie, I can't balance it. *Charlie.*"

Charlie's face twisted, but he didn't look angry. He looked—his mouth was tense and he was chewing on the bottom lip, and his eyebrows were mismatched and neither down nor up.

"You, too," Adam said. "*All* of you."

Charlie swallowed. "I don't want to make you uncomfortable."

It *hurt.* It physically hurt, the little stab in Adam's gut, and he wished he could be brave like Ollie or not care like Phoebe and just blurt it all out in the open and get Charlie to stop thinking...whatever he was thinking. That it was something to do with *him* and not Adam.

"I have PlayStation and huge game collection." Mostly Nat's, but they didn't need to know that.

"Done," Ollie said and Charlie sniggered.

"Yeah, okay," he said and Adam relaxed his shoulders. "I mean, you know. I'll be a bit late. Got squash this evening."

"I didn't know you played," Adam blurted out and there was an odd, slightly too long pause.

"Yeah," Charlie said eventually. "Something like that."

"We'll come at seven," Ollie said. "I'll drag him by the hair. Cavewoman style. Now are we done? *Charlie*, fucking help me!"

Charlie slowly returned to Ollie's chair, bending over her

shoulder to mumble…maths stuff or whatever and Adam sank into the seat opposite Phoebe, to rummage for his lunch in his backpack.

"You're going to tell them about…you know?" Phoebe whispered.

"Yeah," Adam mumbled.

"You okay?"

Adam shrugged and Phoebe reached across the table to touch his wrist again.

"You'll be fine," she said. "It'll be fine. They'll understand."

"Understand what?" Ollie interjected and Adam flinched.

"That his parents are lame," Phoebe said, smooth as yoghurt. "I mean, c'mon, they can't be lamer than my dad."

"My dad's a GP," Adam supplied, wondering if it would be possible to just magically turn straight and date Phoebe instead, because holy shit, she was the best person ever. He decided to go all out for her birthday present next autumn. "And my mum's a lawyer."

"Nah, vicar wins," Charlie said.

"Reverend."

"Whatever," he said. "My dad's lamest, though."

"Your dad's *dead*," Ollie said and Adam blinked.

"Exactly! Lazy arsehole can't even be fucked to play taxi service — how crap is that?"

Phoebe started giggling and Adam smiled. When Charlie flashed him a crooked grin, those blue eyes like oceans in sunlight, Adam's chest seized and for a brief second he couldn't breathe.

Oh, fuck, what was he doing? Letting *Charlie* into his house? Holy fuck. He'd liked Charlie since September and now Charlie was going to see his house and his parents and learn about his disease? Seriously? What the hell was he *doing*?

"I can't do it," Ollie complained and stood up. She shoved Charlie unceremoniously into her seat. "You do it. Feebs, come and get chocolate with me. I need happy in a bar."

Phoebe giggled and bounced up. Adam fidgeted as

Charlie pulled Ollie's book toward him and started filling in the blanks.

"You, um...you like maths?"

"Uh-huh," Charlie said. "S'easy. It's right or it's wrong, no fuzzy gray bits and feelings and shit. It's not complicated."

Adam blinked as Charlie tore through the homework. It was a ten-page paper of trigonometry, like a little mock exam, and yet Charlie was just penciling in answers like he was making it up.

"You're good," he breathed.

"Thanks?"

"No, seriously, you are," Adam said. "How d'you do that?"

"I dunno," Charlie said. "S'just easy for me. Hey," he added and looked up. "Don't let the girls bully you. If it's gonna be too weird, me coming over, I'll make something up to Ollie and not come."

Adam flushed. "No."

"I get it, it'd be weird to—"

"No," Adam repeated. "I want you to come. I need to...I need to tell you, too, and it's just...it'll be easier. Just having to say it once." He decided telling Charlie Phoebe already knew wouldn't be great politics. "I'm...I'm sorry things have been weird. And you'll understand when I tell you. It's just...scary. It's some...personal stuff."

Charlie wrinkled his nose. "Ew, that's the crazy stuff."

"Yeah," Adam mumbled.

"Fair enough," Charlie said and turned the page. "Don't tell Ollie."

"Tell her what?"

"I'm making this up," Charlie admitted. "Teach her to use me like a homework horse."

Adam laughed—and for a brief second, there was no awkwardness and no fear.

\* \* \* \*

When the doorbell rang, Adam nearly dropped his fork.

"D'you want me to get it?" Phoebe asked.

"I..."

"I can," she offered, ducking her head to peer at him. "I can enforce a pajama rule or something. Give you a few minutes."

"Please," Adam croaked, hating the sound of his voice. His hand shot out of its own volition and he squeezed her forearm. "Thanks, Feebs."

She squeezed back before pushing up from the table and bouncing out to the door. Mum was upstairs emptying all the linen out of the airing cupboard and if Adam could have gotten upstairs without passing the front door he would have done. He was fucking terrified.

"You're late! In there, in there, it's pajamas only. And *no*, Charlie, I know you don't sleep naked!"

"How would you know, Feebs? You been staring?"

Adam flushed at Charlie's hoarse voice in his hall. Charlie had never come over before. Adam had never been able to stand the idea of having someone he wanted so badly — and couldn't have — in his house. He'd always ducked out of hosting sleepovers and...and at least that part had been easy, because the rectory was amazing and Phoebe's dad always let them stay over because he preferred them to her sister's friends.

Even the sound of that voice in his hall made Adam's nerves shiver under the weight of an all-too-different anxiety.

The living room door slammed and Ollie shrieked — probably at Charlie — and Adam took the opportunity to zip out of the kitchen and up the stairs. Mum was piling pillows and spare duvets on the end of the landing and he scooped up an armful under the pretense of helping, trying to get his heartbeat under control.

"I've put a casserole in the oven," she said conversationally. "Nobody's allergic to anything, are they?"

"No," Adam said. "Unless you put orange juice in it, then

Ollie might spew."

Mum chuckled. "No, dear. Are you all right?"

Adam shrugged. "Nervous," he mumbled.

"Well, no matter what happens tonight, you've got Phoebe on your side, haven't you?" Mum said and reached across to tap his arm. "And you may well have Ollie and Charlie on it, too."

Adam swallowed. His fingers were trembling around the edge of the duvet. "What if I don't?" he breathed. "What if Charlie freaks out and hates me and tells everybody?"

"If he tells anybody," Mum said, "then you tell everyone he kissed you."

Adam blinked. "Mum!"

"All's fair in love and war, darling," she said quietly and smirked. "I doubt he wants it spread around the school that he kissed you at Ollie's party any more than you want your HIV status spread around. You do have a hold over him."

Adam licked his lips and nodded. Somehow, it…did kind of help.

"Okay," he said.

"Now, I'm going to pull out the futon and set up both sofas—so two of you will have to share the futon," Mum said briskly. "And—"

"Charlie and Ollie can do that," Adam said very quickly. No way would Charlie want to share with him. "They always do at Ollie's house."

"All right, dear, whatever suits the four of you," Mum said. "I'll leave the burglar alarm switched off so it doesn't go off every time one of you needs the bathroom, but no unlocking any of the doors or windows."

"Okay."

"Get that downstairs," she said, piling another three pillows on top of his armload and swatting at his shoulder. "Go on. And don't worry so. It'll all work out fine in the end. It always does, doesn't it?"

*Not really*, Adam thought, but he was wiser than to say it. Working out fine would have been nobody finding out ever and no being bullied out of most of Manchester.

He shouldered the living room door open to find Ollie and Phoebe sitting cross-legged on the sofa, Charlie on the floor in front of it and the girls—doing his hair?

"What the hell?" Adam said.

"Social grooming," Charlie replied.

"Oh, shut your face," Ollie said. "We're combing it because this nest has *never* seen a brush."

"Why would it?" Charlie said. "I don't *have* a brush. I'm not a girl. Ow!" he added when Ollie hit him. Adam smiled, a little of his tension easing, and dumped the pile of bedding on the floor. "Ooh, pillows. Ols? I'm gonna smother you."

"You wish, bitch," Ollie said. She was looking remarkably feminine in baggy tartan pajama shorts and a white tank-top. She'd let her hair down, too, the curls kinked further by spending most of their lives in that messy bun. She looked...shockingly pretty. Prettier than Phoebe. And nobody did prettier better than Phoebe.

"You look nice," Adam told her and she preened.

"See, Charlie, Adam's nice," she said. "You tell me I look awful!"

"I'm practically your husband. I'm supposed to," Charlie retorted. He looked ganglier than ever in a too-large gray T-shirt and black pajama bottoms that seemed to be precariously clinging to his hips and not doing a very good job of it. At all, because if Adam stared hard enough, the material fell in just the right way to show that Charlie was packing in his underwear.

The door banged and he jumped as Mum marched in with the rest of the bedding. "Two of you will have to share the futon," she announced, barely glancing at them.

"I vote me and Charlie," Ollie said. "I wanna get my spoon on."

"Dirty cow," Charlie teased and ducked away from another slap. "Domestic abuse, man!"

"Shut your face before I shut it for you."

Adam let the noise of Ollie and Charlie just being...being

Ollie and Charlie wash around him as he helped Mum set up, then Dad was calling that dinner was ready and his parents had the usual argument of 'eat at the table' versus 'for goodness' sake, Mark, the carpet can be saved if there's any spillages!' and — as usual — Mum won, and —

And suddenly — Adam didn't know when or how — they were all sprawled out on the biggest sofa, Ollie murdering them all at one of Nat's old shooting games, and Adam's tongue was coming unstuck from the roof of his mouth without his brain being involved in the process at all.

"I have to tell you something."

"Can it wait until I blow Charlie's head off?" Ollie asked.

"Hey!"

"It'll only take a — oh, *yes*! Kiss it, baby," she gloated, presenting Charlie with her cheek. He groaned, seized her face in both strange hands and kissed her jaw. "I owned you."

"You usually do," Charlie complained.

"Okay," Ollie said, tossing the controller aside. "What's the big news-slash-secret-slash-thing?"

"Secret," Adam said and swallowed.

"Ooh, nice," she beamed. "Spill, then."

Adam opened his mouth — and nothing happened.

"Hey," Phoebe squeezed his hand. "Go on."

"You know?" Of course, it had to be Charlie who figured it out. It had to be.

Phoebe shrugged. "I kind of pushed a bit far and Adam told me. Adam? It's okay."

"It's not," he breathed. It wasn't. Charlie wasn't going to ever want to come near him again — and it would be *totally* down to the HIV. Completely, one hundred percent disease-related, because Charlie had kissed him, Charlie had wanted to touch him before and —

"Look, it's a big thing," Phoebe whispered to the others and shifted to put an arm around Adam's shoulders. "Adam, it's *okay*, I promise. If either of them get weird, I'll hit 'em!"

"Yeah, right," Ollie scoffed and Adam laughed croakily. "C'mon, Ads. If I can deal with Charlie McCrazy over here, there's no way you got a worse secret."

"Would you have dealt with...with McCrazy if you hadn't known him?" Adam whispered.

"Probably not," Ollie said, to Adam's surprise, "but he's my best mate, isn't he?"

"Aw, how cute."

"Shut your hole," she snapped at Charlie, who pulled a face. "And you're a mate, too, Ads, so spill it and we'll deal, yeah? We'll help out. If someone's giving you shit, I can set McCrazy on 'em. His hands scare small children."

Charlie sniggered and Adam's face shivered under a tremulous smile. "It's not a person," he said.

"Oh, can we guess?"

"Charlie!" Phoebe scolded.

"Are you secretly a girl?"

"What? No," Adam rolled his eyes.

"Do you wanna be a girl?"

"No!"

"S'cool if you do, man. I could use another partner in crime." Adam laughed again, even more croakily. Maybe it'd be easier telling them that. "Not gonna lie, *Rocky Horror Picture Show* looks fun. We could try it out."

"I'm not trans," Adam said. "It's...I'm...it's why I...it's why I shoved you."

Charlie's teasing expression faded. Phoebe's hand started rubbing circles on Adam's back and he swallowed.

"It's...I can't have...have relationships like normal people."

Another pause. Then Ollie very slowly said, "Why not?"

Adam bit his lip. He couldn't do it. He couldn't, but he couldn't *not* now he'd said that much, and Charlie was going to hate him. Adam didn't know if he could deal with that.

"Tell them, Adam," Phoebe whispered.

So he did. "I have HIV," he whispered into the quiet

warmth of his living room, putting his trust in Phoebe's judgment and in Charlie and Ollie to be the people he thought they were.

And nobody moved.

# Chapter Nine

"I have HIV."

Silence.

A long, ringing silence crept over every surface of the room. Adam's hand was sweating around Phoebe's when he grabbed for it and his stomach was churning as if he was going to throw up—and yet nobody moved, nobody said anything, and they were just staring and—

To his horror, his eyes started to itch and burn.

"I—" he croaked. "That's...I..."

Phoebe let go of his hand and hugged him instead, but she didn't say a word and neither did anybody else and... and Adam *felt* it—he could feel this attempt at having a fucking normal life just sliding away from him, and—

"Is this the bit where we group-hug?"

Charlie's voice was quiet and bemused but not...not angry. He didn't sound mad. Adam's chest shuddered and Ollie went, "Yeah I think so," and suddenly he was buried in...in people.

In friends. And his throat cracked and he started to cry.

"Oh, Ads, don't," Phoebe begged. "It's okay. It's *okay*. I told you, didn't I? I said..."

"You *did* know, then?" Ollie asked.

"Only recently."

Adam unstuck his throat. "I was...I was too scared to—you can't just get it off me. It's not like that," he blurted out hastily, fumbling for Charlie's arm and finding his wrist by Adam's ribs. He squeezed it and found himself being squeezed back in a hug. "You won't have—I..."

"Relax, man," Charlie said. His voice had gone from

*be*mused to *a*mused, that little lilt of levity back in it. "It's cool. I mean, you know, sucks for you, but unless you randomly decide to start biting people or this is a date-rape-sleepover thing…"

Ollie laughed. "In your dreams, Fielding."

"Ow! Get off my hair, woman!"

Adam coughed before joining in her laughter, more than a little hysterically. They were still…they were hugging him and bitching at each other, and—and they hadn't freaked out, or…

"I'm sorry," Adam mumbled, clutching Charlie's wrist again.

"For what?"

"For kissing you." He felt sick all over again. "You won't have caught it, I swear. My viral load's really low and I take my medication all the time and—"

"Hey, whoa, okay. Firstly, I have no idea what that means and secondly, it wasn't *that* hard of a kiss. I would have to be the unluckiest person in the universe, and I'm definitely just the unluckiest kid south of Scotland. There's kids in Glasgow with crappier luck than me, so it's cool."

Adam swallowed. "You're not…?"

"Kind of mad you didn't tell me sooner," Charlie whined. "What was I gonna do, beat you up?"

"As if," Phoebe said. "See, Adam? I told you they'd be okay."

"I just…I've…I've been through like a million schools and every time people found out, and it was…"

"HIV is nothing, man, Ollie's got a bad case of the crazy and that *is* infectious."

"*Oi!* Tit! Like you can fucking talk!"

Charlie was removed from the hug and Adam wiped his face on his sleeve and smiled as Ollie wrestled her so-called gay husband to the floor and attacked him with a pillow. Charlie curled up and bitched at her but did very little to defend himself. Phoebe giggled in Adam's ear and said, "Told you," again in a half-comforting, half-smug tone.

"Thanks, Feebs," Adam whispered, starting to feel less… less panicky. He'd said it. He'd said it and they hadn't freaked out and…and Charlie hadn't hit him for the kiss or stormed out, and… "Hey!" he raised his voice.

"What?" Ollie asked.

"Stop smothering him," Phoebe said reproachfully and Ollie sighed and removed the pillow.

"You thank her ladyship over there," she told Charlie sternly and got off his chest to return to the sofa.

"You guys can't tell anyone," Adam blurted out. "You *can't*. If it gets out, then—"

"What do you take us for, idiots?" Ollie demanded then snorted. "Well, okay, what do you take me and Feebs for?"

"Hey!" Charlie protested.

"It's okay, Charlie. You just can't remember dirty secrets to save your life," Ollie threw over her shoulder.

"Eh, true." He shrugged and settled on the floor in front of the sofa, hair re-ruffled after the girls' attempts to tidy it. "And no worries, Ads. Some people might not trust me, but I don't gossip about the important shit."

Ollie opened her mouth then frowned and closed it again. "Yeah," she said and Adam picked at the cushion on his lap.

"So," Charlie said, "is this topic closed, or do I get to ask totally offensive and ignorant questions like a jerk?"

"Um…"

"'Cause, like, I know what it is and I can't get shit from touching you or whatever, but what the hell is a viral load?"

Adam laughed then bit his lip and felt sick all over again. He hated explaining it. People got…people got weirded out more when they really knew about it and how much he had to do and the risks involved, and—

"Okay, Adam, it's okay," Phoebe said, squeezing his hands again. "We're not going to go mental on you, okay? If you don't want to talk about it, then—"

"No," Adam interrupted. "Just…it's kind of heavy. And I don't…I don't want you to…" *To freak out, to walk away, to ditch me at the last hurdle.* Because it was right there within his reach, the opportunity to get to be honest and not lie all the time and keep his friends anyway. And he was terrified of losing that chance at the last second, at coming so close only to have it taken away.

"Heavy's cool," Charlie said. "Ollie can do heavy."

"Yeah, you're plenty practice," she drawled but then ruffled his hair and offered Adam a rare, warm hug. "Go for it, Ads. We're all ears. Edumacate us."

"Um. Okay. Er…" Only…Adam didn't actually have a lot of practice at this, not really, and…

"If you want a starting point, what's a viral load?" Charlie offered.

Adam bit his lip. "Um. Okay. So…so you can take medication to keep the amount of HIV in your blood really low and if you do that you don't get ill, so…you've still got it, but there's so little of it you don't get ill and you…you have less chance of infecting other people and, um, you're healthier. And that's your viral load, how much of it there is, so…"

"So if the load's low, you're better?"

"Yeah," Adam said. "I mean, not better — there's no cure, but…yeah. I'm okay as long as that's low. And mine's always been really low. I was born with HIV so I've always taken my medication properly and everything."

"So, do you have to take like fifty billion pills a day or something?" Charlie pressed. "Are you like a crackhead?"

"Charlie!"

"What?"

Adam laughed and deflected the blow Ollie aimed in Charlie's direction. "It's okay."

"Charlie, stop being a knob."

"I'm not! I'm trying to get it! Anyway." Charlie waved his hand. "Pill popper? Are you one?"

"Um, no, just two. I can take just two pills a day 'cause one of them is two drugs in one pill. Some people have to take more than that, but I just have those right now. But I have to take them at exactly the same time every day, so..."

Ollie snapped her fingers. "Eight-thirty in the morning. Every time you've come to a sleepover, you're in the bathroom at eight-thirty."

Adam flushed. Charlie slowly turned his head to Ollie. "And why," Charlie asked, "did you even notice that?"

"Because of you and your 'bathroom trips' from yonder, nutter boy. Now shut your face."

Charlie snorted. "Poor excuse."

"Shut it!" Ollie threatened, stealing Adam's cushion and hitting Charlie with it.

"Ow!"

"How do you know your viral load is low?" Phoebe asked. The other two had let go, but she was still hugging him and Adam was painfully grateful for it. He felt edgy and raw, as though this was too good to be true and he was going to wake up any minute now.

"You have to keep having tests all the time," Adam whispered. "You can...have spikes, or the medication can stop working on you, so they keep testing and testing. And I have to have the flu jab every year and everything."

"S'it," Charlie said. "You're officially banned from the farm every September."

Adam flinched. "What?" he whispered.

"Not like that." Charlie rolled his eyes.

"His sister Immy gets the summer flu every September when we all go back to school, and she's disgusting," Ollie said and wrinkled her nose. "Seriously, one kid can't hold that much snot. Immy's gross."

"Tell me about it," Charlie grumbled. "I *live* with it. I babysit it!"

Adam smiled nervously. "She really bad?"

"Yeah," Charlie said. "She drips. And she doesn't cover her mouth when she sneezes so the entire room gets slapped with a layer of goo."

"Ew!" Phoebe shrieked.

"Yeah, so – you. Banned. No way am I taking responsibility

for you getting my sister's flu and sending your HIV crazy. Anyway. Are you gonna get AIDS?"

Adam scowled. "I'm trying not to!"

"Ignore him. He's a twat," Ollie said comfortably.

"Well, what's the diff?"

"AIDS is the end bit," Adam said, still frowning. "When your viral load goes up and up and you can't manage it anymore and it takes out your immune system. And if you take care of the HIV properly, it doesn't happen—loads of people don't get AIDS anymore. It's not the same thing."

"Got it, cool," Charlie said easily and Adam slowly relaxed. "So how do you get it?"

"You pop down the shops," Ollie said sarcastically.

"My mother had it when she was pregnant," Adam said shortly.

"What, your mum's got—"

"Not Mum-mum," Adam said and shook his head. "I don't want to go into that."

"'Kay," Charlie said. "So how do you, like, pass it on?"

"I'm not," Adam said desperately. "I'm not. I won't. Like I said, my—"

"No, not—Ollie," Charlie whined. "Translate for me, I'm being a twat."

"He means how would any old HIV-positive guy infect someone else," Ollie said and swatted at Charlie's hair. "You *are* a twat. Ads, you totes have permission to slap him."

Adam smiled faintly and reclaimed his cushion to pick at the threads. "Um. Bodily fluids," he said. "Blood and… and, um, semen. You can't get it through sweat or saliva, and it dies really fast if it gets out, so…you know, that's why you can't get it from touching me. Or kissing me," he added. "That's really rare and you need blood for that."

"Mmm, yummy, bloodstained kisses," Ollie said and she and Phoebe started giggling. To Adam's relief, Charlie's relaxed expression didn't change in the slightest.

"I can't—I mean, I know you were joking, but you wouldn't

get it from being bitten or anything, or—or sharing stuff, like towels or spoons and stuff," Adam continued hastily. This was the worst bit. Everyone always acted as if he was a leper or something, as though they could get it if he so much as sneezed. One kid at his last school had insisted Adam use the girls' bathroom so the boys couldn't catch it.

"Okay, so." Charlie held out his hands and started ticking off. "You're not ill at the minute and you're not likely to be?"

"Yeah."

"And it's pretty much crazy hard for one of us to get it from you?"

"Yeah."

"And you do all your drugs and stuff like you should so your disease count—"

"Viral load."

"—is really low, anyway?"

"Yeah."

"And we have to keep it quiet because other people are wankers?"

Phoebe giggled.

"Yeah," Adam said, squeezing her hand.

"Cool," Charlie said, dropping his hands. "Not that I wanna, you know, downplay the enormity of you telling us or anything, but—I really, really, *really* need some shit food right now."

"There's a first," Ollie said.

"No, I'm serious, I'm really hungry and I dunno why," Charlie said. "Fuck the diet sheet, man. I need crap."

"We have popcorn and fizzy drinks in the kitchen," Adam said, his heart clenching tight and releasing so suddenly he felt high. They didn't mind. They were okay with it and they didn't mind, and…

"Show me the wonders of your kitchen," Charlie commanded, staggering up from the floor. "Fuck, my ankle's dead."

"Bring me sugary things!" Phoebe implored as Adam got

up and he found a real, genuine smile.

"We got marshmallows."

"Oh my *God,* bring them all!" Ollie beamed and Charlie laughed, already halfway to the kitchen.

"She's got a sweet tooth the size of her head," he told Adam as they meandered into the kitchen. "So when did you find out?"

"About what?"

"The HIV." Charlie said it like it was so easy, like it was just a thing and not the disease it was and Adam—

Kind of loved him for it. Not that he'd ever *say* that.

Adam shrugged. "Always knew. I've always had to take the drugs. I was pretty sick as a baby. It's just...always been there."

"Feel free to tell me to piss off," Charlie said, his voice dropping as Adam passed him various things from the cupboards. "And feel free to tell me I'm totally wrong and it's because I'm an ugly minger and shit, but—is that why you wigged out and shoved me into Mr. MacFarlane's shed?"

Adam's heart hiccupped. He could...could save face, could put this crush to bed for good, could lie and say he hadn't meant to say it was why he'd pushed him, kill any chance Charlie would push *back,* and with enough time they'd both move on, right?

But then...Charlie had sat there and clearly, from his questions, had no real idea about HIV, but he'd...he'd not been weird and he'd brushed off the kiss and he'd been so *nice* about it when he had every reason not to be, so...

"Yes," Adam whispered to the cupboard.

"Why?"

Adam swallowed and put the bags of marshmallows on the counter. He turned to face Charlie and folded his arms, licking his lips. "Because of the HIV," he whispered. It felt strange to say it at all and even stranger because he was saying it to Charlie. "I can't have relationships, not with this."

"But if you didn't have it, you'd..."

"I'd have kissed you back," Adam admitted and his gut clenched.

For a moment, there was a silence — and suddenly Charlie was warm at Adam's front and —

And Charlie's top lip was chapped and the bottom one smooth. He tilted his head left instead of right like Adam imagined most people did it, and up so close he smelled of rain and lemongrass and the faint tinge of baking that always hung on his clothes from his mother's homemaking attempts. His fingers at Adam's jaw were cool and rough, but so gentle they were barely there and when Adam let him in and opened his mouth, Charlie tasted of orange juice, sharp and tart, and underneath that, of *want*. Dangerous and alluring. He — he *wanted* Adam and it was so scary and so thrilling to realize that, and —

Adam didn't know he'd closed his eyes until the kiss broke without a sound and Charlie's eyes from this distance were a dizzying, deep-sky-in-early-evening blue. His pupils were huge pools of black, like space itself, and the blue was the event horizon.

"No way everyone with HIV is celibate and alone," Charlie whispered, "and there's no need for you to be, either."

"I..." Adam breathed. His lungs were tight. His hand were flat against the counter behind him and he didn't remember unfolding his arms. He felt caught. He also felt as though he didn't necessarily want to get out of the trap, either.

"Maybe you ought to rethink your policy?" Charlie suggested then pressed a chaste kiss to Adam's cheek and — walked out. Just picked up the bags and wandered back into the living room like nothing had ever happened, like he hadn't just...

Just taken Adam's grudgingly accepted life, turned it upside and shaken the shit out of it.

# Chapter Ten

Adam woke with a start when the front door slammed.

Squinting at the TV, he twisted over under the duvet until he could read the clock on the DVD player. Ten past eight. Dad had gone to the supermarket, then.

The living room was a mess. Phoebe was nothing but a silent lump under a duvet on the camp bed. As promised, Charlie and Ollie had taken the futon when the vicious Mario Kart wars had died down around three in the morning, and Adam could just about see two shadows of dark, almost identical curls on one pillow. The lump there was only one and not two, and Adam pushed himself up on his elbows to blink and frown. They were so *close...*

Huh. Ollie hadn't been kidding. Charlie *did* spoon.

Adam slipped off the sofa, rubbing at his eyes, and made for the door. He could figure it out in a bit. Ten past eight meant he had a pill soon and anyway...he needed to actually *process* last night. Like seriously. He was...he was out. Right? It didn't apply to HIV, but...he was out anyway, yeah? They knew about him.

Charlie knew. And Charlie had...

Mum was coming down the stairs in her dressing gown and slippers when Adam emerged from the living room and she waved his blister pack of pills at him. "Kitchen," she said quietly. "Okay, honey?"

Adam licked his lips — and they tingled, as if the memory of that single at-the-counter-kiss occurred to them too — and smiled back. "Yeah."

Mum chuckled and ruffled his hair, leading him into the kitchen by the shoulder with a firm hand. "You told them, then?"

"Yeah," Adam whispered. The fridge door sounded too loud when he opened it and the glass milk bottles rattled tunefully. He pulled out the orange juice carton. "I told them. And they were...you know...okay." *More than okay.* "They were cool with it." *More than fucking cool.*

Mum made a motion and Adam ducked away from the incoming hug.

"Oh, all right," she said, rolling her eyes. "Is it just you up, or — ?"

Adam knocked back his pill and was about to say yes when there was a muffled thump from the living room. "Um," he said, instead. "Maybe not?"

For a brief second, there was silence — and the door cracked open and Charlie shuffled out in his pajama bottoms, hair stuck up all over the place, feet hidden in socks Adam didn't remember him wearing last night, and...Ollie's sleep shirt hanging open around his torso.

"Uh," Adam said, eyeing it. And the binder. And the shoulders sticking out of the top of it, all lean and lickable. He'd never seen Charlie in any state of undress before, and...er...

Charlie scrubbed a hand over his face, shuffling onto the kitchen tiles with slow, jerky steps. He moved almost stiffly, in little fits and starts. Zombie-like. But his face was open and relaxed, languid in a way Adam rarely saw, and for a moment there wasn't quite enough air in the room.

Mum looked startled, but it was washed away by a smile and genial, "Morning, Charlie."

"M'ning, Mrs. Wood." Charlie yawned then frowned. "Sorry. Um. Can I get a glass of water?"

To Adam's surprise, one of those strange hands emerged from the pocket of the pajama bottoms holding a silver blister packet with only two pills left in it. They rattled as Charlie's hand shook and Adam stared unabashedly. Mum, however, just started running the tap.

"Of course, you can, dear. We have juice if you'd prefer?"

"Water's fine, Mrs. Wood." His voice was deeper than usual, and raspy in a sleep-bruised manner. Adam's heart twisted in his chest, and something horribly…horribly fucking *girly* inside his chest, a sort of weird warm wriggle, made him want to reach out and hug Charlie.

Instead he just watched in mute fascination as Charlie took the offered water and knocked it — and the pills — back like a pro. Like Adam, even.

"What is it?" Adam blurted out and Charlie blinked slowly at him. Then again, faster, and the hazy sheen over brilliant blue was wiped away. A little bit of…something crept in. Alertness.

"Stuff."

"Yeah, but what medication is it?" He wanted to ask what for, but it didn't come out right.

Charlie frowned. "Just stuff I have to take."

Adam winced. "Sorry. Um, sorry, I don't mean to…"

"S'fine," Charlie mumbled, his voice dropping again, and he yawned before putting the glass back on the counter. "M'going back to Ols. She's warm. S'cold out here."

Adam half-smiled, watching Charlie shuffle back into the living room and the door snap shut, and jolted himself out of it when he saw his mother's soft expression.

"What?"

"Oh, nothing," she said and folded her arms around him. Adam was already taller than her, but it didn't seem to be putting her off. She hugged him, running a hand down the nape of his neck, before letting go. Adam scowled but she only laughed. Bloody *mothers*. Seriously! "Don't give me that look. And you didn't say Charlie was t—"

"Yeah, well, he is," Adam interrupted quickly, glancing at the door. He was pretty sure Charlie wouldn't like him gossiping about that.

"Go on, dear, go back to bed for a bit. I know you were up far too late, the lot of you. I'll put breakfast on around eleven and turf you all out of the living room then. How about that?"

Adam nodded, still staring at the closed living room door. He felt fidgety. He'd never really noticed Charlie half-asleep at Ollie's sleepovers, and he'd certainly never seen him without a shirt, and that second kiss...

"Go on," Mum said, nudging him. "What are you afraid of?"

"Ollie," Adam said. Obviously. "You should always be afraid of Ollie."

Mum chuckled. "Mm, I suppose I'm getting that idea. But I'm sure Charlie will defend you."

"I dunno," Adam said. "They're, like...nearly married."

"Well, you'll have to get them divorced if you want to be continuing anything with Charlie."

*"Mum!"* Adam hissed, flaming red, and Mum laughed and pushed him back toward the living room door.

"Get away with you," she scolded. "The look on your face just then, that's exactly what you're after, Adam James Wood." His face was burning. "Go on, get away with you."

Adam put a hand on the doorknob and paused.

"Hate you," he said, because it really *had* to be said when she was being so embarrassing.

"Yes, dear," Mum said blithely. "Go on. Get!"

Adam got.

Sleepovers with Ollie—and Adam was sure it was Ollie who always did this—ended in the tradition that everyone piled into the same bed and they'd watch bad morning telly while they all woke up together. Adam had always managed to get out of it before, mostly due to Phoebe taking pity and stopping Ollie from bullying him into it.

But he learned on Saturday morning that having come out of his little HIV closet meant no more getting out of Ollie's bundles, and...

Okay, so maybe he *still* wasn't liking the morning TV aspect, but...

The futon was enormous and Mum always put a king-sized summer duvet on it. And four bodies under a summer duvet was warm and Adam had been bundled in between

Phoebe and Charlie and…Adam didn't want to give Charlie any ideas or touch too much or whatever, but Charlie…

Charlie hadn't tried to kiss him again after the counter. They hadn't really touched last night after that. Everything had been normal, as though Adam had never said anything and Charlie had never kissed him at all, but now…

Now, Charlie had Ollie cuddled up against his chest on one side and his other arm around Adam's shoulders. And Adam hardly dared to breathe. He was looking at the TV but he wasn't really watching it. Charlie's arm was hot and heavy around Adam's neck and shoulders and Adam didn't know whether to pull away or squirm closer, and the end result was…

He didn't want to move. Just in case Charlie didn't mean for it to be there. And it was nice. Really nice. So Adam didn't want to move yet.

So he just…didn't.

* * * *

The first text arrived not ten minutes after Charlie's uncle dropped by in a battered Jeep for him and Ollie.

*Come over sunday.*

Adam swallowed. It was Charlie. Of course, it was Charlie.

*Why?*

*You n me need to talk, dont we?*

Adam sat down. Abruptly. He was in the kitchen — in theory, helping Mum clean up in preparation for Danni coming over tomorrow with the new babies — but suddenly his legs wouldn't hold him and he sat down with a thump.

*Do we?*

*Yeah. Or were your cokes spiked w/ rum last night? ;) i know n i still kissed you. You get me yet?*

Adam's fingers shook and he had to put the phone down on the table, clench and release his fists and pick it up again. Holy shit.

*Only 1 kiss.*

*Thats two total, anyway wasnt gonna kiss you in front of ols, you or her would have shoved me again ;)*

Adam bit his lip.

*You mean you want to kiss me again?*

*Yeah.*

Adam jolted. He…okay, yeah, he'd *kind* of guessed — hoped maybe — because Charlie had kissed him twice now, but…only twice. He'd not tried anything else last night. And the swift, frank admission…

"What's gotten into you?" Dad asked as he came in through the back door, stamping mud from the garden off his boots.

"Nothing," Adam mumbled, fumbling to text back.

*Are you serious?*

*Do i need to spell it out? i like you, you like me, you said if not for the hiv youd be interested, and i'm saying i'm not put off by it. so come over sunday afternoon after church n we can talk about it. y/n?*

Adam put the phone down again and licked his lips. Go over on Sunday. Telling Charlie didn't change the fact that Adam had HIV, didn't change the fact that he was contagious and couldn't actually…do anything. And what kind of guy wanted a boyfriend who could never do anything? Even kissing was risky and eventually...

Maybe not even eventually, maybe Charlie wanted to do all that other stuff now—he was bound to be more experienced than Adam, right?

But either way, nobody wanted a boyfriend who couldn't do any of that stuff and could give them a disease if he tried it, and Adam's nails were skittering on the wood as his fingers shivered on the edge of the table top. Charlie wanted to talk about it. Charlie wanted...something with Adam.

And Adam wanted it, but...

Maybe it would have been better to make Charlie think he wasn't interested after all?

"Honestly, that man, tracking mud all through the house, don't know why I— What's the matter, Adam?"

"Nothing," he said on autopilot.

"Uh-huh," Mum said, dropping a large box file onto the kitchen table and sliding her thin reading glasses onto the end of her nose. "So why do you look as white as the bits of the carpet your father hasn't tracked his wellies over?"

"It's not that bad!" Dad shouted from the hall.

"Just get the vacuum cleaner and fix it!" Mum shouted back and peered over the top of her glasses at Adam as she pulled piles of paper out of the box file. "So? What's the matter?"

*Dont overthink man. Come over sunday n we can work it out?*

"Charlie wants me to go over on Sunday," he whispered.

"That's nice," Mum said. "Well, as long as you show your face and see Danielle's twins, I don't see why—"

"Mum, last night..."

Mum paused.

"Charlie kissed me again," Adam mumbled.

Mum stopped entirely, her manicured hands frozen on the papers.

"After I told them," Adam said, "me and Charlie came to get popcorn and marshmallows from in here, and he asked if…if I wasn't, you know…would—"

"HIV positive."

"Yeah," Adam interrupted. *Not the time, Mum.* "He asked if I didn't have it, would I have kissed him back and I said yeah and he kissed me again."

"Well, then," Mum said. "And now he's asking you to go over and…"

"Talk about it," Adam whispered.

"Adam."

"I could still give it to him, Mum, I can't…"

"Adam!" He shut up at her sharp tone and her voice softened again. "Realistically, sweetheart? You won't."

"But—"

"You won't," Mum repeated firmly. "I am proud of you for how much consideration you give to your potential partners, but, darling, HIV doesn't mean you have to be abstinent. It means you have to be careful and your partner has to be fully informed and educated on what it all means. And that is *all.* Plenty of HIV-positive people are safely sexually active." Adam's face heated up at the words and their implication. "And you don't need to be any exception. Your tests have been coming back with a minimal viral load since that spell of illness you had when you were five years old, sweetheart. The risk is as low as it's ever going to be and if you've already told Charlie and he seems to be taking it in stride, then it sounds to me like you might have something to talk about."

"But what if I—?"

"And, quite frankly," Mum continued ruthlessly, "you are vastly overemphasizing sex. There's plenty more time in relationships spent simply being together. Your father and I—"

"I don't want to know!" Adam interrupted hastily, clapping his hands over his ears, and Mum snorted.

"It's life, sweetheart. You might have been delivered in a

car seat by a social worker, but the twins certainly weren't."

"*Muuuuum.*"

"So, are you going to go tomorrow?"

Adam eyed the text he hadn't answered. "Dunno."

"For what it's worth, darling," Mum said, scribbling notes on some of the papers in a flyaway manner, "I think you ought to at least give him the chance to say his piece. You do need to be careful, but I think if Charlie is willing to understand, then there's no reason you can't…talk about it."

Adam hummed. "Maybe."

"Which isn't a no," she pointed out.

Adam flushed. "I dunno, Mum. He doesn't know that much about it. I-I didn't exactly recite all the information leaflets last night, you know?" *Too busy being a total girl and crying all over Phoebe.*

"Well, how about you go over on Sunday like he asks," Mum said, "and see if he's willing to come back here and have a proper talk with your father about HIV?"

"Mum!"

"If he's mature enough to sit through that with your father and hear about the proper precautions the two of you would have to take, then maybe he's mature enough that you should think about giving him a chance?"

Adam bit his lip. "But…it'll…"

"Be embarrassing?"

The heat dialed itself up. "Yeah."

"You know," Mum said, shuffling the court papers back into a neat pile and tucking them into the box file, "your father and I discussed this when you were a little boy."

"Mu-um."

"Oh, hush up and listen," she ordered. "We discussed it before you even came out to us. And when you did, we simply changed the discussion to factor in a boyfriend one day."

"Are you serious?"

"Of course," she said simply. "You might have convinced

yourself for years you weren't allowed relationships, Adam, but your dad and I knew better. We planned for it and one of those plans is that your father sits down with you and whichever boy it is you snare first and talks to you both about the precautions you have to take."

"And you *want* me to invite Charlie to this?" Adam gawked. "I don't want it!"

"Tough," Mum said brutally, folding her hands on top of the box file. "I think it'll be a good test for him. If he's mature enough to sit through that, then I think you can boil this down to whether you *want* to go out with Charlie."

Adam bit his lip.

"If you didn't have HIV, would you?" Mum said, in an odd echo of Charlie's own question, in the very same room. Adam eyed the box file and started fidgeting with the clasp.

"Yeah," he mumbled.

"Then why don't you make this talk with your father the test?" Mum asked. "If he agrees and he takes it seriously, then I suggest you go with what you want and go out with him. If not, then he's clearly not to be trusted with this. Yeah?"

Adam's stomach clenched at the thought of Charlie being part of Mum's little 'not trusted' group and churned with the fear that he just didn't get it yet and Dad's talk would terrify him into running away like everyone else always had before.

But maybe Mum was right. Maybe if Charlie *did* sit through Dad's talk and got it, maybe then...

Then it'd be okay? To...kiss him again? Go out with him proper, just them without the girls, and...hold hands and all that girly stuff? Be...boyfriends. Or something.

"Maybe," Adam whispered, staring at his silent phone on the table. He clicked it back into the life and that last text shone up at him. "You think I should go over Sunday?"

"Adam, I think you already know what you're going to do."

He swiped his thumb across the screen as if absently

cleaning it. "Dunno."

"Mm," she said. "Well, you just let me or your father know if he needs to be giving any talks."

"Mum!"

"To quote your sister, Adam—whatever," she said and tapped the box file sharply. "Now, I have to run this down to the office. Apparently, Anderson is going to plead guilty and only decided to inform his solicitor this morning by text message, the inconsiderate berk." Whatever that meant. "I'll be back by two. Do you want me to pick anything up while I'm out?"

Adam screwed up his face, still eyeing his phone as if it was a bomb. "Ice cream and bananas," he said finally.

"Smoothie weekend?"

"Smoothie Sunday. Y'know. If Charlie says no."

Mum laughed and ruffled his hair. "He won't, but I'll get them anyway. See you later."

As she rattled around the hall and eventually slammed her way out of the house, Adam hit the reply function and—painstakingly, letter by letter—typed out a reply.

Only two letters, mind.

*Ok.*

# Chapter Eleven

Adam had never been to Charlie's house and he wasn't quite sure why. Everything just always happened at the girls', even though secretly Adam always wondered why a narrow, three-bedroom terraced house or a rectory was a better choice than a huge farm in the middle of nowhere.

And Stoker Farm was definitely a huge farm in the middle of nowhere.

It lay between Nympsfield and Uley — or as far as Adam was concerned, a drive out to Ollie's house and instead of turning onto her street, turn left and head out of the village into the land of potholes and high hedges. The turning that was marked for Stoker Farm was actually another dirt track that rumbled and roared under the wheels of Mum's car and at the end of maybe a three hundred meter 'road' loomed a squat, kind of ugly farmhouse covered in ivy and surrounded, in the gated yard, by chickens.

Lots of chickens.

"I'll just stop here," Mum said, eyeing them.

Various metal farm outbuildings popped up in a line off to the right, and from there — the minute Mum opened her door — came a frantic barking. A sheepdog skidded into the yard, yipping and howling, and started to chase its own tail.

"What the hell?" Adam asked.

"Maybe you should text Charlie and tell him you're here?" Mum suggested.

"Er, yeah."

He didn't have to. The dog tired of its tail, hurled itself at the gate to growl at Mum then took off around the back of the house and returned shortly afterwards dragging a little girl who was obviously Charlie's younger sister. She was about seven years old, with a lot of flyaway dark hair, and one of her little hands on the dog's collar was...odd. Like Charlie's.

"Oh," the little girl said and stuffed the edge of her jumper sleeve in her mouth.

"Uh," Adam said. "Is Charlie in?"

"Uh-huh." She didn't move.

"Um, could you get him?"

"Uh-huh." She still didn't move.

"Er."

Thankfully, Adam didn't have to try to work that one out. The front door of the farmhouse opened and a bony woman in an oversized jumper and riding boots came marching out.

"Imogen!"

Charlie ducked out behind her, seizing the still barking dog by the collar and grinning up at Adam as he hauled it away from the gate. "Sorry!" he yelled over his shoulder. "Dog's a bit mad. Just jump over the gate while I stuff him back in the milking yard."

Adam hesitated and Mum squeezed his shoulder. "Go on," she said. "Text me when you need picking up. And, Adam?"

"Yeah?"

"Don't overthink things, okay, sweetie?"

"*Mum,*" he whispered, glancing at Charlie's still-staring little sister. She sucked on her sleeve and blinked. Like Charlie, she had enormous blue eyes, only her stare was just creepy.

"Immy, back indoors," Charlie called, loping back across the yard. "Just jump over the gate, Ads. It won't bite."

Adam gingerly slid over the top of the gate and, when the dog didn't make an appearance, dropped to the dirt yard. "Bye, Mum," he called, trying to stop his fingers from shaking. He didn't know what he was doing here. Or what he was supposed to say. Or what he was going to decide to do.

"Don't mind Imogen," Charlie said as they crossed the yard back to the house, the little sister shuffling ahead of them and still chewing on her sleeve. "She's kind of special. She'll get normal once she's sized you up and shit. You wanna go in or you wanna explore?"

Adam eyed the jumper-chewing little sister and the bony woman still standing on the threshold and licked his lips. "Um. Explore," he decided.

"Okay. C'mon, I'll show you the puppies."

"Puppies?"

"Yeah." Charlie casually wandered aside, leading Adam around the side of the house and over another gate. The fields opened up here and a brown wooden barn stood in the middle of the nearest one. "This is just storage. We keep the tractors and stuff in here. We can talk and I'll show you the puppies. And don't look so scared."

"What?" Adam said, startled, and Charlie laughed.

"You look fucking petrified, mate," he said.

"I...might be," Adam admitted, sticking his hands into his pockets as Charlie heaved open the side door to the barn. It was wooden and rotting and the rusty hinges screamed. A dog barked and suddenly another sheepdog was nosing at their knees.

"Hello, Muffle," Charlie crooned, ruffling her ears. "Good girl. This is Ads. You gonna let him see your babies? You okay with dogs, Adam?"

"Generally," Adam said, smiling as the bitch licked his fingers. She was friendlier than the crazy one, he decided, then yapping reached his ears. "There's a whole litter?"

"Five of them," Charlie said. The inside of the barn was gloomy, the remains of a gutted Jeep against one wall, and the yipping came from the hay loft. "God knows why she had them up here. C'mon."

There was a skylight above the hay loft, which was a collection of large wooden crates, small piles of hay and battered sofa cushions. "You come up here often?" Adam asked.

"Yeah," Charlie said after a moment, settling down by one of the crates. Five bundles of fluff bounded against the wood and Charlie clicked his fingers at them. "Shurrup, you lot. Yeah, me and Ollie made a den up here when we were kids. The sisters are afraid of heights, so this is my spot now," he added. There was some unspoken *since* in there, something that Charlie had missed off, and Adam frowned. "Here."

Adam took the offered puppy. They weren't a foot long yet, all fur and oversized paws. It yipped and batted at his fingers, licking his skin in short, sharp bursts.

"You should take one," Charlie said over the discordant yipping. "We sell them anyway. We haven't got the time to train proper farm dogs anymore." And Adam heard it again. The *since*.

"Since?"

"Since what?"

"You..." Adam fidgeted, settling the puppy into the pen created by his crossed legs. "You always sound like you're about to say *since*. Since what?"

Charlie blinked and prized his forefinger free from a puppy that was attempting to gnaw it. "Since Dad," he said eventually.

"Since...?" Adam started then stopped.

"Since Dad died," Charlie clarified and Adam winced.

"Oh," he said awkwardly. He wanted to say he was sorry, but then he hated it when people said it to him. But then he couldn't ask what happened, because that was just... people just *shouldn't*, so...

"Dad used to work with the dogs most," Charlie said. "We haven't the time anymore, so if there's a new litter, we just sell them now. Ask your mum if you can have one."

"We can't," Adam said. "Dad's allergic."

"Shame," Charlie said.

"Mm."

"Get him some of those really good anti-bitch-a-mines and get one anyway?"

Adam laughed. "Anti*hist*amines," he corrected and Charlie rolled those incredibly blue eyes.

"Whatever," he said and lifted one of the puppies to coo at it. "You want to go home with Adam, don't you? Don't you?"

"That's disturbing."

"Yeah, yeah," Charlie said. He dropped the puppy back into the hay and rolled onto his front to peer at Adam, resting his chin in his upturned hand. "So."

And just like that, there were the nerves again—the clenching stomach, the tight chest and the shivery feeling in Adam's hands.

"So?"

"*So.*"

Adam licked his lips and twitched. "Um. So what?"

"So tell me about you, man," Charlie said. "We got no Ollie, we got no Phoebe and you never talk to me. After Ollie's birthday, I wasn't even sure you wanted to be in the same *room* as me."

Adam flushed.

"I mean, I figured maybe you would again after you finally spilled your beans about the whole HIV thing because, you know, I get it, Feebles is like the most unscary person to tell anything ever but you're still doing it. The silent trick."

Adam flushed harder and picked at the hay. One of the puppies, a tiny ball of fuzz with very lopsided ears, pounced on his fingers, but he just shook it off. "Yeah, well," he mumbled. "You make me nervous."

"*I* make you nervous?"

"Well, yeah. I like you." His tongue felt thick and clumsy, but when he dared to glance up, Charlie just smiled a wide, crooked smile that made Adam's heart twitch.

"C'mooooon," Charlie wheedled, and extended a hand to prod Adam in the knee. "Stop being nervous and talk to me. I want to know some new kid secrets, too. It's not *faaaair.*"

He sounded so much like a little kid that Adam managed to muster up a chuckle and shrugged awkwardly. "I just… the boys at my last school were much worse than the girls," he mumbled. The girls hadn't been a picnic, either, but Adam'd been tall since he was thirteen so the girls hadn't gone beyond sneers and whispers and skirting around him in the hall as if he was going to explode.

The boys…

"Yeah, well, take it from me, I can't bully people to save my life and it's not like you haven't got enough dirt on me to bully back," Charlie said loftily and wrinkled his nose. He had freckles building under the skin. They'd erupt soon and they crumpled up like shadows under paper. Adam watched, blinked and tore his gaze away. "If I could bully people," Charlie said, "I'd start with Erica."

"Erica?"

"My other sister," Charlie explained. "She's eleven. That's eleven years I've not had my own dessert at dinner. She thieves it *every time*. She just blinks those big pretty eyes at Mum and *boom*! My ice cream is gone."

Adam laughed again, but there was something a little high and a little too shaky in it. Charlie's eyes were the bluest things he'd ever seen and the way Charlie was looking up at him…it was like he was seeing through Adam and Adam wasn't sure he liked it.

"I…" he said, ready for his speech, ready to tell Charlie why a relationship would be a bad idea.

"Where d'you come from, then?"

Adam blinked—and relaxed. Minutely. This bit…this bit was okay. People didn't mind this bit. "I'm adopted," he said and Charlie tilted his head. Then his whole body, rolling over onto his back and watching Adam upside-down. "I got the HIV from my…biological mother. But my parents adopted me right after I was born."

"The Woods?"

"Yeah."

"So your name wasn't Wood?"

"No," Adam said. "She was a drug addict, the woman, so they took me away." She hadn't been his mother, because there was no way of saying it without sounding weird that wasn't 'real mother' and *Mum* was his real mother. "I wasn't called Adam, either, but I can't remember what Mum said I was called. But she was a drug user and they reckon she used dirty needles. Hence me."

"You came from a dirty needle?" Charlie said incredulously. *"Wow,* man. Seriously? That's amazing. I just came from a dirty old man. How does a dirty needle...?"

"Oh, shut up," Adam huffed and sprinkled hay on Charlie's face.

Charlie brushed it off and sat up cross-legged, grinning. "No way, I want to know how you get a baby from a dirty needle."

"Oh, shut up," Adam insisted. "I got adopted. I don't even remember her. I've never met her." He wasn't even sure what *her* first name was, either, and he had no interest in finding out. His family was a million times better than some druggie with dirty needles.

Charlie nodded, plucking one of the puppies away from an escape route and dropping it back into the crate.

"Do you..." Adam paused. "You know. Your dad. Do you remember him?"

Charlie stared then chuckled. "Well, yeah," he says. "I was nine."

Adam bit his lip, shredding the hay again. "What happened?"

Charlie shrugged. "He just died. He got ill and died. One day he was here then he wasn't anymore."

Adam bit his lip. Charlie's face had closed up again and Adam decided against probing any more. "M'sorry," he said uselessly.

"S'fine. So. Your parents," Charlie said, brushing off his father like he brushed off his face. "Are they old fussy people or are they cool? They seemed pretty okay on Friday."

"They're okay," Adam said.

"Do they know you're…?"

"Well, yeah, they kind of tell you that when you adopt a baby."

"I meant that you're gay."

Adam paused. *Here it goes.* "I…um…"

"Uh," Charlie said. "Relax? You've gone, like, white."

"Sorry, I just…I don't know if…"

"Do your parents know you're gay?" Charlie prompted.

"Does it matter?" Adam demanded.

"Might do. Look, honesty-box confession time? I'm trying to work out what your problem is."

"Excuse me?"

"I'm trying to work out," Charlie said ruthlessly, "why you're so…wary of me. I mean, you keep saying you like me, and I've liked you for ages, but even after I kissed you at Ollie's party—actually scratch that, you got *worse* after the party—look, what I'm trying to say is you go out of your way to avoid me and I'd have thought we've established you don't have to? Only…you know, you still are. I had to persuade you to come here. And climb over the gate."

"The gate was about the dog," Adam tried weakly.

"The rest of it isn't," Charlie said.

"That's the HIV. Not…the gay thing. My family all know about me."

"Okay, your parents are pretty cool, then. So—are you not?"

"With what?"

"Being gay?"

"I—uh…"

"Because if you never liked girls before, and you like me, you're still gay."

"Am I?" Adam blurted out.

It sounded awful, but—*was* he? Charlie was…well… obviously not, um, equipped like Adam was. It was obvious what was marked on his birth certificate, that was all.

"Yes."

Adam licked his lips.

"I know what I look like, Adam, but I'm a boy. I'm getting more boyish the older I get. With my dad's beard, in ten years I'll look more like a boy than you. And you're never getting any boob out of this, so..."

"Good," Adam blurted out, then colored. "Sorry. Sorry, I—"

Charlie just laughed.

"It doesn't—that's not the issue."

"Be honest with me. If it is, I can take that. But be honest. I know what I am. I have no problem with what I am, or with people who do. It's the skirting-around-me bullshit I don't like."

"It's not the issue," Adam repeated firmly. "I mean, okay, maybe it's not as simple anymore, but that's not why. I mean...I don't really care if I'm gay or bi, you know?"

"Okay. So it *is* just the HIV?"

"HIV isn't *just* anything."

"You're still avoiding me like...like...like I have..."

"HIV," Adam supplied bitterly and Charlie pulled a face.

"If I did, would you be avoiding me? In our honesty-confession-box thing?"

In their honesty-confession-box thing? "No," Adam whispered and felt an entirely different kind of sick for it. Like Charlie having HIV would be a *good* thing, like...

"Then...can you stop avoiding me?" Charlie asked. "Can we try actually working this thing out?"

Adam swallowed.

"It feels kind of shitty," Charlie continued. "I mean I know I'm not exactly...I don't know, some gay model I've never even heard of, but whatever. I know I'm weird and lanky and kind of stupid-looking and—kind of stupid in general actually, but—"

"No, you're not," Adam interrupted.

"But I like you," Charlie said. "And in those bits between me turning up and you running away, I kind of got the impression that you liked me, too. And I want to do something about that."

"I…" Adam croaked, and it was like his worst nightmare and his dream come true kind of happening at once and smashing into each other. Because Charlie wanted a relationship, which was Adam's dream come true, but…he wanted a relationship. Which was Adam's worst nightmare.

They couldn't, not with this disease in Adam's blood, not with…

He didn't know what to do. There was a panic rising in his chest and he felt dizzy and he didn't know what to do because Charlie wanted to be with him and it was the worst-best thing ever and…

The burn took him by surprise, then Charlie made a noise and there were tears, and…and a hug. Adam was suddenly wrapped in warm arms. He was being hugged, by someone outside his own family, by someone he knew from school, by someone who liked him and wanted a relationship with him and wasn't afraid to touch him even though the someone knew…

He buried his face in his hands and let go.

"I've never made a boy cry before," Charlie mused next to his ear and Adam laughed through a wet, kind of disgusting sniffle. "Um, why are you crying? I mean, you know, I have sisters, I can do the hugging thing, but…I'm a bit confused here."

"You *can't* like me," Adam croaked.

"Really?" Charlie said. "Well, that's shit. Why not?"

"I'm—I-I can't," Adam said. "I can't have…I can't do anything, not with…not like…not *positive*. I can't!"

"Wait, so…you can't go out and have fun and do all that nice stuff because you're positive?"

"It's not fun. You could…if we…"

"Okay, um, I'm not, you know, saying I'm up for having a roll in the hay right here and right now. I'm saying…you know, we could go out. Date. Kiss. Hug without one of us in pieces. Hold hands."

"Yeah, but eventually…"

"Adam!" Charlie shook him a little without letting go and Adam scrubbed at his face and tried to compose himself. "I like you. You like me. It's that easy. We can, you know, do research. I mean, come on, there's no way every positive guy on the planet is celibate. What the hell, man? You'll be like forever alone and that's really gay, in the totally sad and pathetic closeted twink drinking himself to death in a Wetherspoon's kind of way. Not the awesome sexy let's get shirtless at Pride way."

Adam wrapped a hand around Charlie's wrist. Both of Charlie's arms were around him and he was really warm and there was a sadistic little part of Adam's brain that wanted to say *fuck consequences* and hug him back and soak up all the warmth and ignore it.

"I can't give this to you, Charlie. I *can't.*"

"And you won't if we're careful about it, but we're also jumping the gun, like, massively," Charlie said. "We might hate each other, or you might secretly like to, I don't know, build guillotines for rabbits in your spare time. Let's worry about the whole sex thing when we get there, because I am not man enough to lie and say I am there yet. No way. And neither would you be if your mum's sex talk is anything like my mum's sex talk."

Adam was wavering. He wavered and he wanted to give in and he wanted to not and...

"Come on, Adam," Charlie wheedled close to his ear. "I'm not stupid. We'll be careful. And it'll be ages before we get to the risky business anyway. You keep saying there's no reason people can't touch you normal, right?"

"I..."

"It'll be fun," Charlie whispered, and his hair was tickling the side of Adam's face. "Come on." And he untangled his locked hands to hold one out in front of them, the right one, palm up and those strange fingers splayed wide. Adam's face felt puffy and he was shivery and cold now one of the warm arms had gone, but...

He slid his fingers into Charlie's and Charlie squeezed.

"No problem, right?" Charlie said.

"We have to be careful," Adam whispered.

"Is that a yes-we-can-give-this-a-go?"

Adam swallowed. "I...I don't know."

"No problem," Charlie repeated but in a gentler voice. That softer tone that was so rarely there. The little glimpses of someone a bit more vulnerable under the madcap mania that Adam'd seen but not really managed to find. "Come on," Charlie added, and stood. He tugged on Adam's hand. "Stop leaking tears and stuff. It's depressing. Let's explore more. I'll show you the ruin, too. I think there's some kittens in there, but the mother cat's feral or crazy or infested with crazy fleas or something so we can't play with them."

For a moment, Charlie was framed by the sunlight pouring in through the open barn door and his hair created a dark fluffy halo around that narrow, white face. He looked like some imperfect, hastily constructed imitation of something supernatural. And it made Adam unglue his lips and tongue and say, "Okay."

"Okay what?"

"Let's...I don't know. Give it a go?" Adam whispered.

Charlie paused then grinned and pulled on Adam's hand again. Adam wasn't quite sure what it meant, or where Charlie was really going to lead him—besides the ruin—and yet, for the first time, he decided to just let himself be led somewhere unknown.

# Chapter Twelve

"Dismissed. Mr. Fielding. A word."

Adam scowled. It was Monday, right before lunch, and Bastard Bagshaw wanted *a word*. Of course, he bloody did. Adam was itching to—to—he didn't even know, but to be with Charlie for a bit, having not seen him that morning, or at all since the afternoon at Stoker Farm, and…and had he told Ollie yet, and could Adam tell Phoebe, or…?

"Meet you outside?" he asked, going for casual and instead going red when Charlie glanced up from gathering his books, those blue eyes wide and distracted.

"Eh? Oh! Yeah," he said, and grinned. "Won't be a minute."

"Now, if you don't mind, Mr. Fielding. I wouldn't want to interrupt your busy social life," Mr. Bagshaw drawled.

Adam shut the classroom door behind him and waited at the glass, clutching his folder to his chest and hating the teacher with an intense passion for a moment, basking in warm rage. It wasn't fair. The first day with Charlie…well, *with* Charlie. And Bastard Bagshaw was eating into their lunch hour together. Adam wanted to get down to business, like knowing if they could tell the girls, and maybe once they got out onto the playing fields where the other kids wouldn't see, he'd be able to hold Charlie's hand again for a little bit.

Peering through the glass, he frowned, wondering what Charlie had done. The lesson had dragged in total silence, Charlie staring at the new approach to calculating cosine and Adam staring at the back of Charlie's head. There hadn't been any messing around to break it up, so why—

Adam blinked as Bagshaw handed Charlie a book. A huge fat monstrosity of a book—maths, judging by the numbers on the cover—and one that was rapidly hidden inside Charlie's own folder.

"What's that?" he asked when Charlie finally came out, and Charlie flushed.

"Er..."

"I thought you were getting bollocked."

"No," Charlie said. "Bagshaw's okay. He's, um...he's trying to get me to do the A-level papers in the summer. S'well as the GCSE. Um."

"You're going to do the A-level?"

"Maybe." Charlie went red.

"Wow," Adam said. "What's the book?"

Charlie cracked the edge of the folder open. *An Introduction to Spatial Statistics* smiled back at the pair of them and Adam whistled.

"Wow," he said again. "Feebs was right. You're mental good at maths."

Charlie's red headed into purple. "Shut up," he mumbled. "S'not that hard."

"Yeah, okay," Adam said and bit his lip. "So, um, I meant to ask..."

"Uh-huh?"

"Did you tell Ollie?"

"About the A-level?"

"About...you and me." *Us* sounded a little too strange just yet.

Charlie grinned. "Nope."

"Um, is it...okay...to?"

Charlie snorted. "Ads, if I didn't think you'd freak out and break my wrist, I'd hold your hand here. I don't fucking care."

Adam smirked around the teeth he was digging into his lip. "I don't think I'm there yet."

"S'cool," Charlie said. It just rolled off his tongue, so calm and casual that Adam wanted to hit him and kiss him all at once and it was a weird feeling.

"I'm just...not ready for everyone to know," he said quietly. "I mean, not the girls. They don't count. They're fine, but — everyone else, you know?"

Charlie caught his elbow, and Adam was suddenly hauled sideways into the boys' toilets at the end of the corridor — the ones just shy of the science block, always empty at lunchtime because they were farthest from the canteen, and sure enough they were empty now. Just as well, when Charlie pushed him up against the door and kissed him hard enough that Adam couldn't breathe and didn't want to. Charlie's hands were fists in the front of Adam's blazer and his mouth was hot as a branding iron — and Adam had thought he'd known butterflies in his stomach before, but he hadn't.

"Um," he breathed when Charlie let go.

"S'up to you," Charlie said. "Long as I get some covert snogging now and then, yeah?"

Adam grinned, cupping the back of Charlie's neck and grasping a handful of that rule-hating hair. "Yeah," he said and pressed a fleeting kiss to the edge of Charlie's mouth. His heart felt shivery. His blood felt too hot in his veins. He wanted to just get under Charlie's skin and figure him all out, but...he couldn't.

For more reason than one.

"The girls'll be waiting."

Charlie groaned.

"C'mon."

"Bully," Charlie accused but let go proper and Adam opened the bathroom door again, hoping he didn't look as flushed as he felt. "We could have taken five minutes."

"It wouldn't have been just five," Adam mumbled and Charlie laughed as they passed through the doors out onto the edge of the playing fields. "You're a bad influence."

"What, me?"

"Yeah, you," Adam grumbled and laughed when Charlie batted his eyelashes. "Oh, shove off."

"Some snog *you* are," Charlie griped then put the fingers of his left hand in his mouth and whistled. Piercingly. "*Oi! Ollie!*"

She waved. Despite the chill in the air, she and Phoebe were sprawled out in the grass by the bleachers at the athletics track and Adam hunkered down by Phoebe as Ollie engaged in her customary way of greeting Charlie and rugby-tackled him.

"You okay?" Phoebe squinted at him. "You look flushed." Her long hair was undone and everywhere — apparently in the midst of a tweaking, judging by the hand mirror she was holding.

"Er," Adam said. "Yeah. M'fine."

"Why're you two so late?" Ollie demanded once she'd let Charlie out of his headlock. He flopped down on the grass beside Adam and promptly turned over to grin at her upside-down.

"Bagshaw," he said.

"Urgh, what'd you do?"

"Nothing!" Charlie protested. "Oh, my God, what is it with you people suspecting me?"

"Because we're always right," Phoebe teased, sticking out her tongue. "I'm screwed, by the way," she added dramatically. "Miss Young's off sick again — she's *so* pregnant — and Mr. Ashburner's covering French. I haven't practiced any of the vocab."

"You could practice it now," Adam suggested as he pulled apart his sandwiches to investigate whether Mum or Dad was guilty. Ham and cheese. Mum, then — Dad liked to think himself inventive. "What?" he asked when Phoebe gave him a dirty look.

"As if," she said. "I'll say I threw up and go to the nurse's office after lunch."

"Your mum'll — speaking of lunch, Mum gave me this for you," Ollie interrupted herself, tossing a Twix at Charlie. "Ooh, and speaking of lunch, guess who's dissecting a frog afterward?"

"Are we taking bets on who's gonna chuck it?" Charlie asked, peeling open the Twix.

"You know it."

"I bet a cinema ticket on Rachel."

"Rachel A. or Rachel B.?"

"B. Obviously." Charlie snorted.

"No way, it'll be Grace, she's…"

Adam tuned the girls out when Charlie offered him half of the chocolate bar. When Adam took it, Charlie slid their hands together. Adam squeezed, willed his stomach not to churn quite *that* violently — because he sort of maybe had a boyfriend now — and bit down on the chocolate.

"I still vote Rachel B. She's a total pussy," Charlie insisted around his own chocolate, then crumpled up the wrapper in his free hand and tossed it at Ollie. "She'll puke or faint. Ooh, can I change my bet to faint?"

"Nope," Ollie said easily. "I take faint. Feebs?"

"Grace."

"And Ad — whoa. Whoa, whoa, whoa. What is that?"

Adam flushed red as Ollie pointed at their joined hands. And pointed, frankly, like she'd seen a cockroach.

"What is that?" she shrieked again. "Charlie!"

Charlie blinked and lifted their joined hands. "I think," he said slowly, "it's Adam's hand. Ads? Is that your hand?"

"Yeah," Adam said, and Phoebe started giggling.

"Let me clarify. Let me just outline this and wrap it up and shit," Ollie said. "Specifically, what is Adam's hand doing touching your hand?"

"Ummm…" Charlie said, turning their joined hands over again. "I *think* it's called holding hands. I think. I mean, you know, I might be wrong, but I'm pretty sure — ow!"

"Tease!" Phoebe said, retracting the hand she'd used to hit him. She hugged Adam's other side, beaming from ear to ear. "Dating! You're dating!"

"Well, um —"

"Yep," Charlie said then was forcibly dragged away from Adam by Ollie, being bundled over in the grass and pummeled in the chest. "Hey! Bitch!"

"You didn't tell me you're dating!" Ollie hollered. "You're such a dick! You suck!"

"Umm…" Adam said.

"Don't mind them," Phoebe said and tugged on his arm. "When did this happen? You both kept it quiet—that's not fair!"

Adam felt his face burning again and very carefully kept his gaze on Charlie and Ollie wrestling in the grass. If he looked at Phoebe, he'd probably have a stroke. "Yesterday," he said.

"*Yesterday?*" the girls cried in unison and Charlie yelped as his arm was twisted behind his back.

"Lay off, Ols!"

"We worked it out," Adam said, as Ollie started demanding compliments in exchange for Charlie's arm, which she had jammed into his back. "I went up to Stoker Farm yesterday and we talked about it and…yeah."

"And, yeah, you're dating?" Phoebe prompted.

"Well…"

"Yes, now get this crazy witch off me!"

Phoebe laughed and clambered up to push Ollie off. Adam hauled Charlie back toward himself once the girls had started their own shoving match and found that hand again to hold it.

"Okay?" Charlie asked lowly, and Adam grinned.

"Yeah," he said. It might take some getting used to, being teased about dating and stuff, but…it was okay. It was more than okay.

"Sure?"

"Uh-huh."

"I'm not convinced!" Ollie yelled.

"Oh, piss off!" Charlie whined.

"You're having us on!" she insisted. "C'mon, pucker up!"

"Not a chance. It'll be on Instagram in about five seconds!"

"Grope hard or go home."

"Ollie!"

"Nope." She folded her arms over her chest and Adam groaned.

"We might as well," he said.

"Okay, fine, but—phone."

Ollie sighed and handed her phone over. Charlie tucked it into his pocket.

"And I'm taking revenge."

"You what?"

Adam glanced across the field. They were way out on their own and nobody would see if they were quick about it.

Charlie was mid-protest when Adam kissed him. But he shut up pretty fast, so…yeah.

\* \* \* \*

"You."

Adam was getting used to being yanked into bathrooms. "Ollie?"

"No, it's Tinkerbell," she said snidely, and folded her arms. She was dressed in her kit, ready for the after-school hockey practice, and somehow it was even more intimidating than the usual blazer-and-black-trousers combination. Maybe it was the cap pulled low over her curly hair, making that sharp, tan face even sharper.

Adam could feel his guard going up and tried forcibly to lower it.

"You and Charlie a thing now?"

"Uh. Yeah."

"You don't sound sure."

"I don't know if you're gonna hit me."

She snorted and rolled her eyes but uncrossed her arms. "Look," she said. "I like you, but fact is? Charlie's my bestie. He and me, we're like married. We've been together since we were five and you don't change that."

"Er…"

"I don't want to sound so trite and shit, but…you two get

into a fight, even if it's 'cause Charlie's being a fucked-up prick, I'm not on your side, okay?"

"Um, okay."

"And...you've got to be ready for Charlie," she said. "He's...he's my best friend and all, but he's not exactly right in the head all the time, yeah? And if you...if you put him through all of this shit to get close to him and cut and run first time you see him really lose his shit then you can cut and run *now* and not make me have to see him through it with an episode on top of it."

"Ollie, I don't know what you're talking about," Adam blurted out. He got it, okay? Charlie had had some weird mental stuff happen—he was bipolar or whatever—but... "He got mad at me the other week. That's why I eventually told you all about it. And..."

"No, he didn't."

"Sorry?"

Ollie heaved a sigh. "Look, Charlie's...he's not well, okay. Upstairs."

"Will you and Phoebe stop talking in riddles?"

"You're not the only one who doesn't want things aired all over the place," she snapped. "There's rumors and shit but nobody—not even Feebs—nobody but me here knows how bad he really got. Okay? He didn't just have a little freak-out. He got *really* ill and I—"

She stopped. Sharp and abrupt, the way...

The way Adam recognized from himself. The way he'd stop if someone conned him into talking about his old schools and old friends a little too much. And a cold feeling began to work its way up his spine.

"I figured for a while I was gonna lose my best friend," Ollie said quietly and that just floored Adam. She spoke quietly. Ollie didn't do quiet. She was kind of like Charlie— okay, a lot like Charlie—in that she either said nothing at all or she was mad-crazy-hyper and screamed it. "And he's... he's better, but he's not okay and you don't put him back there."

"I don't know what you mean," Adam said, "but I never thought I'd ever date anybody. Charlie...he just kept pushing, you know? And I let him. That says something, right? I don't know where it's going, but..."

"Don't change your mind and lock him out again," she ordered.

Adam swallowed. "What happened, Ollie?"

She pursed her lips and exhaled heavily through her nose. "I'd like to tell you," she said. "I could use the help, you know? But he won't let me."

"Charlie?"

"Yeah. He gets embarrassed and stupid about it. He was sick. It wasn't his fault, but he gets stupid. Kind of like you."

Adam flushed. "It's different."

"It's not really," she said. "There's *no* way that you could catch what he has, but...it's not that different. Sick's sick, you know."

"What was he sick with?" Adam asked. "Phoebe said it was...mental."

"Mm." She was frowning. "I can't tell you, Ads. I keep telling him to tell you and if you can get it out of him then do, but I can't tell you. For a while I was the only person he'd ever talk to and I won't betray that. 'Cause if he found out I told you, I won't be able to do anything next time."

"Next time?"

She grimaced. "Well. Some of it has a next time and some of it doesn't and...look, you'll have to get it out of him. I just can't."

For a moment, a weird understanding sat between them — which was kinda strange. Adam had never really got Ollie. He liked her well enough — she could be crazy fun — but she was Charlie's friend, not his. She wasn't anyone else's friend the way she was Charlie's. He had been genuinely surprised when Phoebe had dropped, a few weeks after Adam had joined the school, that Charlie was gay and not Ollie's boyfriend. Charlie and Ollie were like one person sometimes and so Adam had never felt close to Ollie like he did to Phoebe. It wasn't possible, not the way Ollie's loyalty so blatantly lay with Charlie all the time.

But at that moment, an understanding existed.

"You'll be late for hockey."

"You'll be late for him," Ollie said and grinned. "I heard rumors of going back to your house?"

Adam flushed. "Yeah. Well. Y'know. Video games and a widescreen TV."

"Uh-huh, sure."

"Oh, shut up," he mumbled and she laughed, stepping aside to let him out of the bathroom.

"Get gropey, then I can interrogate him tomorrow," she advised and Adam's face burned.

"Shut up, Ollie!"

They parted ways at the courtyard, Ollie peeling off toward the gym and Adam heading up toward the bike sheds and bus stops. Phoebe and Charlie were sitting on the wall behind the bike shed, heads together to peer at her phone screen and sniggering.

"It's a cat on a skateboard, look," Phoebe offered, but Adam ignored it, lounging against the wall and smiling when Charlie obnoxiously ruffled his hair. "Stop being so hands-off, you two!"

"Fag-hag," Charlie sneered.

"Shut up and snog," she said, raising the phone.

"We did earlier. Should have got your porno picture then."

Adam hit Charlie's knee. Charlie laughed and suddenly ducked his face to kiss the top of Adam's head. Phoebe's phone clicked.

"Awwww," she cooed.

"That's all you're getting. Exhibitionist whore."

"You're the one who showed off in public," she teased and slid down from the wall. "Mum's picking me up. I figured you two might want to go home together," she added.

"Go on, then, shoo," Charlie said and she laughed. The moment she vanished around the corner of the shed,

Charlie grinned that wide, shit-eating grin and Adam bit his lip. "C'mon, then."

"C'mon, what?"

"Nobody can see us."

Adam felt his mouth twitching into an answering smile. "Can't reach you up there."

"So get up here."

"No. You come down."

Charlie snorted. "Dude, come on, get your arse up on this here wall."

Staring up at that lofty expression, flyaway hair and crooked smirk, Adam found it both impossible to believe and impossible to doubt that Charlie was anything more complicated than what was right in front of him. That there was some damage beyond his odd hands and gangly limbs.

That there was anyone more fucking beautiful, and shut up, it was not girly.

Adam planted his hands on the wall either side of Charlie's hips and stretched, rising right up on his toes to reach and curling his fingers into the crumbling old stone and pushing hard for that last inch.

The kiss tasted like summer was coming.

# Chapter Thirteen

*Come over after school? :) x*

Charlie had taken to putting kisses on his texts and Adam swore it was only because they made him blink and fumble for a reply. Charlie was *sadistic*.

*You could stay the night, have our own private sleepover ;) x*

The fumble was replaced by a flush, and it wasn't exactly convenient. He was in the middle of chemistry, for God's sake.

*Haven't got an overnight bag or anything.*

*Who needs one?? x*

Adam swallowed. Yeah. Uh. How about no? Of course, he needed one because Charlie had no idea—
Scratch that. Charlie was sadistic—he'd just covered this. Of *course* Charlie knew he was being tempting. And he was being an arse.

*You're tempting me when you shouldn't.*

*Tempting would be telling you i sleep in the nude ;) x*

Adam stared intently at his textbook for a long minute before daring to slide the phone back out from under the desk and replying, *You're evil. I could come over for the evening?*

*Shall take what i can get ;) Meet you by the bike sheds after school? x*

"Mr. Wood, I know you're texting."

Adam jumped and groaned, dropping his phone into his bag hastily.

"People don't stare at their crotch and smile without good reason, Mr. Wood," Mrs. Dunstable — a teacher who got free facelifts by scraping her hair into the tightest buns possible at the top of her head — drawled. The class sniggered. Adam ground his teeth and prayed for lightning to strike and obliterate her.

But no such luck. Maybe he should start going to church with Charlie.

"Sorry, Mrs. Dunstable," he mumbled and wished for the whiteboard to fall on her instead. Seemed he had to start small with these prayer thingies.

She harrumphed and returned to the joys, the rapturous wonders, the — uh — astounding pleasures of ionic bonding and the stupor re-settled over the room. Adam picked at the skin of his hands and stared at the diagrams in the book without really seeing them. He wanted to go, but... Charlie had wanted him to stay the night. Which meant Charlie wanted to do stuff. And Mum had said Dad needed to give them some weird talk thing, but Charlie wanted to do stuff *now,* and...

And Adam wasn't ready for stuff, or for an excruciating talk from Dad.

But then maybe Charlie just wanted to do light things. Kissing and stuff. And anyway, he was hardly the biggest guy in the school. If he got too handsy Adam could always shove him into a shed again, right? And now Charlie knew about the — about Adam, properly like, maybe he wouldn't want to do the heavy stuff anymore, anyway. Once he was sure Mrs. Dunstable was far enough into her droning, Adam inched his hand back down toward the bag. He'd text Mum and ask her if he could go for the evening. *Then* he'd worry about what to do if Charlie wanted to go too far.

* * * *

"Do you pray?"

Charlie was sitting on the wall behind the bike sheds, alone and cross-legged, a book open in his lap. He blinked at Adam's question, those blue eyes wide and blank, and very slowly shook his head.

"You go to church and stuff. You used to pray, right?" Adam insisted, heaving himself up on the wall.

"Er. Yeah. When I was like…six. Do I want to know why you're asking?"

"I prayed for lightning to strike Mrs. Dunstable and nothing happened. So I prayed for the whiteboard to fall on her and *still* jack all."

Charlie sniggered.

"Do you have to clock like…loyalty points on prayers?"

"Yeah," Charlie said. "Fifty Hail Marys gets you a low-level plague. Two hundred gets you a smiting. And if you get fifty Lord's Prayers, you can have yourself a biblical apocethary."

"Apocalypse."

"Whatever. It's all crap."

"I thought you went to church?" Adam asked. "Ollie said you do."

"Meh," Charlie said. "I go to the church. I don't go *to* church."

Adam didn't understand the difference but shrugged it off. "Um, Mum said I could come over for the evening."

"Cool," Charlie said and shut the book. "Did you make notes in English?"

"Yeah."

"Great. I'm stealing them. I can barely read normal English, never mind fucking Shakespeare."

"*Hamlet*'s okay," Adam protested, and Charlie wrinkled his nose.

"Yeah, okay," he said. "Better than *Romeo and Juliet*. Forsooth and all that. Hey, when we've been together two weeks, let's have a murder-suicide party."

Adam laughed as they dropped down in unison, Charlie stuffing the book very haphazardly into his bag. "So, um, do you have plans?"

"You, me, my room, some DVDs turned up loud..."

Adam gripped the strap of his bag tightly. "We can't..."

"I know," Charlie said. "I haven't forgotten, sheesh. You're sex mad, you are."

"I'm not!"

"You are, s'all you think about," Charlie teased. They fell into step as they passed the long line of bus stops. "Sex, sex, sex. Can't a guy get a hug without some sex?"

Adam shoved him. Charlie staggered into the plastic glass of a bus shelter, cackling.

"After the shed, that's nothing, mate!"

"Oh, fuck off," Adam jeered and Charlie laughed as he rummaged for his bus pass. "Seriously, I should call Mum and go home. You're evil."

"Guilty as charged," Charlie said and beamed. "S'what you like about me, though."

Adam reddened.

"See? I got you hook, line and sinker, Ads," Charlie said and waved Adam ahead of him onto the bus in some piss-poor imitation of a gentleman.

"You only like me because I'm better at English than you."

"Immy's better than me," Charlie snorted as they headed up onto the top deck and took over the seats right at the front. Adam was starting to like Charlie's bus. It was always empty because all the kids who lived out beyond Stoker Farm got fetched and carried by their parents and everyone closer rode their bikes.

"You're not bad..."

"I'm hopeless," Charlie said. "Can't read worth shit. The letters jump all over the place and I think a word's another word. I gave up in primary when I kept misreading 'she'd' as 'shed' and the other kids laughed at me."

Adam blinked. "You're dyslexic?"

"I dunno."

"Sounds dyslexic."

"I dunno," Charlie repeated and shrugged. "I'm just shit and it's boring, anyway. S'not like maths. All that pissing about with what the author meant — maybe they just meant what's on the fucking page, yeah? And *poetry*, urgh."

Adam laughed. "It's not that bad."

"It's bullshit," Charlie said. He was lounging and in the quiet emptiness of the bus, Adam slid their fingers together. Charlie squeezed before continuing his tirade. "I meant, where's poetry ever gonna get you? Stacking shelves in that sonnet structure thing?"

"Iambic pentameter?"

"Whatever."

Adam grinned, stroked his thumb over the back of Charlie's hands and stared at the way Charlie's fingers shifted. He couldn't get over that they moved so normally when the rest of his hand — the left more than the right, he supposed, but still — was so strange.

"Stop staring."

"Can't help it," Adam said but tore his gaze away to stare out of the window instead as the bus jerked forward down the road. "Um, you're not out, are you?"

"As what? Gay or trans?"

"Either?"

"Trans, yes. Gay, not so much, but it's not exactly secret either. I wouldn't be up for any PDAs in the kitchen, if that's what you mean."

"Okay," Adam said. "Just your room, then?"

"Or the hay loft."

"Or the hay loft," Adam agreed. "In our honesty-box-confession thing you said once..."

"Uh-huh?"

"Well, honesty-box-confession time and I know it sounds really stupid and girly and crap, but..." Adam chewed on his lip and dared to look at Charlie from under his eyelashes. "I want to steal some more kisses."

"Can't steal what's yours," came the easy reply and a flood of warm heat washed through Adam's stomach and chest. It felt like happiness tinged with yearning, or anticipation without the anxiety.

As the bus crested the ridge and started out on the single-track roads to the outlying villages, Adam realized that it was raw desire.

\* \* \* \*

Adam had never been into the farmhouse at Stoker Farm. He'd never seen the threadbare, once-red-now-pink carpets, or the fine layer of cat hair on everything, or the way every nook and cranny in place was filled with muddy shoes and coats. He'd certainly never seen Charlie's room, with its heavy blackout curtain and whiteboard on the back of the door covered in messy equations, bracketed by band posters on the walls.

And he didn't care. Because the minute Charlie had shut the bedroom door behind them, Adam was stealing one of those kisses. It was quick to start and slow to finish, Adam's hands cupping Charlie's neck and—who knew where Charlie's hands went, really. Adam was too focused on the exact contours of Charlie's lips and the way Adam felt as if he couldn't breathe.

It was that need-to-breathe that broke it and Charlie grinned against Adam's cheek. "What film d'you wanna ignore?" he whispered.

There was a bang downstairs and a voice bellowed Charlie's name up the stairs. Charlie took in a lungful and Adam backpedaled only just in time to avoid getting an eardrum blown out.

"*What?*"

The answering roar was in such a thick Gloucestershire accent that Adam missed it entirely, but Charlie didn't bat an eyelid.

"Got a mate round!" he yelled back and a…bellowed sort of grunt noise was the reply. "Sorry," Charlie said. "Uncle Keith. So? What film d'you wanna ignore?"

"Was that English?"

Charlie snorted. "I dunno. Probably not. Told you my uncles are stupid."

"You don't talk like that."

"Because Dad talked like a normal human being and passed it on," Charlie said loftily and planted both hands in Adam's chest to shove him. "Stop molesting me and pick a DVD. G'wan."

Adam pulled a face but did as he was told. Given Charlie's position on English, he wasn't surprised to find the bookshelf by the window jammed with computer games and DVDs, though he *was* surprised to find a couple of audiobook cassettes, obviously ancient.

"They're Dad's," Charlie said when Adam asked, and pointed at a framed photo on the computer desk. "That's him."

It looked like a winter picture, a head-and-shoulders shot of a very fat man in a woolly hat and heavy coat. He was red-faced, his nose and cheeks covered in spidery lines from burst blood vessels. Adam recognized it from his own grandfather — a heavy drinker and a man who liked his meat pies.

But under the fat and the lines, he looked a bit like Charlie. Same big blue eyes, the same crooked angle to the smile, the same shape to the jaw. His hair was hidden by the hat, but his eyebrows, enormous and fuzzy, like a couple of caterpillars engaging in a bit of foreplay above his nose, were jet-black.

"He looks like he was fun," Adam said diplomatically. He didn't figure saying Charlie's late father was a fat, mostly ugly bloke would go down well.

"Yeah, he was," Charlie said, his voice a little faint. "He was a laugh. He was pretty epic, too. It sucks now he's gone."

"What happened?" Adam asked, his own voice barely above a whisper.

There was a long silence and, when Adam turned back from the desk, Charlie had folded his arms around himself.

"Charlie..."

"Heart attack," he said suddenly and shook his head. "It caught up to him and he had a massive heart attack."

"I'm sorry..."

"Shit happens," Charlie said, a little harshly.

"My granddad had a heart attack," Adam offered and tried to lighten the mood with the story. "He was watching the wrestling and there was a guff call and he jumped up to shout at the telly and dropped dead."

Charlie snorted and started sniggering.

"My nana's still mad at him for it," Adam continued, watching the way the tension eased from Charlie's shoulders. "Every Christmas, she complains it'd be easier having all these guests if he hadn't died. She calls him inconsiderate."

"That is pretty rude. Wrecking the match and all."

"Yup," Adam said, starting to relax. "When she got rid of his slippers and chair and everything, when she moved to the bungalow, Mum was saying she couldn't get rid of it all and Nana was just like 'well if he wanted to keep them, he shouldn't have bloody died, should he?'"

Charlie laughed properly and Adam ran his fingers along the DVD cases before finding a Marvel one and pulling it out. "I suppose that's fair."

"That one," Adam said, handing the case over. "Then we can watch the good bits and...ignore the other bits."

"So, every time the villain starts bleating?" Charlie asked, popping it open. "Sounds like a plan. Doesn't he have a huge special effects-y bit near the end?"

"I dunno."

Adam didn't care. He wanted—okay, he *really* wanted to be able to just go with it and everything, and he *wanted* like he'd never wanted anything before but —

Right this minute, fuck the stupid film. He wanted to kiss Charlie again. To touch him — his hair and his arms and his...body — and explore. Find out if his hands were the only weird thing about him, find out what he packed with, find out if he had leg hair or not and was it dark like his head hair. He wanted Charlie in this raw and clumsy hot feeling in his chest and it wasn't like he was going to be watching like *any* of the film when he felt like this, right?

So Adam shucked his school blazer and shoes and perched on the bed while Charlie fumbled with the TV. The room was, unsurprisingly, a chaotic mess. And there was a scary number of...well, numbers. Maths books and stuff.

"You're a maths nerd."

"Yeah, well," Charlie said as the film flickered into life. "Numbers are easy. They're not all fucked up and complicated."

"Trig is."

"Trig's easy," Charlie snorted, shrugging off his own blazer. "Shift up."

Charlie's bed was a narrow single, but Adam didn't mind. It left not a lot of room and a perfect excuse, Charlie's arm ending up under Adam's shoulder. Adam barely waited past the shadowy opening scenes and sinister, growling dialogue before twisting over, cupping Charlie's face in his hands and kissing him.

This position — namely on top — was kind of odd, in that Adam wasn't exactly used to having a hand in the small of his back at that angle, but good, too. He was in control. Charlie just smiled against his mouth and wound a hand into his hair and that was it. Adam was in control here and he could explore a little. He found the exact right angle and when Charlie hummed and pulled Adam's shirt free from his belt, Adam felt suddenly daring and shifted over a little more to drop one leg between Charlie's thighs.

He was making out. With a boy. In said boy's bedroom. With *Charlie*.

Then Adam's brain decided to do away with thinking altogether and, when sliding a hand down Charlie's chest and side did nothing more than elicit another hum, Adam relaxed. This was fine. This was more than fine and what the hell had he been nervous about? Charlie's hands were warm — one still in Adam's hair and the other on his back now, under his shirt and above his waistband.

Adam shifted when Charlie's hand pushed higher. "D'you want me to take it off?"

"F'you want."

Charlie's voice was deeper than usual and his eyes were hazy — Adam suddenly felt far too warm and his fingers shivered on the buttons of his shirt. But here, with Charlie's fingers still massaging his scalp as he worked, Adam felt bold. Charlie didn't care. Charlie wasn't pushing. He was just enjoying and that mean Adam could just...

*Go with the flow. As Nat would say.*

And Charlie's hands weren't warm, they were *hot*. And the look on his face — Adam suddenly felt invincible, like nothing could touch him. There was no illness, there was no risk, there was just that look in Charlie's eyes, as if he'd seen something completely incredible...

Then Adam touched the gap between Charlie's trousers and his shirt and found his hand pushed away.

"C'mon, fair's fair," he mumbled but Charlie just chuckled and twisted them sideways until they were sharing the pillow, still — mostly, with breaks for air — joined at the mouth. And it was so nice that Adam let it slide for a little bit...only to find, when he touched the gap again, the same thing happened. "Charlie?"

"Not yet," Charlie said.

Adam frowned. "I can't...you know, you can't get —"

"I know, Ads..."

Adam stopped the hand that was wandering up his chest and squeezed the knuckles. "Charlie? We gotta match."

Charlie colored.

"What's up?" Adam pressed. He didn't know why he

had the urge to worry at it like this, but something wasn't adding up. Charlie was so easy with his affection, Adam already knew that. The girls both groped him all the time and he'd even Frenched Phoebe under the mistletoe at Christmas. And he was letting Adam touch him just fine, so why not…?

"I'm not ready to strip off in front of you yet," Charlie said eventually.

"It's just your shirt."

"Yeah, well, it's a shirt I'm not ready to lose yet."

Adam blinked and wondered if this fell into Charlie's lost year, or if it was related to his…identity.

"Look, um…can I just put my foot in it? Like, royally?" They were still lying facing each other and Charlie's hand was still caught in Adam's. Adam twisted it round to rub his thumbs over the knuckles and massage it. "If, um…if I didn't have HIV, you'd still…"

"I'd still not be taking this off yet," Charlie clarified, tugging on the collar. It was plenty rumpled and the sight of his long throat disappearing into the cotton was — to be perfectly honest — rude. It was mocking him, Adam was sure of it.

"I know what you've got there. I won't touch."

"It's not that," Charlie started then blew upward into his hair. "Don't ever repeat this, ever. On pain of death."

"Okay?"

"I'm not exactly my body's biggest fan. In — not dysphoria ways. Like. Even if I had been born right, it would still suck."

Adam frowned. "You're…body shy?"

"I'm gangly and weird."

"You felt fine to me."

"Yeah, well."

Adam squeezed the captured hand. "Well. You shouldn't be."

Charlie's jaw worked and Adam bit his lip.

"Um…this *may* not be the time to bring it up, but…but

145

my mum says my dad wants to talk to us."

"Er…"

"About…sex and stuff."

"Oh, shit." Charlie's color rapidly left his face again and Adam bit his lip.

"Like…what we can and can't do, and how to be careful. And stuff. On Sunday. Can you come over Sunday morning?"

There it was. Mum's test. And his own, in a way, because Adam hadn't expected Charlie to be shy when it got down to things and he had the unpleasant feeling that Charlie wasn't being totally honest and it *was* the HIV and…and that would hurt. After the sleepover and the kiss in the kitchen and everything he'd said, that would *really* hurt.

"Afternoon," Charlie said. "Got church in the morning. But okay."

"Really?"

"Yeah," Charlie shrugged. "Be embarrassed as fuck, but yeah, okay. Makes sense if we're gonna…eventually."

Adam toyed with the hem of the cotton. "You'd *have* to let me see if we did."

"Why d'you think I said eventually?"

Adam wriggled across the gap and kissed Charlie's lower lip, pulling on the smile that threatened to disturb it. "Let's get back to that, yeah?"

Charlie laughed and kissed him back. After a few seconds, the tension eased again and Adam found that nice angle where his nose *just* touched the side of Charlie's. But he made a note, even as he spread his fingers and explored a lean waist and perfect arse. Body-shy his left foot. He was getting fed up of all this shy stuff and determined — stubbornly, stupidly, Wood-family-trait determined — to shake it off.

Charlie Fielding had nothing to be shy about and it was about fucking time he learned. Twat.

# Chapter Fourteen

Adam hadn't exactly felt great when Mum had called him down for breakfast that morning and he felt downright sick by the time one o'clock rolled around and he heard the heavy grind of tires pulling up on the road outside. Sunday afternoon, after church, just as Charlie had said.

Adam wanted to call it off. They could just hold hands forever. They didn't even have to kiss, right? They could be like those kids in America who got purity rings and said they wouldn't do anything until they got married, then just…never get married, ever. Yeah? It'd be a better option than the wasps' nest in his gut, anyway.

"You look like you're gonna hurl," Charlie said when Adam opened the door.

"Might do," Adam said weakly.

"Er. So. Don't?" Charlie offered. He shut the door with a snap and cocked his head. He hadn't changed from church and was still wearing his black trousers and pale blue shirt, open at the collar. "Relax, Ads."

"Look, um…before…before we have to do this," Adam stammered, "I just want to say if it's too big…you know, too much, I won't blame you for walking away."

"Okay," Charlie said. "If you accept that I'm offering the same get-out-of-jail-free card when I finally get the balls to fill you in on why I'm not exactly the best option either."

Adam frowned. "That's different."

"You don't know the full story. 'Course *you* think it's different."

Adam bit his lip. "But…"

"That's the deal. Take it or leave it."

Adam nodded. "Okay. No blame if…if one of us changes our minds."

"About those things, anyway. If you dump me for other stuff I won't be happy," Charlie said and held out his little finger. "Swear on it?"

A proper smile worked its way onto Adam's face. "What are you, five?"

"What does that make you, perv?"

Adam rolled his eyes and locked his finger around Charlie's. Charlie squeezed, slid his hand the rest of the way to hold Adam's and grinned.

"C'mon. This is going to be horribly embarrassing and I am never going to be able to look your dad in the eye like… *ever*, but it's okay. I agreed to come, didn't I?"

Adam swallowed against the urge to throw up. "It's… people get weirded out when they…"

"Well, I got plenty of my own weird," Charlie said easily. "Ads, gimme a chance here, yeah? You let me in once and I didn't wig out. Just…do it again. One more time."

Adam exhaled through his nose. "I know I said you could stay the night, but if you don't want to… I haven't told Mum yet, so if you want to…to go home after…"

"Relax before I hit you."

It jarred a laugh out of Adam's chest, then there were cool hands cupping his jaw and sliding fingers behind his ears and he was being kissed — but not like how Charlie usually kissed him. Charlie was energy and excitement when he kissed. It was like getting a laugh pressed to Adam's skin. This kiss was gentle and soft — so soft it barely made contact — and it was like a switch being flipped. Just like that, Adam felt okay again.

"How'd you do that?" he breathed when Charlie let go and Charlie's smile was as soft as the kiss and twice as sincere.

"Magic. C'mon. Let's go get the sex talk."

* * * *

Dad was reading the paper in the kitchen.

Dad had been a doctor – a GP for over thirty-five years – and taken early retirement when Mum had been offered the new job down here. He spent his whole retirement doing the housework and pottering around in the vegetable patch at the bottom of the garden. And he looked the part these days, too, with his threadbare green jumpers and checked shirts. Adam loved his dad, but…he was *Dad*, you know? Mum was always the go-to about the big stuff. Dad had been the go-to for homework help and – when Adam had been a little kid – finding cool bugs in the garden or at the park. Dad was 'what's for tea?' and 'what's the speed of sound?'

Not 'how am I supposed to have a relationship with another boy when I'm diseased?'

So, Adam curled his toes inside his trainers, embarrassed before Dad had even looked up from the business pages, and sank into one of the seats opposite.

"That time already?" Dad asked mildly and folded up the paper. "Afternoon, Charlie."

"Hi, Dr. Wood."

"Sit down, both of you," Dad said, reaching under the table for a plastic bag. He tipped it out unceremoniously and Adam's face burned red as a handful of leaflets and a box of assorted condoms bounced onto the surface. "Let's get this over with, shall we? Charlie, I'm told you're aware of Adam's status?"

"Uh-huh."

"How much do you know about HIV?"

"What he told me," Charlie said. He turned his hand over so his palm faced the ceiling, and wiggled the fingers. After a moment, Adam slid his fingers into Charlie's grip. "I'm not right bright, though, so…"

"You *are*," Adam snapped.

Charlie wrinkled his nose and Dad chuckled. "Well, then. You know what HIV is?"

"S'an STI," Charlie said promptly. "Kills off the immune

system and stuff."

"I won't bore you with the medical details," Dad said, "but suffice to say HIV is very serious and there's no cure. If you manage it properly, you can have a perfectly normal life. If not, it can lead quickly to severe health complications."

"Like AIDS?"

"Like AIDS," Dad agreed. He was doing his doctor face—glasses on the end of his nose, peering over them at Charlie—but Charlie didn't seem to care. His fingers were relaxed and Adam hooked his thumb around Charlie's. "With the right drugs and constant, consistent treatment, HIV is not the death sentence it used to be. Adam has lived sixteen years without any major issues."

Charlie glanced at Adam, who just shrugged. He hated discussing it. He felt miserable and wanted to go, but...but if he left, and Dad just talked to Charlie, Adam wouldn't be able to tell if Charlie was...

Okay with it. Or not.

"Now, there's nothing can be done for Adam in terms of curing him," Dad continued. "He will always have HIV, whether or not it ever actually makes him ill. Which means he cannot—ever—become complacent, and if you're going to be in a relationship with him, neither can you."

*Here it goes.* Adam braced himself.

"Okay," Charlie said. "Adam said something about counts."

Dad frowned.

"Viral loads," Adam mumbled.

"What's that got to do with it?" Charlie asked.

"It's the amount of HIV present in Adam's blood," Dad said. "Simply put, anyway. It's quite easy—imagine we were to fill a vial with Adam's blood and inject it into you. If there's a lot of HIV in that blood, it would almost certainly take hold and you would be infected. But if there was very little—which is when the viral load is low—your chance of infection is enormously reduced."

"Even if I got exposed?"

"Even if," Dad confirmed.

"So…"

"Adam gets tested every few months at the HIV clinic in Gloucester," Dad said. "His viral load has been consistently undetectable or near-undetectable for many years, so his chances of infecting another person are very small. But the chance is still there."

Adam gripped Charlie's hand hard. He knew this bit, from years ago. He'd told a friend once, when he'd been about eight. The friend had been okay, but when the friend's parents had found out…Adam had walked in on Dad trying to explain all of this to Stevie's irate mother and it hadn't worked. Any chance was too high. He hadn't been allowed to play with Stevie again.

And it had all started. Adam knew this bit and he hated it.

But Charlie's hand was still relaxed. "So, I'm guessing this is the safe sex lecture."

"Mostly," Dad agreed. "But it's also about what you *can* do, and not just sexually. You can't transmit HIV through the skin or saliva — so sharing your food, sharing towels, that's all fine."

"I can still steal his food at lunch?"

Adam blinked. "You don't steal my food at lunch."

"Yeah, but I could, right? You know, in theory."

Dad chuckled. "Yes, if you felt like it. I can't promise Adam won't pose a risk if you try taking his crisps, though."

Adam scowled. "Dad!"

"Noted," Charlie said, smirking. Adam wrinkled his nose. "So it's just, what? Blood and sex?"

"Blood and some sexual activity, yes," Dad said. "I hope I don't have to specify that you don't share drug paraphernalia."

"Drug what now?"

"Needles," Adam said.

"Yeah, nooooo," Charlie said. "With my brain? I'd either invent, like, perpetual motion machines, or my brain'd explode and leak out of my ears."

"Probably the second one," Adam offered.

"Anyway, Mum'd kill me."

"Good for your mother," Dad said dryly. "In essence, I would advise against sharing anything that is used inside the body, aside from the mouth. Needles are the most obvious, but sex toys—"

"*Dad!*"

"Also fit the bill. If you do use toys, they must be maintained very hygienically. The risk is microscopic with toys, but it is there, unlike skin-to-skin touching."

Adam let his forehead hit the table. Charlie sniggered.

"Adam, I don't like having this conversation any more than you do. Now. Boys. I hate to ask, but it is relevant—are you sexually active?"

"Not yet," Charlie said and Adam made a faint noise in the back of his throat. He wanted to die. Seriously. Somebody just burst into the house and shoot him, right this minute.

"In which case, get yourself in the habit of regular STI checks at a clinic," Dad said ruthlessly. "Let's not pretend either of you are always going to be one hundred percent rational when it comes down to it. And even if you did manage to religiously use protection every single time, protection can fail. Condoms break. At some point, Charlie, you *will* be exposed to this illness, so it's a good idea to keep getting regular testing. God forbid you do catch it, but if you do, early detection is a must."

Charlie screwed up his face. "Uh…"

Adam's guts tightened up into one solid knot of pain.

"Where can I go that aren't going to freak 'cause I'm underage?"

Dad paused. Adam could hardly breathe. *What?*

"I mean, I'm fifteen. I tried to get some condoms from a clinic in Bristol once—I was curious, you know?—and they just kept on and on asking me really awkward questions about why I wanted them."

"I see," Dad said. "Well, don't quote me as a doctor, but lie."

"Lie? About my age?"

"Until you're sixteen, I would recommend stating you need an HIV test only," Dad said. "It is perfectly reasonable to state your friend has HIV and you were exposed to his blood. Adam's mother and I would be perfectly willing to vouch for your story, but I would prefer you were regularly tested for the virus. Get into the habit now, before it becomes genuinely necessary."

"Okay," Charlie said. "But I can't tell my mum. She'd freak out."

Dad raised his eyebrows.

"Seriously," Charlie said. "I can't take my mum to the clinic with me or anything. She'd go ballistic and, like, ban me from ever standing in the same room as Adam again."

Adam grimaced. Charlie squeezed his hand.

"You're in the same year group, aren't you?"

"Uh-huh."

"So when do you turn sixteen?"

"July twenty-ninth," Charlie said promptly. *Only a few months away now.*

Dad hummed. "Well. Perhaps it would be easier to wait until you are sixteen, but that would mean no risky sexual activity until then. I'll leave you two to work it out, but, Adam, I want to hear the result of that discussion."

Adam reddened and decided they'd wait just to avoid that. "Er. 'Kay."

"Now for the painful part," Dad said, opening the box of assorted condoms. "Some sexual activity carries no risk. As I said, the virus dies very quickly outside the body. Masturbation — mutual or otherwise — is fine provided you don't have open wounds or ingest any bodily fluids."

Adam closed his eyes. This was his worst nightmare. Oh, dear *Jesus,* they were sitting at the kitchen table and he was holding Charlie's hand and Dad was talking about hand jobs.

"Oral sex is very low-risk, but the risk is there, particularly if you suffer from bleeding gums or mouth sores," Dad continued in that dull doctor-drone of his. Adam felt as though his face had been set on fire. Charlie just sat there like he was listening to the rules of cricket. How was he so fucking calm?

"So…protection?"

"Yes," Dad said. "You cannot catch HIV if you are receiving oral sex, but you must be much more careful if giving it. A condom is the rather obvious solution…"

Adam. Wanted. To die. *Now*.

"The risk is minimal, particularly if you stop before orgasm," Dad continued blithely. "You would have to be incredibly unlucky to become infected from pre-ejaculate, but don't allow orgasm in the mouth, or swallow the result."

"I'm going to die a virgin," Adam announced.

Charlie laughed — much to Adam's surprise — and said, "Come off it, Ads. I'm practically getting permission to —"

"Shut up!"

"I hate to be indelicate, but I do have to speak about vaginal sex, as well as anal."

Adam glanced aside. Charlie, to his surprise, simply shrugged.

"Okay."

"You need condoms for both. End of story. Anal sex carries the greater risk, purely because the anus tears more easily and so the risk of exposing blood to semen is greater. But that can happen with vaginal sex as well, so always use protection. Always."

Dad was just tearing through it and Adam both hated it and appreciated it. He didn't want to be here, or hear it — any of it, because *God* — but at least it would be over soon, right? And Charlie was still here and not freaking out, and that was…that was good.

"Anal. Ew."

Adam grimaced too and Dad chuckled.

"It may not appeal now, but I have no doubt that eventually you will want to try it."

"Jury's out on that," Charlie said doubtfully.

"Well, you're getting the talk regardless."

"So if we use condoms, I can't get it?"

"Not if you use them correctly. They need to fit properly, they need to be of good quality and if you use latex, do *not* use an oil-based lubricant."

"Why?" Charlie asked.

"Oil weakens the latex and can break it," Dad said evenly. "This leaflet is on proper condom usage, but I'll run through it quickly with you. Adam, you'll need to experiment with different types to find ones that fit properly and are the right size, and you do *not* have sex until you know which ones are right. Always check the expiry date—again, the latex can be weak or brittle if it's too old—and don't put it on until you're erect or it won't fit properly."

Adam nodded jerkily. Charlie was eyeing the box.

"Can I take that?"

"Well, they're not for me," Dad said and Charlie dragged it across the table toward himself. "If you use good quality condoms, and correctly, and use plenty of lubricant and preparation, then your risk of infection will be minimal."

"What if it does break?"

Adam flinched. Dad glanced at him and smiled gently.

"If the condom ever breaks, you need to get to a hospital or a specialized HIV clinic immediately. There are certain emergency drugs which can be given to patients very recently exposed to HIV. They make you very ill in the short term but can prevent the virus taking hold and kill it before it takes root. You need to do that *immediately*. The time window is measured in hours after the exposure, not days. And Adam." Dad's gaze fixed on him, the stern doctor in place of the blasé, I've-seen-this-all-before one. "Listen to me carefully now. If that *does* happen, you need to tell me or your mother immediately. We know where we can take Charlie for the fastest treatment and I need to know you will do that."

"Yes, Dad," Adam whispered. His throat felt dry.

"We will not care if you have been having sex. We will

not care what you have been doing. The important thing in that event will be to get Charlie the retrovirals he needs and I need you to promise me you will come immediately to your mother or me if you think — for whatever reason — that Charlie has been exposed."

"Promise," Adam breathed. It wouldn't happen. It *wouldn't*, he wouldn't let it, not ever, and...

"Accidents happen. People forget. Sometimes you just get a duff condom," Dad continued. "That's how your mother and I had the twins."

"Dad!"

"Well, at least I can't get you pregnant," Charlie told Adam and grinned. The color had faded from his face and he looked so chilled out that Adam envied him.

"Oh, shut up," Adam mumbled.

"And, Charlie, I need you to promise you will be frank and honest with Adam and with us if you think you've been exposed."

"Yes, sir." Adam — and Dad, actually — blinked at the sudden somber tone of respect.

"Yes. Well. Good." Dad coughed, thrown. "And if either of you have any questions or concerns, then I am happy to discuss them. You can also go to your GP."

Charlie snorted.

"Don't you like your doctor?" Adam asked curiously.

"Nope," Charlie said. "I wouldn't tell her if I got squashed by a tractor and my legs were hanging off."

"Then you can always talk to me," Dad said. "There are also a lot of helplines you can contact if you wish." He pushed another leaflet across the table. "Realistically, there is no reason you cannot enjoy a perfectly normal and healthy sex life. You just have to be more careful about it and you have to be very honest with each other. It's normal for HIV to impact how people relate to each other and what they would like to do. As long as you're both honest about that, then there is no reason you can't enjoy yourselves."

Adam could feel his lungs tightening up.

"But I do urge you both to think about it. Making a mistake would have serious consequences. I personally think you're too young to be making these decisions, but I'm also a realist. It's perfectly normal to want to do this, but you need to use your brains and not your balls with this one, boys."

"Dad!" Adam exploded. Charlie just exploded into laughter. "I can't believe you just said that!"

"It's true," Dad retorted. "I would encourage you to wait until you're older and have more time to adapt to this, but there's no shame in feeling any urges or in indulging yourselves. Don't rush headlong into things, but don't feel any shame for wanting to either. And if either of you need any more information, there are plenty of resources, including Kathleen and me."

Adam swallowed. "Can we go now?" He wanted to bail—hard—and he sensed that Dad was winding down.

Dad seemed to take pity. "Go on, then. But talk about what I've just told you. Do some more research on the internet if you feel the need then, if you've got any questions or concerns, come back and talk to me again."

"We will," Adam mumbled, already getting up.

"Thanks, Dr. Wood," Charlie said, gathering up the leaflets and the condoms. "One question. What's HIV stand for?"

Dad chuckled. "Human immunodeficiency virus."

"Ye-eah, I can't spell that," Charlie said. "Thanks."

"C'mon," Adam urged, catching Charlie under the elbow and hauling him towards the hall. Bailing time. Seriously, *way* beyond bailing time.

He dragged Charlie up to his room, slammed the door and collapsed on the bed.

"Fuck," he told the ceiling and Charlie laughed.

"That was hilarious."

"That was *humiliating.*"

"That, too."

Adam sat up. Charlie was standing in the middle of the

room, turning the box of condoms over in his hands.

"I meant what I said."

"What?" Charlie asked.

"If you want to…to go…to not see me anymore…"

Then Charlie grinned and it was as though something clicked in Adam's head. Charlie was here. And he wasn't going to walk away.

# Chapter Fifteen

"So?" Charlie said.

They were sitting on Adam's bed, side-by-side and backs to the wall, and Adam hadn't said a word since they'd fled Dad. He swallowed, fidgeting with the denim of his jeans over his knees, and...well, yeah, he didn't really want to look Charlie in the face right then. That talk had been awful and...yet Charlie was still here.

"It's big," he whispered.

"No kidding," Charlie said and dropped the box of assorted condoms onto the duvet. "Have you read the back of that?"

"No," Adam mumbled.

"There's flavored ones in there."

"Oh."

"Why would they be *flavored?*"

Adam sighed. "If...if it's too much — ever, I mean, if you ever want out 'cause of this, then...then I get it." He did. He'd be miserable, but he'd get it.

Charlie snorted and Adam's tight chest snapped and released. "I just sat through that talk with your *dad.* Trust me, I'm not doing that for nothing."

Adam laughed and Charlie dropped a hand onto his knee and squeezed.

"Gimme some credit, yeah? I like you. And it's more than about what's in your jeans. I mean, don't get me wrong — I am *never* having that discussion again. Holy fuck, I would rather go to my actual doctor, but — I get why you wanted me to. And I need to know this stuff if we're gonna do this, right?"

"Yeah."

"It's heavy, I get it, but…it's no different than you needing to know I can't be allowed to get drunk without someone around to stop me going mental. Not really."

Adam mustered up a smile and stroked Charlie's fingernail over his knee lightly, paying particular attention to that middle finger. He was getting used to the odd appearance of Charlie's hands. Maybe.

"Do you want me to go?"

Adam snapped his head up. "No." Charlie's face was soft and thoughtful and Adam bit his lip. "I just…I don't like talking about it. Or hearing about it and how…how different everything has to be."

"Well, it's not *that* different," Charlie said. "We're supposed to use condoms, anyway, right? Or you might get me pregnant and I'll drop out of school and we'll give the baby some horrible name like Teyanna-Reece."

Adam stared.

"Yeah, I'm secretly a chav."

"That would explain a lot…"

"Hey!"

"You said it!" Adam defended himself and Charlie sniggered. "Um. Can you?"

"Can I what?"

"Get pregnant?"

"In theory. On the pill, though. The whole monthly bleeding thing is — not good."

Adam shivered.

"Anyway," Charlie said, bumping Adam's shoulder with his own. "You keep your viral count down, we use condoms when we actually do anything that poses any kind of risk and I'll get tested all the time. It's not that hard."

Adam squeezed Charlie's hand.

"G'wan, get your laptop and let's do some research of our own. Like where the next-nearest clinic is, because I am not going to a clinic where your dad knows half the staff."

Adam laughed as he crawled across the bed to stretch for

his laptop on the desk.

"Anyway," Charlie continued, "when we have a baby, you gotta knock up Feebles. She has better hair than me."

"Oh, thanks."

"It's true! She has supermodel hair. She's gonna have our kids."

"Just for the supermodel hair?"

Charlie laughed, opening the condom box and spilling plastic packets onto the sheets. He was cross-legged on the pillows and Adam mirrored his position when he returned with the laptop.

"M'gonna have to make something up, too," Charlie said, sifting through the packets. "S'like I told your dad. Clinics don't like underage kids asking for stuff."

"How would you know?" Adam asked. "Why'd you go asking for condoms, anyway?"

Charlie went red. "Uh. I may have...precluded..."

"Procured?"

"Got."

"Procured."

"I may have *got* some condoms at Christmas."

"Why?" Adam asked curiously.

"Um. Wishful thinking?" Charlie said and groaned. "Okay, look, I...kind of...that school trip to London in November? To see Parliament?"

"Yeah?"

"That's when I started to proper like you."

Adam bit his lip and smiled as he unlocked the computer and fired up the browser.

"I mean, I liked you a bit anyway, but in that kind of — you know, 'look at the fit new kid' way. Then we went to Parliament and you and Feebs were having a nerdy spaz-fit at all the ornate stuff on the walls, and...yeah."

"Thanks," Adam said, his face burning.

"Yeah, well, if I were straight, it would've been Feebles."

"So...you *are* gay?" Adam hedged.

"I dunno. Maybe."

"Maybe?"

"Yeah. I dunno. Like…I find…girls are pretty and stuff. And sometimes I think I'd like a relationship with a girl and there's girls like Phoebe where I kind of wish I *was* into girls, because she's totally awesome and I would so be there if I was into it, but…I'm not. Physically, you know. Girls don't do anything."

Adam blinked. "So, you're like…emotionally attracted to girls?"

"Yeah, maybe."

"But…not sexually?"

"Nope. That's all guys."

Adam tilted his head. "Huh."

"S'weird."

"A little bit, yeah, but…you're…you know, you're emotionally attracted to me, right?"

"Uh, *yeah.* Even I know better than to chase a positive guy just to get my rocks off, Ads."

Adam snorted. The acerbic comment should have hurt, but it didn't and he laughed then spontaneously leaned across the space created by their yoga-fanatic-crossed-legs thing and landed a sharp kiss on Charlie's mouth. Charlie blinked. Then a smile washed across his features. "What was that for?"

"Oh, shut up," Adam groused. "C'mere."

Charlie shuffled round to look at the laptop, picking at one of the condom packets.

"Those're the nearest clinics," Adam said. "Why d'you have to lie, anyway? Did you have to lie to get the condoms?"

"No," Charlie said, "but it was about forty minutes of trying to explain to a nurse I just wanted them for curiosity's sake and I wasn't being touched up by a creepy uncle or something."

"What?"

"I'm fifteen, man. I'm not meant to be banging yet," Charlie said and rolled his eyes. "Fat lot *they* know."

"Have you?"

"What?"

"Ever...you know?"

"Had sex?"

"Yeah."

"Nah. Ollie and I were gonna once, but even kissing her felt weird," Charlie said and grimaced. "We didn't even French. It was just too weird. But, anyway, going and asking for an HIV test without my mum present, that's going to be a *loooooong* conversation."

"Why not take your mum?"

Charlie's eye roll and shake of the head made Adam's gut cramp.

"You told Dad she'd freak out."

"She would."

"She...wouldn't like me?"

"Nope."

"Does she know you're...?"

"It's a phase," Charlie said brutally. "This is all a phase. I'll grow out of it. It's what happens when your dad dies and you're left with a couple of useless uncles as father figures."

Adam winced and tried to change the topic a little bit. "Your uncles are really that bad?"

"Yeah, I'm surprised Uncle Keith can walk and talk at the same time. Makes me look clever. I guess we could...you know, not put me in that...position — um, put me..."

"At risk?"

"Yeah. Y'know. Not do it. 'Til I'm sixteen. Then I can tell them to naff off and gimme the tests."

"Okay," Adam said, a little relieved at the time window. Not too long, but enough time to...get used to it. Decide how far he wanted to go, and...what he wanted to do. It'd be good. Right? "So no sex until you're sixteen."

"Well, you know...no *anal*..."

Adam screwed up his face. "Ew."

Charlie sniggered. "Well, yeah, it's not...you know, the most amazing-sounding thing, is it?"

"I'm not sure I'll ever do it—doesn't it *hurt*?" Adam asked.

"The guys in porn don't seem to think so," Charlie said. "Hey, while you're on there," he added, peeling apart a condom wrapper, "go on the NHS website and find out if you can get HIV from a strap-on."

"What?"

"How else do you think I'd ever get to be on top?"

"Oh. Uh. I guess. I think you can. It's a sex toy, right?" Adam said, wondering how to phrase that. He decided on just reading through the risk factors and how to avoid it. Some list somewhere would say it. No *way* was he typing in 'can I get HIV from a strap-on'. Ever.

"Check it out. It's a ribbed one," Charlie said, unrolling the condom onto his fingers. He wiggled it like a sock puppet and Adam snorted with laughter. "Have you seen *Red Dwarf*? There's a bit where Lister says he went condom fishing in the canal and he caught this massive condom 'cause it was all swelled up with water. Reckon they do that?"

"Well, yeah, it's just like a balloon, isn't it?"

"I dunno. I've never tried it," Charlie said, shaking the condom off again. After a minute, he brought it up to his mouth and blew—and Adam collapsed as it blew up *just* like a clear balloon, with the weird little tip on it still pinched out.

"Fucking hell!"

"You could get a footlong in there," Charlie said proudly, pinching it to keep it swelling up. "Look, the little dimple bit's still there. Is that where the sperm-killing stuff goes?"

"Yeah," Adam said. "Seriously, didn't you do sex ed?"

"We got taught how to put them on cucumbers and that sex is this filthy dirty thing you only do when you're an adult with the person you love," Charlie recited faithfully and grinned. "One thing private schools *suck* at, man. Did you get proper sex ed?"

"Sort of. Half the class were pregnant, but they at least explained properly. This doesn't say what the risk is from strap-ons, but it says you can from dildos, so I guess so."

"I'm guessing your dad meant hand jobs from 'mutual masturbation'. Yeah?"

"Uh-huh."

Charlie eyed him. "That was fast."

Adam shrugged. "It's risk-free."

"You sound certain."

Adam went red. "I once asked Dad if I could pass it on if I masturbated and someone else handled my clothes or my bedsheets. And he said it dies too fast outside the body, so I can't."

"Wank, Adam," Charlie said. "The word's wank. Masturbate," he echoed scornfully, ripping open another packet. "So I can get my hand down your pants, nice to know."

"Not right now you can't," Adam muttered, scrolling through the information pages. "It says here, um, you should put a glove if you want to, um..."

"A *glove?*" Charlie echoed. "The hell do I need gloves for?"

"Um, you know..." Adam wiggled his fingers.

"What, fingering? I need to glove up to finger you?"

"Charlie!" Adam flushed scarlet and Charlie grinned.

"So, basically, I can't put my skin near your arse," he said.

"Oh, shut your face."

"No glove, no love."

"Charlie, I'm gonna hit you."

"Oh, *dude*, blowjobs with condoms. What's that feel like? Look it up. And *that's* what they have flavored ones for!" he said gleefully and abandoned the condom he'd found for another one. "Oh, cool, here, this one's strawberry — seriously, where did your dad get all these weirdo condoms? D'you reckon there's any proper kinky ones in here?"

"For someone who doesn't know where the spermicide goes, you know way too much about those," Adam said, clicking through a couple of links. "There's nothing about, um, blowjobs with a condom on."

"Yeah, but that's totally the answer," Charlie said. "'Cause even without swallowing you're gonna produce stuff, anyway, all the pre-cum stuff, and rubber tastes fucking awful, so that's why they flavor 'em." He tore a packet open and — to Adam's horror — licked the condom.

"Charlie!"

"What? It's a flavored one. Sort of. Not convinced it's strawberry. Here, try that."

Adam eyed it then unrolled it and gingerly tasted the tip. And gagged. *Urgh,* what the hell? It tasted like — "That's like...like a latex glove someone smeared sweets on!"

"Now *there* is a weird kink," Charlie said, taking it back and licking it again. Somehow, the sight of him doing so without flinching at Adam having licked it felt...nice and Adam curled his bare toes into the sheets. Even if it was, you know, Charlie licking a condom. "Meh. I think you could get used to it. Gonna experiment with flavors, though, definitely, that's *not* strawberry. Oh, hey. Hey, Ads, look."

Adam looked — and started sniggering helplessly. Charlie beamed, two feeble-looking condoms dangling from his ears like enormous, disturbing earrings.

"What are you *doing?*"

"Next pop sensation, man! Katy Perry'd looking *amazeballs* with these earrings. Check it out!"

And he jumped up on the bed and started dancing. Or... having a seizure. Or something. The condoms swung in time with his shoulders and Adam rescued the laptop, laughing too hard to protest or stop him.

"You're mental!"

"Totes! C'mon, dance with me!"

"No way!" Adam said, but it didn't faze Charlie, who started jumping and playing air guitar to something Adam couldn't hear. The condoms amazingly stayed in place, tucked over his ears, and through fits of laughter Adam managed to seize Charlie's belt and yank him down to the mattress in a tangle of laughter and limbs.

"Bastard!"

"No!" Adam ordered, pinning Charlie to the bed in a bear hug. "You'll break my bed!"

"Ooh-er."

"Bad!" Adam scolded, still sniggering. "You're awful. Holy fuck, you're awful."

Charlie beamed, wriggling until they were chest-to-chest, and quite suddenly Adam was being kissed. Not…not deep or intense or…anything really, because they were both grinning and it was a bit lopsided because they weren't quite on the pillows and there was a weird rubbery smell because one of the, um, rubbers was on Charlie's cheek. Adam drew back, biting his lip lightly, and removed the condom.

"Thanks," he said.

"For what?"

"Doing this with me," he said. "S'not so weird and scary with you…being a tit."

Charlie laughed. "Oh, cheers."

"You know what I mean."

Charlie's smile was a little less manic than usual and there was a knuckle stroking the side of Adam's face. "Yeah," Charlie said. "I really like you, yeah? And we'll work this all out together, one way or another. Don't get so freaked out all the time."

"If I infected you…"

"You won't," Charlie said flatly, "'cause we're gonna be sensible. First time in my life."

Adam laughed.

"Oh, you think I'm kidding."

"I don't, that's the best bit," Adam said and squeezed Charlie tight in a hug. "Just—thanks. You know. It's weird and embarrassing and really shit, but you're making it fun and mental and stuff."

"S'me."

"I think I need it to be you," Adam admitted.

"Now we're in bed and covered in condoms…"

"Charlie…"

"Can I get handsy yet? You won't let me get handsy."

"Define 'handsy'."

"Do weird shit with my hands."

"How weird?"

"What d'you want, a dictionary?" Charlie asked and squirmed an arm free to drop it around Adam's waist. "Step one, a hug that's *remotely* comfortable."

"Step two," Adam said quietly, unable to tear his glance away from those blue eyes. It was like looking out of a plane straight down into an ocean. The fall would kill him, but… but he couldn't back up. Or he'd already jumped. "Do all this research and stuff."

"Step *two*," Charlie corrected. "Is I get one of my crazy hands under your T-shirt again. Can I?"

Adam blinked, then licked his lips and nodded. Charlie's gaze flicked down to his mouth, and then—then there was another kiss and they were turning over until Charlie's weight—solid, but not heavy, firm, but not unyielding—was pressing Adam down into the duvet and a pair of very hot hands were on the bare skin of Adam's waist.

"This okay?" Charlie murmured against his mouth and Adam hummed and tangled his fingers into Charlie's hair. He'd never imagined he'd get to do this. Find a boy who understood, find the courage to take the risk, find someone else to take the risk *with* him, never mind *this* boy. Never thought he'd get to just…have snogging sessions in his room, or blow up condoms, or…*joke* about it. He'd never been able to *joke* about it.

*Bang!*

"Adam!"

"Fuck!" Adam yelled and shoved. Hard. Charlie tumbled off the bed with a startled yelp and there was a sickening crack as he hit the carpet. "Mum!"

Mum stood in the open doorway, chuckling and shaking her head. "Oh, honestly, Adam, I've walked in on your sisters doing worse. Are you all right, Charlie?"

"Urgh, my *nose*," Charlie mumbled, hauling himself back onto the bed, and—

Adam froze. Red. Blood. There was blood on Charlie's face. His nose was bleeding. He was *bleeding*.

"I'll get you a tissue, dear," Mum said, disappearing.

"Ow," Charlie said, surprisingly clear. "Damn it. I thought that'd cleared up."

Adam pulled himself into the wall as tightly as possible and hugged his knees, staring. Oh, fuck. Charlie was bleeding.

"Adam?"

He shook his head and held out a hand when Charlie tried to inch closer. "No, stay there," he whispered.

"It's just a nosebleed, Ads."

"Stay *there*."

Charlie's expression shifted from bewilderment to something a little gentler. "*You're* not bleeding."

"Just stay there," Adam begged. He hated blood. It made him feel nauseous. He wanted to be sick just seeing it, and seeing it coming from *Charlie*…

"Here you go, dear."

"I'll go and wash my face," Charlie said quickly, taking the tissues Mum offered him and vanishing. Adam swallowed and slowly uncurled, and Mum's sigh was heavy.

"Adam?"

"M'okay."

"It's all right, darling, it'll only take a minute. He's not broken it."

"It just startled me." Scared him, but he knew better than to say the word.

"I know. Is Charlie staying the night?"

Adam snapped his head up to stare at her.

"Not in your room, he's not," she said firmly. "You're sixteen — you don't need to be sharing your bed yet. But am I making up the spare room and setting him a place at the table for dinner later?"

"Um…if…if he wants."

"Do you want him to?"

"Yeah," Adam admitted. Bloody nose aside, it was…it

was okay, this. Tonight. It was nice. And he didn't really want it to end—like ever.

"All right," Mum said, then raised her voice in a shout. "Charlie, I'll make up the spare room for you in a minute. Will you be needing a spare toothbrush in the morning?"

"Um. Please, Mrs. Wood!"

"Mrs. Wood," she muttered, and made a scoffing noise. "Honestly, he's as bad as you." Adam smiled gingerly as she ruffled his hair. "I'm popping out to get things for dinner in twenty minutes, sweetheart. Give us a shout if either of you want anything from the shops."

She got up to go just as Charlie reappeared, and closed the bedroom door. His face was clean and a wodge of tissue poked out from the pocket of his jeans. "So, I'm staying the night?"

"Yeah," Adam said. "Sorry about…pushing you off the bed."

"Meh, I'll live," Charlie said, crawling back onto Adam's bed and flopping upside-down again. Slowly he nudged his head onto Adam's lap and Adam absently stroked his fingers through that wild hair. He was beginning to realize that it wasn't quite curly, but more…wild. Loose. Flyaway? "You don't like blood?"

"No."

"Fair enough," Charlie said and held up a condom packet between finger and thumb. "Bet I can blow one of these up bigger than you can."

A slow smile spread across Adam's face. "No, you can't."

"Pfft, yes I fucking can."

Adam laughed and reached for one of the many packets scattered across the bed. "You're on."

And despite the rubbery taste of the condom, despite the fact Charlie *did* have better, um, blowing skills than him, despite his mother having walked in on him snogging a boy, Adam felt…

Felt as if just for one single evening, he was allowed to be normal.

# Chapter Sixteen

That half term was the best and weirdest one ever. If Adam wasn't out with Charlie and the girls, he was out with just Charlie. They went to the cinema in Stroud twice and Adam couldn't remember a single thing about either film. It was weird, because...well, Adam had a boyfriend and he wasn't sure what to do with him. He'd never even entertained the idea of having a boyfriend before. He was positive, for God's sake — he wasn't allowed boyfriends. He'd never thought it was ever going to happen, not unless he met something else who was positive, and there weren't exactly millions of positive teenagers kicking around Gloucestershire, right? He'd resigned himself to it years ago. He wasn't allowed to have boyfriends.

Except he had one. And it was kind of...weird.

He was dating. Proper dating. As in, he went on dates. And it was really, really weird.

It was the way it would come out of nowhere. One minute the four of them were lounging around Phoebe's house, or playing football in Ollie's back garden and everything was just like usual and the next minute Charlie would hug him, or put his head on Adam's lap or something. He'd squeezed Adam's thigh on Ollie's sofa on Tuesday afternoon and Adam had nearly decked him in reflex.

"You're twitchy," Charlie had said and laughed, but it didn't change the fact that Adam felt kind of stupid for taking so long to adjust.

It wasn't that he didn't like it — he loved it! — it was just that it was...not normal, you know? He'd seize up in surprise if Charlie hugged him without warning and that one time Charlie had kissed him in front of the girls, Adam had almost shoved him again. It was like…a double dose of strange. *Twilight Zone*-type stuff. Because not only did Adam have a boyfriend, Adam had a boyfriend who was cool with being handsy in front of their friends. And Adam had never really imagined that, either, because everyone knew gay plus kissy in public wasn't allowed, right?

Charlie *was* affectionate in public. The minute they were well away from the villages, he just let rip. On the Thursday of half term, they all went to Bristol—or rather, the girls dragged them to go shopping and Charlie's mum had given him fifty quid to find some new trainers—and Charlie had kissed him in right in the middle of Cribbs Causeway. During half term! The place had been packed out and Charlie had just out and kissed him!

It was throwing Adam for a loop. A nice loop, but a loop all the same.

Faintly, Adam suspected Charlie was doing it on purpose, because it meant that whenever they went anywhere—alone or together—Adam got stupid nervous and daft excited. He'd get worked up and his fingers would stick and his tongue get stuck. And Charlie would just laugh and hold his hand, or smile and kiss him—

Yeah. Charlie was definitely doing it on purpose.

*Git.*

* * * *

"For the record," Charlie said when Adam answered the phone, "I got these dental dam things with weird patterns on, kinda like a ribbed rubber, and they feel pretty fucking amazing."

Adam groaned and flopped backward on the sofa. It was Sunday evening and they were back at school tomorrow—and he didn't know whether he was hoping Charlie's affectionate streak would last into school or not. The attention was incredible, but…he kind of didn't want school to know yet, either.

"They do!" Charlie insisted. "It's like…weird pressure changes and stuff when you rub, and—"

"TMI," Adam said.

"You're gonna touch it eventually."

"*Still* TMI." He swapped the phone to the other ear. "What are you calling me for?"

"I'm bored."

"And I'm your choice above Ollie?"

"Now you're not shoving me into sheds, yeah—but don't tell her."

"I dunno," Adam mused, around the wide idiotic grin Charlie's admission had sparked off. "That sounds like good blackmail material."

"She'd kill me. And you'd be minus a boyfriend and back to square one."

Adam curled his toes at the word. *Boyfriend.* Fucking hell, he had a boyfriend and the boyfriend knew it and said it and…

And Adam was turning into a total girl lately.

"Actually, I did call for a reason."

"Which is?" Adam asked acerbically.

"Well, I'm not gonna be in school tomorrow, so…"

"You're not?" Adam blinked. "Why not?"

"Got an exam."

"You've got an *exam*? In what?"

"Maths," Charlie said. "You know, the A-level and all that stuff Mr. Bagshaw wants me to take. There's an early exam sitting at some center in Cirencester and I have to go there if I want my result before the GCSEs. 'Cause if I get a good grade, I can apparently skip out on the GCSE—anyway, not important, thing is I won't be back in time even for afternoon school."

"Okay. So?"

"So, I won't see you tomorrow."

"So?" Adam prompted again.

"So, can I come over this evening?"

Adam glanced toward the kitchen. Danni had dropped the twins two weeks ago and had brought them over today. It was a big messy family muddle, and…

"Okay."

And who cared? They were all focused on the new babies and Adam was bored of new babies. They didn't even do anything.

"Awesome. In which case, can you let me in?"

"What?"

"I'm on your front gate."

"*What?*" Adam yelped and abandoned the phone. What the hell? It was raining and everything and Charlie had just shown up and not even rung the bell? Was he nuts? Okay, yes, he was blatantly out of his tree, but—

He wrenched the door open and the porch light snapped on. It wasn't even quite dark yet, the sky a deep steely gray, and the shadow sitting on top of the garden gate grinned.

"Get in here!" Adam cried.

Charlie laughed, sliding down from the gate and bouncing across the garden. His hair was plastered to his head and his jacket was literally dripping. He toed off his shoes on the mat and his socks made a squishing sound.

"What were you doing just sitting out in the rain?!"

"Rain's nice."

"Stay *right* there. Don't move an inch," Adam ordered and bolted into the kitchen. There were towels in the dryer, fresh and warm. He'd seen Dad put them in before dinner.

"Adam? What's wrong, dear?"

"Charlie's here," he blurted, grabbing a couple of the bigger towels from the tumble dryer. "And he's been sitting out on the gate in the rain 'cause he's a tit!"

"Who?" Nat asked.

"Oh, yes, Adam has a new boyfriend," Dad said, like it was just the sort of thing that could be mentioned in passing.

"In the rain? It's bucketing it down!" Mum cried and put down her glass of wine. She followed Adam back into the hall, where Charlie was still standing on the mat. "Has something happened? Here, put your jacket on the banister and get those socks off."

Adam threw a towel over Charlie's head and caught the jacket that was tossed at him. "What's happened?" he demanded and wide blue eyes gave him a bewildered look under the white fabric.

"Nothing," Charlie insisted. "I *like* the rain. It's cool."

"Well, you can't wear those wet clothes," Mum said firmly. "Adam will loan you something to wear. Go and get changed and I'll put all that through the dryer."

"Yes, Mrs. Wood."

"Who're you, then?"

Adam flushed scarlet as Nat appeared in the hall and eyed Charlie obviously from head to toe. She had lime green hair this week and Charlie blinked at it in silence for a good half-minute.

"Is this your new boyfriend, Adam?" Nat asked with that evil smirk of hers.

"Oh, shove off, Nat."

"You have to introduce us!" she insisted.

"No, I don't. Charlie, upstairs," Adam added, shoving Charlie in the back.

"Nice to meet you, Charlie!" Nat yelled after them, so Adam snatched the towel back off Charlie's head and threw it at his sister.

"You suck!"

"That your sister or your aunt or what?" Charlie asked as Adam pushed him into his bedroom and started rummaging in his chest of drawers. Charlie was scrawny. There was no way Adam's jeans would stay up on him, but Adam was pretty sure he had some old drawstring jogging bottoms in here somewhere.

"My sister," he said. "Natalie."

"Cool."

"She's as crazy as you," Adam grumbled and shoved some clothes Charlie's way. "There. Get changed."

Charlie paused.

"What? Do it, or I'll tell Dad you got dizzy and he'll go into doctor-mode."

"Um…can I use your bathroom, then?"

Adam blinked. "To *change*?"

"Or can you, you know. Gimme a minute?"

Adam frowned, oddly hurt. "You…want me to leave the room?"

"Just so I can get changed."

"M'not gonna jump you."

"I wouldn't mind that," Charlie mumbled then reddened. "I just don't really fancy just stripping off right in front of you."

Adam was thrown—rudely—back to their aborted make-out session in Charlie's room and flushed. "Okay," he said and bit back the urge to push the issue. Maybe after Charlie had changed. "Um, you can use the bathroom."

Charlie vanished. Adam took a deep breath and steeled himself, deciding that maybe since they were starting to push the HIV boundaries, it was time to start pushing some of Charlie's weird body-issue ones, too. Body shy, Adam's *arse*. Charlie had nothing to be body shy about, from what Adam could feel, and Adam had to form a plan of attack. And Adam had learned from his sisters—and his mother, truth be told, but he wouldn't tell her that—that the best attacks were usually the ones that didn't have to be planned in huge detail and put into careful practice. Not when it came to people.

He frowned and slipped out of his room to knock on the bathroom door. "Charlie?"

"Uh-huh?"

"Unlock the door a sec?"

"M'changing."

"Yeah, I know. Unlock the door?"

There was a pause.

"You know," Adam lowered his voice, hoping to God that Nat had gone back into the kitchen, "if I'm going to know how amazing a dam feels on you, I'm going to have to see you."

Silence.

"Unlock the door?" Adam coaxed.

*Clunk.*

Adam barely cracked the door enough to get inside before shutting it behind him and locking it again—last thing they needed was Nat barging in or something—and offering Charlie a smile. He'd changed into the jogging bottoms, but was still wearing his damp white T-shirt, his hair messy from where he'd roughly dried it.

"Let me see?" Adam pleaded, touching his fingers to the hem of the wet cotton. "I'll have to eventually."

"Doesn't mean I have to like it," Charlie grumbled and Adam frowned.

"Why don't you want me to look?"

Charlie shrugged. He always shrugged crooked, his left shoulder higher than the right, and his head lolled briefly towards that side. It was rhythmic and charming and Adam stepped close enough to feel the heat coming through the damp clothing.

"I like the way the rest of you looks."

Charlie grimaced. "Yeah, well, you're weird."

"Am not," Adam protested. "You've got amazing eyes and this big brilliant smile and…"

Charlie was going red and Adam dared to press a tiny kiss to the corner of his lips.

"Is it—is it the gender thing?"

"No."

"Really?"

"Really. I'm actually…kind of okay with that bit. I mean, maybe not the tits, but…you know, your dad was saying vaginal sex and yeah, I'd like to try that."

Adam frowned. "So—what is it?"

"I just—don't want you to."

"Charlie? I mean…I have to ask, okay? I have to, 'cause…I know I don't know everything and it's okay that you're not ready to tell me everything just yet, but…I know *enough,* you know?" Adam paused, then took a deep breath. "Do you...do you have scars you don't want me to see?"

Charlie blinked. "Scars?"

"You know..."

"Oh," Charlie said and grimaced. "No. I never...no."

"It's just...some stuff Phoebe once said. You never self-harmed?"

"Well..." Charlie rolled his eyes. "Some of the stuff I did — okay, most of it — it was harming me and I knew that, so... yeah, I suppose technically I did self-harm, but not cutting. Or burning or anything like that. No scars."

Adam relaxed...sort of. As much as he could after that admission. "So?"

Charlie exhaled heavily. "I know it's stupid and I shouldn't be so weird about it. I'm working on not being so — off."

"Well, you're not allowed to judge your appearance," Adam said. "You go that color when I say the total truth about your face, you lose your right to judge how you look naked."

Charlie laughed then shifted on his feet.

"I'll make you a deal," he said. "I'll-I'll let you see, just this once, just for a minute, if...if you let me put my hand down your jeans."

Adam stared.

"You — want to touch me?"

"Let me think...*yeah.*"

Adam grinned and stepped back, making a 'go on' gesture with his hands.

"Deal?"

"Deal."

Charlie took a deep breath — and stripped the T-shirt off.

Adam didn't even give him time to drop it on the floor — he pushed forward again immediately, knowing exactly how to disrupt Charlie's discomfort, and kissed him hard against the bathroom door, both hands splayed on Charlie's bare hips. His skin was warm and incredibly smooth. When he inhaled in surprise at the kiss, powerful ribs surged against Adam's fingers and it was a heady feeling. One of his hands came up to cup the back of Adam's head and just like that the tension leaked away and Adam felt a strong heartbeat and the gentle sweeps of muscle under that inviting skin.

But he didn't look. He kissed and didn't look. Baby steps, you know? It had worked before and it was working now. And Adam knew all about baby steps to doing something he was scared of.

"You feel fine to me," Adam whispered against Charlie's mouth — and there were fingers tugging at his fly, and he groaned when heat passed into his jeans.

And into his *underwear*.

"Holy hell," Adam groaned. It was a deep, guttural sort of noise and Charlie's lips caught the edge of it. His hand was hot and clever and determined and this was nothing like masturbation. Nothing like it at *all*.

It was over embarrassingly fast and Adam had to press his forehead to Charlie's shoulder and just breathe for a minute. It felt as though he had to rearrange his soul back inside his own body.

When he opened his eyes, Charlie was giving him an... unreadable look. There was something soft and distant in those brilliant eyes and Adam tilted his head. "What?"

"Thanks," Charlie murmured and the kiss was barely a breath, a mere clasp of lips that parted slowly as though they were clinging together. Could lips hug? It was like a hug more than a kiss, so slight and gentle that to call it a kiss was exaggerating.

"Like I said," Adam breathed, catching Charlie's gaze and holding it. He could feel something...shifting around them. The air was too close and he felt almost dizzy. The room was bending. "You look fine to me." Charlie's skin under his fingers was the most intense thing Adam had ever touched.

Charlie's lips twitched — a tiny movement that...Adam didn't know what it did — caused a ripple in the space-time continuum, what? — but something changed.

"Can I put my shirt on now?" Charlie asked and Adam laughed, letting go and stepping back.

And it felt as if...as if something magnetic was trying to pull him forward again, as if he *couldn't* let go, and as if...

As if he'd suddenly — quite suddenly — had it all ramped up a notch.

He watched Charlie slide the borrowed shirt on and run both hands through his wet hair, and Adam's heart punched sideways in his chest as he realized what the shift had been. The shiver in his fingers was gone. The churning in his stomach whenever Charlie smiled was gone. His crush was gone.

And in its place was something far, *far* more powerful.

# Chapter Seventeen

"Shut your ugly face!"

"His face isn't ugly!" Adam interrupted. Ollie stuck her tongue out, but the distraction was enough—Charlie tackled her into the grass and shook her, jeering about her alleged crush on her next-door-neighbor's son. Adam settled back. Job done.

He'd embarked on a new campaign—stop letting Charlie get away with derogatory comments about himself. He didn't go *overboard* or nothing, but, you know. Correcting him sometimes. Telling him he looked good, or he'd done good. Using him to help with maths homework—which was totally part of the plan and nothing to do with Adam not wanting to do it himself. Whatever it took, you know? Sacrifices for the one he—

*Well.*

Phoebe had caught on and he'd outright told Ollie, but Ollie and Charlie had that weird sibling thing going on, so she ragged on Charlie anyway, sometimes. But sometimes was okay. Adam could battle against sometimes and, really, the challenge would be to get Charlie to believe it, not Ollie to say it.

And boy, was that going to be a challenge.

"*Oi!*" Phoebe rapped the top of Adam's textbook. "Stop staring at them and help me!"

Exam season had hit and with it, leave from school to study. Adam didn't *really* feel the need—he found GCSEs too easy, to be honest—but Phoebe was the type to panic about exams even if they were exams she'd ace. So he'd agreed to study for their history paper with her.

He was regretting it. Study sessions were in Ollie's back garden, because she was the only one without siblings or parents or random animals always hovering around, and that meant Charlie was there. In the sunshine. Wrestling with Ollie in the grass. Barefoot and wearing only a thin T-shirt and a pair of jeans.

Yeah, Adam was…regretting this study session thing.

"Focus!" Phoebe snapped then sighed. "Guys! Cut it out! You're distracting us!"

"You so have a crush," Charlie told Ollie, leaving her with that parting shot and retreating to Adam. He sprawled out in the grass, all freckled skin now that summer had finally arrived, and twisted to stare at Adam upside down. "How's it going?"

"You're like a cat," Adam decided, stroking Charlie's hair. It was hot from the sun and he dropped his hand farther to rest on Charlie's stomach. That was part of the plan, as well. Charlie wasn't—and Adam wasn't either, really—used to being touched. Not…nicely, anyway. He was used to being wrestled with and pounced on, but not so much…hugging and that kind of touching.

Adam intended to rectify that, too. And it was nice to be able to touch in front of the girls and not get teased now. They were getting used to it, along with Charlie

"Huh," Phoebe said, looking down Charlie's body and frowning. "Go figure."

"What?"

"I never paid attention before, but your feet are normal."

Ollie sniggered. "Congrats, Charlie!"

"Oh, shut up!" Phoebe huffed. "I meant I thought they'd be like your hands. I never noticed they're not before."

Charlie shrugged. "Nope. Just the hands." He wiggled his toes—all ten of them, unlike his hands—and stretched his head back to peer at Adam again. His eyes were enormous from this angle and Adam smiled. "I'm bored."

"Yeah?"

"Yeah. When're you done?"

"Not for ages."

Charlie screwed up his face. "Jesus, how much history can there *be*?"

"About a hundred and fifty years in this paper."

"And how much have you done so far?"

"About ten."

"*Urgh,* kill me. I'm bored."

"I got that the first time," Adam said mildly, rubbing his hand over Charlie's biceps. A huff, a shift and suddenly Charlie's head was in the middle of Adam's textbook. "Hey!"

"You don't need to study. You told me so this morning," Charlie pointed out.

"Adam!" Phoebe scolded.

"I'm helping you!"

"And neglecting me," Charlie said and pouted. "That's ten whole years. A *decade.* You can take a break now."

"Why aren't you studying?" Adam asked.

"Because I don't need to for maths, ICT and science, I'll fail English anyway, geography isn't for another month and we're all fucked when it comes to French."

"True," Ollie said.

Adam didn't know whether to bollock him for dissing his own abilities in English and French, or kiss him to reinforce the good thing he'd acknowledged his skill in the other subjects. Hmm.

"Okay, me and Feebs will make a start on Henry VIII — any bit you're not interested in, Adam?"

"All of it?" Adam suggested. "Um, the diplomacy section. That's easy."

"Okay," Ollie said. "Me and Feebs will get going on diplomacy and you and Charlie go to the shop and bring back ice creams."

"Orders," Charlie said, holding out his hand. It was a ritual to write ice cream orders on Charlie's hands and the first time Adam had seen it, it had seemed creepy because of — well, because of his hands. Now he felt a weird surge of *don't touch his hands* when Ollie cupped the palm to ink her choice on the back.

"We should just tattoo our ice cream orders here," Phoebe suggested as she added hers.

"You change your mind too much," Charlie said and hauled himself up off the grass. "C'mon, Ads."

"Put your shoes on!" Phoebe called after them, but Charlie just latched and unlatched the side gate.

"Why?" he yelled over his shoulder. "S'just over the green!"

Then they were alone. Ollie's village was quiet and Adam simply smiled when Charlie took his hand and swung them as they crossed the road, both barefoot. The potholed tarmac was hot and gritty and the grass on the green cool and soothing.

"I'll kiss you later," Adam said decidedly.

"Not complaining, but why?"

"For not being...for admitting you're actually good at some subjects at school, instead of insisting you're stupid."

Charlie groaned.

"Stop it. You're doing good, don't ruin your winning streak."

Charlie laughed. "Okay, then. So, I get kisses if I'm not all up in my own face?"

"When you're right about how epic you are, yes, you get kisses."

"Huh. Good therapy technique."

"Thanks."

"Wonder why Dan never tried it."

"Dan?"

"My counselor."

The sudden show of openness startled Adam, but he knew better than to show it and just laughed instead. "I hope your counselor isn't snogging you!"

"That's my point—if he was, maybe I'd be better by now."

"No kissing your counselor," Adam said. "I own those kisses now."

"My counselor's?"

"*Yours*, dipshit. They're mine."

"Possessive, much?"

Adam heated. "Actually…I kind of wanted Ollie to let go of your hand when she was writing her order down."

"Holy shit, you *are* possessive."

"Yeah. So—your kisses. Mine."

"Yessir," Charlie said as they climbed over the church wall and cut through the graveyard to the little lane beyond where the shop-cum-post-office-cum-tearoom was. Their hands drifted apart in the shadows of the tombstones, but when they disturbed a cloud of butterflies on a purple bush by the dovecote, Adam gave in to temptation and reeled Charlie in by the T-shirt for a quick kiss.

"For…not being all up in your own face," he said.

Charlie's smile was softer than usual. "Come back to mine once you're done studying?"

"For what?" Adam asked as they crossed over the road and into the cool interior of the shop.

"Therapy," Charlie said, making air quotes, then peered at the back of his hand. "Okay. Phoebe wants a screwball and Ollie wants a white Magnum. Racist cow."

Adam sniggered as he fished them out of the cooler box. "I thought you hated reading?"

"I do. Look." Charlie turned his hand around, and showed Adam two letters, a smiley face and a symbol. *WM :)* and a swirly thing that was either a tornado or a badly-done whirlpool. "Are there Calippos in there?"

"Orange ones."

"Deal. And you coming over after studying?"

"You never told me for what," Adam said as Charlie rummaged in his jeans for change. The elderly lady behind the counter gave Adam an odd look—usual, in villages so tiny—but called Charlie 'sweetie' and asked how his girlfriend was.

"She's fine, Mrs. Lundy," Charlie said breezily. "Exams, so we were sent to fetch the treats."

Adam chuckled as the door clinked shut behind them. "Girlfriend?"

"You give up correcting them after a while," Charlie said. "So? Coming over?"

"For what?"

"For...therapy. Positive reinforcement for you, that you can get within ten feet of me without giving me lurgy, and positive reinforcement for me, that..."

Charlie trailed off. Adam waited through the whole graveyard and prompted him at the wall.

He wasn't expecting the answer.

"Positive reinforcement for me that I can strip off in front of you and not feel like a fuckwit. Deal?"

"...Wow. Deal."

* * * *

They walked back to Stoker Farm from Ollie's that evening. Half an hour over fields and Adam realized they were close when a sheepdog came bolting out of the tree line just below the ridge and started worrying Charlie's shoelaces.

"Evening, Spaz."

"Spaz?"

"I shit ye not, her name's Spaz," Charlie said, and ruffled the dog's ear. "She's not ours. Hawthorns. Over there." He lifted an arm and pointed to the faint outline of a house, four fields away and tiny. "She's a lovely animal, aren't you?"

The dog sniffed at Adam's laces then decided Charlie was the favorite. She followed them across two more fields, then dropped back and disappeared as they approached the rear yard.

"You like dogs, then?"

"Better'n I like people sometimes," Charlie admitted. "Hay loft?"

Adam grinned.

They hadn't been up here since...since the first time, and the puppies were gone, but the nest of old cushions and hay was still warm and weirdly comfortable and Adam wasted no time in pulling Charlie into the nest and kissing him. Hard.

"S'at for?" Charlie murmured.

"Being you," Adam offered and felt Charlie smile against his mouth. "You're...you're trying. I know you are. And I'm glad you are."

Charlie shrugged and freed himself to settle down, sprawling out on his side and facing Adam. "You made me want to try."

"I do appreciate it," Adam said.

"Can we...?"

"Can we what?" Adam prompted.

Charlie huffed. "Can we experiment a bit? You said your folks are away next weekend visiting your...granddad?"

"Nana."

"Are you going?"

"No," Adam admitted. "That nana doesn't like me."

Charlie blinked. "You what?"

"She's Dad's mother. She's an old witch," Adam said and wrinkled his nose. "Apparently, I'm not her grandkid 'cause I'm adopted."

"Yeah, you are, it just makes you the evil psycho grandkid who's gonna stab all the other grandkids in their sleep."

Adam sniggered. Charlie's grin was wicked for a minute, then it faded.

"So, you'll have the house to yourself?"

"Friday and Saturday night, yeah."

"Can we use it, then?"

Adam blinked. "As in...?"

"Experiment," Charlie said. "With the condoms and everything. Not—not all the way or anything, but...start figuring it out?"

Adam's heart beat in his throat. Charlie wanted to...try stuff out already? "You'll, um...you'll have to take your shirt off," he said.

"Right now?"

"Well, I wouldn't say no, but...that weekend. If you did come over and we did...experiment a bit."

"Okay."

Adam blinked. "Yeah?"

"Yeah." Charlie's shrug was relaxed. "It's getting harder not to just...grope you and I'm a bit worried you'll clock me one if I don't give you fair warning. Or shove me into a shed again."

Adam groaned. "You're never going to let me live that down, are you?"

"Nope."

He laughed and suddenly Charlie was a little bit closer and his hand was on Adam's waist. "What kind of experiment?"

"I'll be crude if you make me say it."

"So?"

"I want to find out what someone else's dick feels like in my mouth," Charlie said and Adam sputtered. Holy *shit.* That wasn't crude, that was — Adam's face. On fire. *Again.* "I warned you!"

"Hardly!" Adam protested. "Oh, my God." But...under the shock and instinctive *what the fuck* recoil, there was a tiny part — okay, maybe a bit more than a tiny part of him — that sat up and paid attention. What would Charlie's lips around him feel like?

"Would you let me?"

Adam bit his lip. "Maybe."

Charlie dropped his hand and tugged at the front of Adam's jeans. "It's okay if you don't want to."

"I know it is," Adam said, a little sharply, and Charlie's mouth quirked up at one side in a smirk. "Sorry. I just...I'm still getting used to this."

"And I'm not?"

"*Touché,*" Adam said. "And you want to start trying out the condoms?"

"Uh-huh. And ribbed ones are *great.*"

188

Adam laughed and flushed. "Um. Well. Maybe we can... start with those."

"And...advanced warning..."

Adam tilted his head, pressing it a little farther into the cushion. Slowly, he curled his fingers around Charlie's on his jeans. Charlie's thumb was rubbing the button as though polishing it and it was faintly nice and even more faintly... nice, you know?

"I've been thinking about other stuff too."

"What other stuff," Adam whispered. It wasn't quite a question.

"Getting in your lap, and—getting you inside me."

"*What?*"

"Yeah," Charlie said, and he didn't even look embarrassed. "I dunno. I just want to. So, you know. Fair warning."

"I dunno about that," Adam said, chewing on the edge of his lip. "I mean, the risk's higher with that."

"S'okay," Charlie said. "S'just a warning. Doesn't mean I will. Might change my mind, and, anyway, it's up to you."

Adam squeezed his hand and removed it from his jeans. Charlie dropped them in the hay between them and smiled.

"Look at that," he said. "A sex talk and you didn't freak out."

"And you said you'd take your shirt off if we did anything."

Charlie grimaced. "Yeah, true."

"Progress all round," Adam said loftily and tugged. "C'mere."

Charlie wriggled over in the hay until he was within hugging range, so Adam hugged him. "This is nice, too," Charlie admitted.

"Mm. Um. Charlie? Don't get weirded out?"

"Depends what you're gonna do."

"I want to...I want to ask you something."

"Yeah?"

Adam twisted a coil of dark hair around his finger. "What...what happened in Year Nine?"

Charlie froze.

It was as though Adam had electrocuted him, or just killed him stone-dead or something—he went completely rigid in Adam's arms, and not in a good, cool way. In a bad, what-had-he-said, Charlie-was-gonna-flip-his-shit way.

"I just," Adam started then stopped. Then restarted. "You never told me and Ollie and Phoebe drop hints, but they won't tell me and I…I need to know, Charlie. It's still hanging over you, what happened, and I want to help."

"I—"

"Just let me in, yeah?" Adam coaxed. "I let you in about the HIV. Let me about Year Nine."

Very slowly, Charlie's hands found their way to Adam's chest. And pushed. He pushed himself away, half-sitting up in the gloom, and when he just kept rising, Adam took hold of his shirt and held on.

"Please?"

"I…Ads…"

"Please," Adam whispered. "I won't tell anyone anything if you don't want me to, Charlie, but let me in?" He wanted to know. He desperately wanted to know, to separate out rumor from fact, to tease out what Phoebe knew from what Phoebe supposed and to get the detail he was *sure* Phoebe didn't have. Because if there was one thing Adam knew about Charlie, it was that *nobody* knew some things about Charlie. Charlie sat down again, back turned. Adam shifted his hold to the front of Charlie's shirt and pulled, tugging him once more against Adam's chest. Maybe…maybe it would be easier this way? If Charlie didn't have to see? He didn't seem to like looking at himself, sometimes, and… and Adam had a bad feeling there was a lot of staring at Charlie in Year Nine.

Shut up. It made sense.

"Please," he whispered and Charlie squeezed his hands.

"I…I might flip my shit or cry," he said hoarsely.

"S'okay."

"I mean…I might *really* lose my shit, Adam. I'm not…I'm

not normal. You know, in the head. I'm fucked up in the head."

Adam kissed the side of that fucked-up head. "It's okay," he repeated. "M'not going anywhere."

"Maybe you ought to."

"And maybe not," Adam whispered. "You stuck around to hear about my HIV. So I'll stick around to hear this. And we'll deal with it, yeah? You and me. Whatever it is."

Charlie shook his head and Adam took a breath to try again — and Charlie beat him to it.

Charlie opened his mouth and — for the first time — started to really talk.

# Chapter Eighteen

"I was nine when Dad died."

Adam said nothing. Charlie wasn't looking at him — or anything else. He was staring off at the ceiling and Adam thought maybe he wasn't seeing anything at all.

"He just died."

"Just died?" Adam prompted quietly when Charlie went quiet again. When Charlie said nothing more, Adam released his death hold on the shirt, draped his arms around those broadening shoulders and pressed his nose to the side of Charlie's head above the ear, into that nest of fluffy hair.

"He just died," Charlie repeated. "Here, at the farm. It was in October, nearly November. He didn't come down from the top field and it was getting late. Mum sent me up to call him in — he liked training the dogs up there, see, he'd lose track of stuff. So, I went up to top field and he was lying in the mud by the Jeep. And he weren't dead yet. He looked at me, and he was just…gurgling, you know? Like he was brushing his teeth. And the dogs were all barking and whining and I took off to get Mum. Just turned and legged it." Charlie's voice was rough and short, that aggressive tone he took sometimes when he was getting riled up. The one he'd had out on the playing fields when they'd argued, before anything was going right at all.

"Only I was a right fat kid back then — took after me dad, that's what everyone said — and it took me ages. And the farm being where it is, we had to call the helicopter ambulances, the yellow ones."

"Air ambulance?"

"Yeah." Charlie paused and folded up his hands to curl

around Adam's wrists. His fingers were chilly. "Took ages. All of it took ages. And he died."

Adam opened his mouth, wanting some…some detail, maybe, but it was so macabre, and…

"He died up there. Heart attack. I heard Uncle Keith say something a few days later. Died before the chopper got to him, right in the mud where I left him. And Uncle Keith said if I had been a bit faster, Dad would've made it."

Adam's jaw dropped. "What? Charlie—"

"And I believed him."

"Charlie, *no.*"

"I did," Charlie said ruthlessly. "I was just nine, I was this fat, useless nine-year-old who couldn't run fast enough. It was downhill all the way, Ads. It should never have taken me so long."

"Yeah, but Charlie—"

"Can you just…listen?" Charlie interrupted harshly. "It's hard enough saying this and I already have a counselor. Just…shut up and listen."

Adam shut up and listened.

"I believed him, okay? And I was nine, and…I always got on better with Dad than with my mum. Always. Right from when I was little and coming out as a boy when I was seven made it worse because he was so chill about it but Mum wasn't. So, we were close, me and Dad, and me and Mum weren't. And Dad dying…it never helped that. She was busy with the girls, you know? Immy was just a baby and Dad was gone. One minute he was there, the next he wasn't and…you ever lost someone, Ads?"

"No," Adam whispered faintly. *Not like that. Not somebody close like that.*

"Well, it's…the stuff that stays the same that gets to you. That got to me," Charlie said. "We still had Sunday dinner just the same. Dad's boots were still by the door. I was still going to school. The funeral was on a Thursday afternoon and I went to school on Friday. It was like we buried him and things just carried on. Everything just carried on like normal, 'cept for the weeds that grew up behind the old Jeep."

Adam pushed his face into that hair and held on tight. His throat felt choked.

"And I guess that got to me more than Dad dying. I felt as though something *should* have changed, you know? But there was nothing. Nobody said or did anything at all, everything just carried on. I felt as if I was the only one going around with this huge hole in my chest, as though I was the only one who missed him. And usually when I had a hole, I ate. Like Dad. Was how I got fat. Only...you know, I had Uncle Keith's voice in my head, saying Dad died because I was fat."

Adam bit back an angry denial and shifted his legs so he could bracket Charlie's hips and ribs and squeeze him with all his limbs at once. Charlie's left hand dropped onto Adam's knee, the little finger curling loosely into the denim, and the sigh nearly rattled the blinds over the window.

"So, I didn't anymore."

"Didn't what?" Adam whispered.

"Eat." A minute passed in silence, then the angry tone was back. "Was like, if I'd just been a normal kid, not a fat kid, I would've been quicker and Dad would've been okay. So I couldn't fill up the empty hole with food, which is what I always did when I hurt before. I couldn't do it that time. So I stopped eating, started running. Ran all over the farm. I'd do laps of the top field, just...run and run and run. Started losing weight, started getting fit..."

Adam had a bitter, ugly feeling that he knew where it was going.

"When I ran, the hole wasn't there. I couldn't feel it over everything else. So, I ran more. People started commenting. Started saying I had a problem — and I wasn't stupid, Ads, I knew I had a problem. I'd hear Dad gurgling in my head if I wasn't running. It got that bad I couldn't sit still in classes because I could just hear him blaming me for his death, see the way he'd looked at me, and...I dunno. I don't think I snapped. It wasn't that fast, but I started going really crazy."

Adam licked his lips, desperate to speak, but simply wrapped his arms around Charlie's chest and held on, imagining he could keep all the pieces of Charlie together that way.

"That hole in my chest where Dad had been started getting bigger and it hurt at all the time. I started veering between being so angry with myself for not being good enough — and I've never been good enough, you know? I have crazy hands and I'm kind of thick and Erica was always so clever, even when she was tiny, and I was just this...useless fat kid. And I was so angry with myself for being that way. And I was angry, or I was...like, empty. In my head too, not just my chest and my stomach. I'd go from angry to nothing, just like that."

Adam swallowed. "Then what?"

Charlie shrugged. "Just kept getting worse. We're talking, you know, years here, but it *really* got bad after I turned thirteen. I'd flip my shit over Ollie buying us too much popcorn at the cinema, you know? Stupid bad. I'd have screaming arguments with Mum if she tried to shut me in the house to stop me running. I threw things when she argued with me. I once got in a fight, a proper fist-fight, with Uncle Harry it got so bad. I'd just...if I saw her, I'd freak out. I started getting angry at her for just not being my dad, you know? I was mad at anyone who wasn't him and I took it out on her in those rows. All the time, just constant rowing. I started lashing out at everyone — wouldn't talk to other kids, wouldn't go to the teacher. God forbid you criticized what I was eating. I even hit Ollie once — she hit me back, too, twice as hard, it fucking hurt..."

Adam didn't laugh. He knew he was meant to, but he didn't. *His* chest hurt, never mind Charlie's.

"And it all just kept escalating and escalating. I could feel I was out of control but I didn't know how to stop it and I didn't care. I didn't care how bad I was treating my mum, because she wasn't Dad. My uncles weren't Dad. Nobody was going to bring my dad back and I was the one who let him leave in the first place."

Adam squeezed tight, pressing his chin into Charlie's shoulder. He wanted to say something, but he didn't dare interrupt.

"Then in Year Nine…"

Adam held his breath.

"It was just another row with Mum," Charlie said quietly. "Lots of screaming and shouting, her saying I was offing myself and I needed to get my act together, me screaming she needed to leave me alone and she always preferred the girls, anyway. The usual. And I shouted that I was so useless I'd killed Dad and Mum shouted Dad had killed himself…and I lost it. I just totally lost it. I know it's totally gay but my dad was my hero, Ads. He didn't kill himself. I mean, yeah, his diet was shit and he was stupidly fat, but he didn't mean for it to happen. He didn't want to leave us. It wasn't *him*."

Charlie's voice was cracking and Adam burrowed as close as possible, pressing his lips into Charlie's hair and whispering, "'Course he didn't want to go," desperately. Ollie had tried to warn him, but he hadn't imagined…

"I didn't mean to do it."

Adam blinked. "Do what?"

Charlie shrugged.

"You…didn't mean to do what?"

Charlie shrugged again and sighed. "Told you I'd just flip out, right? Well, I flipped out. Just took off, ran away from the house. I was wigging out, my head was all over the place, and I saw…I saw that double-decker bus that goes around the villages, you know, the Uley bus…"

"You didn't."

"I did," Charlie said bitterly. "I took one look at it and thought 'you ought to be dead, not Dad.' And I just walked right out in front of it."

Adam flinched.

"I was in hospital for months," Charlie said, "and there

was this one doctor who right from the start was saying if they didn't sort out my head, there'd be no point in sorting out my legs. Only I didn't want to know at first. I was just caught up in being angry and...you know, I figured they couldn't understand, they didn't know what it was fucking like."

He trailed off and Adam shifted his chin over Charlie's shoulder until they were as close to cheek-to-cheek as he could get. He wanted Charlie to turn around, but then... maybe Adam would want to turn his back for this too. It was so *raw*.

"Then Dan came to see me."

"Who's Dan?"

"My counselor," Charlie said and snorted. "Sort of. I mean, he is, but it's not...you know, let's sit in this office with weird squashy chairs and talk about it stuff."

Adam hummed.

"I was good at physio," Charlie said and Adam started.

"What?"

"No, it's relevant, listen. I was really good at the physio. I broke both my legs so I had to do physio and I was okay with that, you know? And the doctor, I dunno, maybe he noticed, but he stopped trying to get the children's psycho trick..."

"Psychiatrist."

"That. He stopped arranging appointments with her and this guy Dan started coming to physio instead. And he was kinda cool, you know, he'd give me proper tips like if I got really mad to rip up paper, stuff like that. He didn't actually try to talk to me about *why* for ages. Then when they said I could go home, they said I'd still have to go and see Dan."

Adam bit his lip. "Do you still see him?"

"Yeah," Charlie said quietly. "Every Saturday and some Wednesdays. We play a game of squash down the leisure center, and talk about stuff."

"Does it...help?"

Charlie snorted. "Not tried to chuck myself under any

buses."

"Don't," Adam breathed.

Charlie shrugged. "Yeah. The medication helps too."

"For…"

"They said I have a personality disorder. I don't really know what it means. They talk about all this shit but it's… you know, it's my brain. It doesn't work all divided up like that. I don't get it. But the drugs are technically for bipolar people. The doctors tried me out on them and they stop me getting so wound up—usually, anyway—and Dan's helping me sort out all the feelings shit and not…not get so up in my own face."

"You really don't get it," Adam mumbled, and Charlie started.

"You what?"

"You. You don't get it. You're scary good at maths and you keep up with Ollie which is like superhuman and you're funny and you're kind and—I can count literally on one hand the number of guys who've been comfortable with me. I'm gay and I have HIV. You know how many guys didn't freak when they found out?"

"How many?"

"You. That's it."

Charlie huffed.

"I don't get it," Adam said. "Why you're so…up in your own face, I mean. You're fucking brilliant."

"Ads…"

"You are."

"I'm nuts."

"You're amazing," Adam corrected. "You're just…you're fucking amazing. You got through all that shit and okay you're kind of crazy sometimes but it's a fun crazy and… and I've never liked anyone as much as I like you. Not ever."

Charlie's cheek creased against his own and that thin hand squeezed his knee. His kneecap felt oddly exposed in the gap between Charlie's fingers, but his grip was solid.

"Thanks."

Adam squeezed back, hard as possible, until Charlie smacked his knee.

"Ow! Jesus, Adam."

"Shut up," Adam said. "Charlie."

"What?"

"If you...you know. Need to vent or...talk or anything..."

There was a pause then Charlie's hand slid sideways to cup the very bottom of Adam's thigh where it joined his knee, and pressed. "Yeah," Charlie said. "I know. And thanks for that, too. It's...it's been a long time since I really had anyone but Ollie to talk to."

"You don't talk to Phoebe?"

"You can't tell Feebs things like you chucked yourself under a bus. She'd cry all over me or something."

Adam laughed — inappropriate though it was — and fisted both hands in Charlie's T-shirt. "No more buses."

"I don't *mean* to go off the rails."

"Well...I'll help you stay on them."

"I never said it, but I'm sorry for going off at you after Ollie's party. You know, at school and everything."

Adam shrugged. "S'okay."

"Not really."

"Yeah, it is," he said. "Y'know, you had every right to be all...confused and shit."

"Hurt," Charlie supplied. "It hurt."

Adam bit his lip. "I'm not sorry," he admitted. "I figured it was better than you maybe getting this, and...honestly, I figured it was better than the secret getting out. I never thought I could just tell you."

"Yeah, well. Here we are."

Adam hummed and bit his lip. "Did you...do you want me to not tell anybody? About the stuff you've just said."

"Not really," Charlie said, to Adam's surprise. "I don't really care. The whole school knows I went completely batshit. Why d'you think all the teachers send me to the head when I get in trouble? Everyone else gets to stand outside the classroom, but they figure I'm too whacked out to be left unsupervised so I get the head's office."

"Stop it," Adam said sharply.

"What?"

"Stop saying things like crazy and batshit. You're *not*. Your dad died, Charlie. You're kind of allowed to go off the rails a little bit after that."

"What, years later?"

"Yes," Adam insisted. "Especially when you were blaming yourself and not dealing with it well at the time, anyway." He shook his fists, still clenched in Charlie's T-shirt, and huffed. "You *might* be a bit stupid, actually, 'cause you don't get how you're fucking amazing and—"

"Fucked *up*, maybe."

"Stop it or I'm gonna slap you."

"Pft, you wish."

"I'll tickle you."

"Don't you fucking dare," Charlie warned.

"Are you really—?"

"No."

"You are!"

"No... I'm—fuck!" Charlie yelped as Adam buried his crooked fingers into Charlie's stomach and ribs and tickled. Mercilessly. Adam had sisters, so he knew *just* how to torture and he clung on with both legs to Charlie's thighs as he found all the ribs and hip bones, the flat stomach muscles and the tight sides, and—

Got headbutted.

"Fuck!"

"Serves you bloody right!" Charlie panted, scrambling away.

"Fuck you!" Adam declared and lunged, tackling Charlie back into the hay. They scuffled, Charlie trying to push Adam away and Adam intent on pinning him down and tickling again—

Until...

Until suddenly he had one of Charlie's arms pinned above

their heads and the other trapped between their chests and they were face-to-face. And Charlie's eyes were like...like falling into an ocean from a passenger plane from thirty thousand feet up or something.

The kiss was sudden but softened instantly. Charlie's lips were chapped and warm and familiar now in a way that sent a thrill down Adam's spine and burrowed into his stomach in a coil of warm anticipation. That he *could* do it was still just as startling as the fact that he *was* doing it. Charlie's mouth was wide and gentle. His wrists, still squeezed tight in Adam's hands, twitched and shifted but made no real attempt to move.

It was like a tsunami crashing down, the sudden surge of raw emotion, and Adam felt as though he had been hit by a savage tide and was sliding away into the sea — but it didn't matter, because he was hanging on to Charlie and Charlie had to be sliding, too.

"Tell me," Adam whispered against Charlie's mouth. "Tell me how you came back from the edge."

He half-knew and half-didn't, what he was asking. Charlie's eyes had darkened to the stormy North Sea in winter, but the half-lidded, glazed expression was something softer and more tempered. The proverbial storm in a teacup or something.

"S'gonna sound daft," Charlie mumbled.

"Say it, anyway."

"Immy."

"Imogen?"

"Yeah," Charlie whispered and twisted his wrist until Adam let go. But the hand didn't go far, dropping into Adam's hair and playing with the strands. Charlie looked...dazed and calm. *Beautiful*, some voice in the back of Adam's head whispered, but he quashed it as being too girly. Amazing, he decided. Charlie looked amazing.

"What'd she do?"

"Family visit," Charlie said. "I dunno why it got to me, but she brought me a picture. Insisted the nurse stuck it up by my diet sheet on the wall, said if I kept looking at it I'd remember to come home and not go away like Dad did."

Adam hardly dared to breathe.

"And I felt like such a shit," Charlie murmured. "I felt like such a heel making my little sister think it was going to happen all over again. It was all she knew about Dad, that he'd gone away and that was why Mum was sad sometimes, why I was angry sometimes. And I must have made her ask if I was going away, too. And I just suddenly...wanted to not be there, to do something to calm down even if it didn't make it better. I just wanted to be okay, so I could tell Immy I wasn't going away."

Adam found his voice. "M'glad."

"Sometimes, now...so'm I."

"Good," Adam breathed, and it seemed like they were wrapped up in something fragile that would break if he spoke too loudly. "You shouldn't be ashamed of it, Charlie. What your brain does. It's not your fault."

Charlie hummed, then frowned. "If I can't be ashamed of it because it's not my fault..."

"Uh-huh."

Charlie blinked, and the glazed distance vanished. His gaze sharpened and it was like a knife through Adam's mind.

"Why are you ashamed of the HIV?"

# Chapter Nineteen

It was nine o'clock in the evening before Adam called Mum to come and pick him up and…he didn't want to go, really, but he couldn't stay, either. Charlie had been quiet for ages after his confession and Adam hadn't wanted to leave him like that. But—

"I have an exam tomorrow," he said on the threshold of the barn, the sinking sun throwing a shroud of gray over the farm. "Ten o'clock. But…are you free after?"

"Uh-huh."

"Will you be here?"

Charlie shrugged. "Probably. Auntie Liz is visiting. I'll probably end up babysitting if one of the girls doesn't kidnap me."

"Well, I'll text you and I'll come here and we can…hang out and stuff."

"And stuff," Charlie said. "Thanks for this evening, Ads. I think I needed that."

Adam hugged him tightly. Charlie hadn't—quite—cried, but there was red around the blue in his eyes and he wasn't right. And Adam didn't quite know how to tell him to be all right, either.

"Ads."

"Tomorrow we can—"

"Ads. I'm okay."

Adam bit his lip. "You sure?"

"Yeah," Charlie said and smiled. It wasn't quite as bright as usual, but it wasn't forced either. Adam licked his lips and Charlie—glancing quickly around the yard—kissed him. "Go on. You've got to be…a historian?"

"Religious studies," Adam corrected.

"Eurgh. Fine, go be a monk. Whatever. Kick arse. I'll see you tomorrow."

A car horn sounded beyond the outer gate and Adam kissed Charlie one last time before letting go. He didn't like it—it felt wrong to leave him after Charlie had just totally bared his soul like that—but he had to go. And Charlie's question—*why are you ashamed of the HIV?*—just kept niggling in the back of his head.

Adam hadn't answered and had changed the subject, but...the question wouldn't go away.

"Had a good day, dear?" Mum asked as he slid into the car and Adam hummed. "Adam?"

"M'fine."

"So why the long face?"

Adam shrugged. "Charlie...Charlie let me in on a few things tonight."

"Oh?" Mum asked as she reversed out into the lane and started down the narrow, bumpy track back towards home.

"Like...like how when his dad died, Charlie got really messed up."

"Ah," Mum said. At the junction that split Adam and Phoebe from Ollie and Charlie, she paused. "Want to get a KFC and talk about it?"

Adam eyed her.

"We won't tell Dad," she promised.

Adam smiled. It had been a long time since they'd gone in cahoots about dirty takeaways. Dad *hated* fast food. And Adam...kind of missed being eleven, sometimes, and sneaky trips to the McDonalds on the pretense of helping Mum with the food shopping.

"Okay."

She turned left instead of right, the indicator clacking loudly in the quiet car, and said, "So what did you find out?"

"Stuff."

"Adam..."

"He's got a personality disorder," Adam blurted out. "He has to take drugs or he goes a bit...you know, a bit out of control and stuff."

"And what did you say to that?"

"He said more than that," Adam said, ignoring her. "He said...he said there's loads of arguments at home and one day he had a huge row with his mum and ran away and... and he was so messed up he walked right out in front of a bus. On purpose."

"When was this?"

"A couple of years ago."

"What did he mean to do?"

"He said...he said he was thinking that he should have died, not his dad, but then he said he didn't mean to do it," Adam mumbled.

"Is he still suicidal?"

"I don't think so." No, in fact. Adam was sure he wasn't, but...but the way Charlie had just come out with it and the fact he'd done it at all...could someone be fleetingly suicidal like that? Could they want to, and just not want to? Was that what a personality disorder did? "No."

"And how are you feeling?"

Adam blinked. "Me?"

"You're the one he told," Mum said evenly. She'd not been to court that day and she looked more mumsy in her red jumper with her hair let down. "And it's not easy to hear that kind of thing about someone you love, sweetheart."

Adam fidgeted. "It hurt," he said eventually.

"Mm?"

"That...you know, it's *Charlie*. And he's all...he's really different and—and he's not like anyone else I've ever met and it's amazing and...it really hurt, the way he talked about himself. Like he was pathetic or something."

"It does hurt," Mum agreed softly, "when someone quite brilliant thinks they are less than what they are."

Adam paused.

"I imagine you're feeling now what your father and I feel

every time you shy away from other boys your age, Adam."

"Mum…"

She pulled over. Quite abruptly, too. She just pulled the car over tight against the hedge and flicked the hazard lights on.

"Mum—"

"When you and Charlie sat down for that talk with your father, I was so *proud* of you, dear. I've always worried — ever since that first school — that you would let life pass you by because you were too afraid to try again. I've always been upset by your simple pig-headed refusal to see yourself for who you really are, Adam."

Adam felt his face burning. *"Mum,* Christ…"

"And you should be proud of Charlie right now, too," she continued, speaking over him like he hadn't bothered. "I imagine it's taken him a lot to let you in and what's in our heads is never the easiest of things to share."

Adam squirmed.

"Did you make plans to see him again soon?"

"Tomorrow," Adam mumbled.

"Then I suggest you take your time tomorrow. He's going to be feeling pretty vulnerable right now."

"I had a campaign," Adam blurted.

Mum quirked an eyebrow.

"I was…I was trying to get him to stop calling himself thick and stuff. You know. Positivity and stuff. Only…the way he was talking about his uncles and his mum and stuff, I don't think it's easy there, so…"

"So don't see him at the farm," Mum said and chuckled. "Invite him over, darling. Have the house to yourselves — I'll be in the study, and you know your father won't be coming out of his rhubarb patch for another month after having to talk to you and your boyfriend about safe sex."

Adam sniggered and Mum smirked.

"Between you and me, I've spent years bullying your father into taking up that responsibility when the time came," she whispered and Adam snorted. He could imagine. Mum just totally overruled Dad, like, *all* the time. "Now — onto the important things. KFC, or do we go the extra couple of miles for a McDonalds?"

Adam worried at his bottom lip.

"Adam?"

"McDonalds' milkshakes are better," he decided and fumbled his phone out of his pocket.

"All right then," Mum said, switching the hazard lights back off and easing the car into gear. "But you ate at Stoker Farm, didn't you? That's what we'll tell Dad. You had a perfectly balanced meal."

"Yes, Mum." Adam wondered, as he scrolled through his contacts, whether Charlie was properly over his eating thing. Maybe that was why Ollie was always bringing extra food to school for him. But then he'd eaten marshmallows at that sleepover at their house, so…so maybe he was a little bit over it?

He'd have to check. But first —

*YOU ARE AMAZING xxx*

*???*

*You are totes amazing. See you tomorrow :) xxx*

*ILU2 x*

Adam smiled and figured he'd just have to up the campaign a bit. Starting now.

* * * *

"Be right back," Adam said to his mother, jumping out of the car and vaulting the farm gate. He'd texted when he'd come out of the exam, but he was beginning to realize Charlie always needed physically dragging somewhere that he was supposed to go.

And finding first. Ringing the bell got him nowhere.

Ringing the bell while knocking did nothing. Even opening the door did nothing and who didn't lock their front door? "Hello?" he called into the empty hall.

"*Oi!*"

Adam jumped as a man came barreling through the kitchen door, boots clomping loudly on the tiles. One of the many cats slithered around Adam's ankles and shot into the house.

"Who the hell are you?"

The man was tall and wiry, with graying fair hair and a thin mouth. He also had hands like spades and was scowling.

"Um, I'm Adam, I'm—I'm Charlie's...friend," Adam stammered lamely.

"Huh," the man grunted, then—without moving an inch or breaking eye contact—bellowed, "Charlie!" at the top of his lungs.

Someone shouted.

"Get down here!" the man shouted.

An explosion of noise reached Adam's ears—door off wall, feet on stairs, yowl of cat getting out the way—before the kitchen door banged open and Charlie appeared in a lanky, wild-haired, oversized-clothes tumble.

"Oh!" he said, and grinned. "You're early. C'mon, gimme a sec."

He seized Adam's wrist and towed him around the man and up the stairs. Adam awkwardly hopped over the cat, dodged a pair of boots halfway up the stairs and finally managed to twist his wrist around to a more comfortable position when they reached Charlie's room.

"What the—?"

"Yeah, one sec," Charlie said, scooping the baby up off the floor. "I've been babysitting. Auntie Liz!"

He disappeared with the baby and Adam perched gingerly on the corner of Charlie's bed. Some cartoon was playing on the TV and there were baby toys all over the floor, but Adam just toed them aside and settled in for a minute. There was a book on the side table and Adam picked it up curiously, wondering if Charlie had decided to read something for once.

And groaned. It was a book on mathematical theory. Seriously? He found the bookmark—a dog-eared photograph—and opened the book to find a page of equations staring back at him. Holy shit.

He turned the photograph over and blinked. It was — well, it *had been* of all four of them. At Christmas—he recognized the decorated classroom window behind him. Only Charlie had cut it in half so the girls were missing and it was just... them. Just him and Adam.

"Okay, that's—hey!"

"You have a picture of us as your bookmark?"

Charlie went bright red as he shut the bedroom door with a snap. "Yeah, well..."

Adam grinned. "That's cool."

"Yeah?"

"Yeah," Adam said and bit his lip. "Y'know, we could always...take a proper picture instead of you having to cut up photos all the time."

Charlie flopped down onto the bed. He sprawled everywhere, Adam was starting to notice, and his T-shirt rode up to show off a tiny strip of stomach above his jeans. Adam bit his lip again then ran a thumb along the strip, watching in fascination as that warm skin jumped and tightened. "Lay off," Charlie said, pushing Adam's hand away. "Did you decide if you're kidnapping me, then?"

"Yeah," Adam said. "For today. Maybe tonight, too."

"Bring my PJs?"

"Bring your PJs," Adam advised and Charlie laughed.

"Gotcha. One sec."

He bounced up again to rummage around the haphazard room and Adam leaned back on his elbows to watch. "Bring a dose for the morning," he advised gingerly and when Charlie only made a vague 'uh-huh' noise, he relaxed. Charlie seemed okay. "I have plans."

"Yeah?" Charlie asked, throwing things into a bag. "Like what? And lead on."

Adam heaved himself up off the bed. "Like...Ollie once said you'd learned how to spoon."

"Yeah, I'm a good spoon."

"Prove it," Adam challenged and Charlie laughed.

"You're stealing me to spoon?"

"Yeah."

"Okay," Charlie said as they clomped down the stairs. He kicked the boots down too. "I guess I can live with that. Uncle Keith! I'm going out! Might not be back 'til tomorrow! Oh hey, going in style?" he added when he opened the front door and saw Mum's car.

"Uh-huh," Adam said. "I figure it's a long walk home from mine, so you'll have to stay."

"Guessing your exam went well? You're in a good mood."

Adam shrugged. "Yeah, guess so." It was more relief, but he didn't fancy saying it. He'd worried all morning if Charlie was actually okay or not. And he was acting so normal — for him, anyway — that it was putting Adam well at ease.

Plus, it helped that they could slide into the back seat together and Adam could hold one of those weird hands. Mum didn't care.

"Hi, Mrs. Wood."

"Afternoon, Charlie. Have you had your lunch, or do the two of you want to stop off on the way home?"

"Don't really do lunch," Charlie said and Adam frowned.

"We'll raid the fridge," he said, deciding that maybe he could let lunch slide — there was spooning to be had, after all — but at least something would be on the table. Metaphorically speaking.

Charlie snorted and tapped the back of Adam's hand with his free one. "Don't start fussing, man, Ollie does that enough for, like, four people."

Adam huffed, eyes drawn to their joined fingers. He frowned, turning them over to examine Charlie's pale, spidery hand. Mutant spider, anyway.

And an idea occurred.

Scratch spooning. He was going to explore.

* * * *

Adam fetched Cokes, snacks, and—*just* in case, you know?—his iPod for some background music before heading back upstairs—to find Charlie lying on his bed.

"Make yourself at home?"

"Don't mind if I do." Charlie was lying on his front, propped up on his elbows and leafing through one of Adam's magazines, shifting his socked feet in the air. "Never took you for a metal fan."

"Yeah, well," Adam said.

"So?" Charlie asked and propped his chin on his hands to grin at Adam. "Any ideas? 'Cause I got one."

"Oh?"

"You're a bit far away."

Adam laughed, shutting the bedroom door with a snap. "Yeah?"

"Yeah, mate, I'm not getting up, this bed's comfy. C'mere." And Charlie reached out a hand.

His left hand.

Adam had never touched his left hand before and that gap between the remaining fingers was suddenly stark and staring him in the face. He stared right back, fascinated. Did it hurt? Did it even work? He couldn't recall having noticed if all of Charlie's hand worked before, and suddenly—

The hand hovered and started to drop. Adam blinked, startled, as Charlie's face started to close and the smile vanished.

"Sorry," Adam said and caught the hand before it dropped entirely. Or rather, the wrist. "I just…I've never touched this hand, I don't think."

"Yeah, well, it's not diseased," Charlie said sharply then grimaced. "Look, I get it, they're weird."

"No," Adam said. "I just... Does it hurt?"

"What? No. Why would it hurt?"

"I dunno," Adam mumbled and slid his hand from wrist to palm. Charlie's palms were rough, hot and dry. Like... desert rock, or something. Charlie seemed to hesitate for a minute, then curled those two fingers around Adam's hand and pulled him down to sit on the bed. "Did...what happened?"

"Nothing," Charlie said. "S'just like you. Born that way."

"Don't—"

Charlie took a deep breath.

"No Gaga!" Adam yelped and clapped a hand over Charlie's mouth. Charlie cackled and licked his palm. "Ew! Rank."

"Please, you like my tongue," Charlie said, and stuck it out. Adam smirked, then recaptured that left hand, turning it over. Charlie's hands *were* weird, no two ways about it. The right hand had just one middle finger where the middle and ring fingers should have been. Three sets of knuckles, three fingers, no extra tendons. It was like a real-life version of the hands on *The Simpsons*. Adam always stared at that hand, because his brain liked to try and tell him he was seeing things and there really were two fingers instead of one.

But this hand—the left hand—was different. And Adam had never explored this hand before. The palm was normal. All the knuckles and tendons and muscles and everything. And the thumb and index finger were present and accounted for, but—

There was just this *space* where the middle and ring fingers should have been. The skin was smooth over the top of the knuckles of his hand, no sign of any scarring or surgery. And his little finger was half the size of the one on his right hand, bent in the middle into a little hook and the nail so small it was almost invisible. It looked broken and paralyzed, just sticking out on the end like that, and Adam very—*very*—carefully stroked a fingertip over it.

And jumped when Charlie curled it in and laughed.

"It's not dead."

"It *looks* dead," Adam blurted out, then reddened. "Er. I mean..."

"Yeah, I know, but it's not," Charlie said. "It's always been a midget, but it's all snarly 'cause I broke it when I was nine. Mum was dead against me having it cut off as a baby and apparently it can fuck your hands up if you do it later, so boom. Random finger on the end there."

"It's not random," Adam said, and paused. "Um. Does... it hurt?"

"What?"

"This bit." He pointed at the gap between the index and broken pinkie, and Charlie squinted.

"What d'you mean?"

"Well...does...what does it feel like?"

"Touch it and find out."

"No, to you," Adam said. "I mean, is it...just like your palm or the back of your hand, or..."

"It's sensitive like my palm," Charlie said, "but it doesn't hurt at all. It's just, you know. Part of my hand."

Adam rubbed a little harder at the gap and Charlie's voice caught in his throat. "Shit, sorry," Adam said. "Did that hurt?"

"Er. No. Not exactly."

"Not exactly?" Adam prompted.

Charlie grimaced. "Feels...nice, actually." He flushed again and Adam laughed.

"Really?"

"Shut up," Charlie said and tried to take his hand away. Adam hung on and started rubbing his thumb into the space instead. And Charlie *shivered.*

"Oh, my God."

"Shut up!" Charlie repeated, staring valiantly at the ceiling. Adam grinned and rolled over him to sit on his hips and capture the now-amazing hand in both of his.

"You have a hand kink!"

"The nerves are really close to the skin there," Charlie whined and Adam laughed, bending his head and licking the gap. "Fuck! Get off! Sadist. Fucking *bully*."

Adam slid his fingers around Charlie's as though interlocking his own with the missing ones. And it felt *weird*, really fucking weird, to have that space of nothing and the little hooks of Charlie's remaining fingers tucking into his. He shifted to clamp Charlie's index finger between two of his own and adjusted.

"That's weird," he said, and Charlie laughed.

"You're holding hands with a boy — that's pretty weird," he said and twisted over onto his back to grin at Adam upside-down. His hand twisted too and slid free easily. Adam scowled. Those missing fingers were going to be a pain in the arse for keeping Charlie under fucking control. He could just escape. Bastard.

"Not fair," he said petulantly and Charlie sniggered.

"C'mere."

Adam eyed him, upside down and sprawled out, and an idea occurred. "Huh," he said and Charlie barely had time to frown before Adam buried his hands in that mad hair and leaned down to kiss him. Upside-down. It always worked in the movies, right?

Well…

Well, yeah, it *worked*. And it was…it was *nice*, Charlie's little noise of surprise and the cool new angle his hand was at when it came up to clutch Adam's hair. That was good. But it was also…a bit…

Adam broke it off and sat back. Charlie blinked comically at him. "What?"

"Is it weird I miss your face?" Adam said.

"Er…"

"Like…there's no nose bumping mine. It's weird."

"You are seriously freaky, you know that?" Charlie said seriously and Adam snorted. "So kiss me the right way up, freaky-tits."

"Freaky-tits?"

"I dunno, maybe, didn't pay too much attention to 'em last time you took your shirt off…"

Adam laughed, crawling around and dropping himself unceremoniously onto Charlie's hips and chest. "Better?"

"Yup. Mostly."

"Mostly?"

"You're no fairy princess."

Adam rolled his eyes and kissed Charlie again. The right way up, this time — the heat of his face, the brush of his nose alongside Adam's, the slowly-getting-familiar grooves of his mouth. And teeth and tongue, when Charlie cupped the back of Adam's neck and opened it up properly, letting Adam in.

And this was starting to feel —

*Natural.* The solid frame of Charlie's hips between Adam's knees. The taste of him, sharp on the tip of his tongue and sweeter and softer at the back of his mouth. The way he'd breathe when Adam ran the tips of his fingers over the hidden shells of his pale ears. Even — much as Adam hadn't really noticed before — the way that Charlie's hands on his back, shoulders, neck, face — even the way they felt slight and absent was beginning to be familiar. Adam was warm and at ease, exploring the creases and hitches in Charlie's lips with his own, mapping the corners of his mouth and pulling his bottom lip with his own teeth just to feel the catch in Charlie's chest.

"Can I?"

Adam heard his own voice as though it were far away and when Charlie shrugged, it was like the world shrugged with him. But a shrug was permission — sort of — and Adam inched his hand up under Charlie's T-shirt as though that was how people had sex. Because — it was kind of that big, you know? There'd been so many false starts, so much conviction he'd never get to do this and least of all with Charlie Fielding…

"Nuh-uh," Charlie mumbled when Adam tried to break the kiss and look, and kept him reined in by the hair. Adam didn't mind. He kept his eyes closed, drinking in kisses and heat like he survived on them, and maybe blind was the better way of doing it after all because blind, he could feel the steady wash of heat rolling off Charlie's skin, feel the smooth binder expanses over steel-hard ribs and muscle, trace the soft rise of his collarbone escaping from the top. He wanted to see and yet—

Touch was heady on its own, especially as he raked his nails gently down the surface of the binder and Charlie hissed in a way that had Adam adjusting his position and fumbling with the zipper on his jeans to relieve some of the pressure. "C'mere," Charlie breathed again, but Adam was struck with a strange urge and buried his face in Charlie's neck instead to feel a jumping pulse and taste salt-tinged skin. "Fuck!" Charlie snarled, tightening a hand brutally in Adam's hair and Adam laughed.

"Just like that?"

"Fuck, yes. What are you, a vampire?"

Adam laughed again and bestowed another one on the other side, bracing himself with hands on the bed when Charlie arched, mad powerful and weirdly hot, and—

Adam stopped.

Hand still right up under Charlie's T-shirt, he stopped and pulled back at the first touch of Charlie's fingers at the waistband of his jeans. "I…"

"Please?" Charlie asked. His eyes were dark for once, the blue washed away by inky black. "I've got a condom in my bag. I just…I wanna taste you."

For a moment, the world flexed. Charlie's fingers were stroking the front of Adam's jeans, maddeningly light and Adam wanted so badly to say yes and yet—

A wariness stopped him. And in the next beat, he realized it was nothing to do with him and nothing to do with Charlie and everything to do with…with having Charlie's mouth on him there.

He swallowed, the realization earth-shattering. He was nervous and it was about totally normal shit. He wasn't ready for it and that was *all*. It wasn't about him—it was just…just *stuff,* just general stuff, like what if he wasn't any good and what if Charlie didn't like it and would he have to do it to Charlie too and—

"Not yet," he breathed and Charlie's hand slid back up to his waist. "I'm…I'm not ready yet."

"'Kay," Charlie said and Adam leaned down to kiss him again. Those hands ended up in Adam's hair again, and—

And it wasn't no. It was—not yet.

# Chapter Twenty

The newfound peace? That feeling they were settling into something and it would all be okay and Charlie could be the superhero that didn't care about HIV and Adam could be the superhero to keep Charlie grounded? That feeling?

It didn't last.

It shattered the following Tuesday.

* * * *

"I'm telling you," Charlie insisted as they dropped down off the bus, "that it's true."

"No way," Adam denied, swinging his hand casually into Charlie's and squeezing. "She likes Josh Denbar."

"I'm telling you what I saw!" Charlie retorted vehemently. "She's totally gaga. She didn't stop staring for the *whole* exam."

"Lies."

"You seriously have no faith in — the fuck?"

Charlie interrupted himself and dropped Adam's hand in the same instant as they turned the corner onto Adam's lane and saw the front door open. Mum was standing on the step in her court suit, arms folded and frowning, and there was a tall, thin woman with long hair in a ponytail on the front path, arms moving erratically as she talked.

"Oh, shit," Charlie said.

"What?" Adam asked. "Is that your — ?"

"Mum!" Charlie yelled.

The woman turned. Adam hadn't seen her close up before, and...she really didn't look much like Charlie, apart from the skinny thing. And maybe the baggy clothes habit. But she was mousy-haired and round-faced and…scowling.

"Charlie!" she snapped—literally, she snapped her fingers—and beckoned. "We're going home. Come on."

"Why?" Charlie called. "What's happened?" He stopped dead at the garden gate and Adam hovered uncertainly. Did Mrs. Fielding know? About them? Charlie'd said…

"Just get in the car, Charlie."

"But what's—?"

"Mrs. Fielding, we can discuss this calmly and civilly like responsible parents—with the boys—or…"

"There's nothing to discuss," Mrs. Fielding said. "Your son could have given Charlie a terminal illness and—"

Her voice *vanished.* The roaring in Adam's ears was too loud to hear her and he groped blindly for the gatepost. How the—what did she know? *How* did she know? She… she couldn't, there was—

"Mum, what the hell are you talking about?" Charlie's voice was loud and startled.

"I found those leaflets from the clinic!" Mrs. Fielding snapped.

"What leaflets?"

"The ones in your room, Charlie!" she shouted. "You'd highlighted the relevant passages and I know you don't have it, so it didn't take too long to put two and two together. For goodness' sake, how *stupid* can you be?"

"Mrs. Fielding, let's go inside and discuss this. I—"

"I told you, there is no discussion," Mrs. Fielding retorted and folded her arms over her chest, frowning at Charlie. "How utterly stupid can you be, Charlie? I thought this self-destructive idiocy was finally over then you go and do something as stupid as carry on with a—"

"I'm not being stupid," Charlie snarled. "I'm not—we talked about it and we did all this research and—"

"You're fifteen," she snapped. "You are far too young to have the faintest idea…"

"I know what I'm doing," Charlie said slowly. His fists

were clenching at his sides, and Adam gingerly stroked his fingers over the knuckles on the right one. Mrs. Fielding's eyes flicked down and her mouth pursed.

"Get in the car."

"I was going to spend the evening here. I texted you. You said it was fine."

"And now I'm saying it's not. Get in the car."

Charlie's voice was hardening. "Why not?"

"Because you are not throwing your life away on some silly fling with an infected—"

Adam flinched. Charlie walked straight through the gate like it wasn't there, the metal bouncing off his hip, and almost squared off to his mother, chest expanding and shoulders locking into a tense, broad poise.

"It's not," Charlie said slowly, "a silly fling."

"It's a teenage affair with a boy you barely know."

"How would you know?"

"Don't talk back to me, young lady."

Charlie *twitched*. Visibly twitched. Then his chest swelled.

"Young *man*. And he's not fucking contagious because he takes his pills and I'm not crazy because I take mine. What more do you want?" he spat. "I didn't just jump in, Mum. We've talked about it and—"

"You are fifteen years old," Mrs. Fielding snarled back in the same slow, tight voice.

"Old enough."

"You're a child," she snapped. "You've always been a child, Charlie! Ever since your father died, you have been completely out of control—what is it? Do you *want* to end up like him? Do you *want* to kill yourself out of your own bloody stupidity? Because this will kill you if you carry on with this…this *boy!*"

"I'm fucking happy!" Charlie shouted back. "I know that's a really weird fucking emotion for you, that *anyone* could be happy, but I am! I'm actually fucking happy and I've been doing better for the last like year, but you're too busy having a go at Erica and Immy and Uncle Keith to bother fucking noticing!"

"Don't you dare use that tone with me, you ungrateful little—" Mrs. Fielding yelled and Adam's breath caught. Charlie didn't look like her, but the temper was the same, the speed with which everything was blowing up.

"What tone? The same tone you fucking took with Dad every day he was alive? It wasn't my fault!" Charlie bellowed. "It wasn't me who left him at the top field. It was you who drove him there—you couldn't fucking *stand* each other and—"

The crack was loud, like a gunshot in the movies, and Charlie's head snapped sideways under the impact of his mum's hand. Her wedding ring flashed in the sun and there was a sudden, sharp silence as Charlie staggered back, his expression wide-eyed and shocked.

Very slowly, Charlie brought a hand up to his cheek and stared at his mother.

Silence.

Then his face twisted and Adam lunged.

"No!" he yelled, catching Charlie around the waist and hauling backwards as Charlie leaped for his mother, a raw shriek of pure *emotion* tearing through his throat. It was a scream and a curse and a cry all at once. It made the hairs on Adam's arms stand on end and Mum was shouting for Dad and Adam was pulling Charlie towards the front door.

"Inside, no, c'mon, inside," he gasped. "Charlie, leave it, c'mon, *leave it!*"

Charlie fought against him, but Adam was stronger and he bundled them both inside as Dad came running down the stairs.

"Mrs. Fielding's outside and she slapped Charlie," Adam said breathlessly over the sound of Mum shouting. "C'mon—Charlie, c'mon, let's go into the kitchen."

"You fucking *bitch!*" Charlie bellowed at the top of his lungs then quite suddenly sagged in Adam's grip and allowed himself to be pulled into the kitchen. He was breathing hard and Adam clung on, arms locked around

Charlie's chest, half afraid Charlie would bolt if he let go and half afraid he'd collapse.

An engine started and the front door slammed. Gingerly, Adam let go and when Charlie didn't move, Adam tried to turn him around. Charlie refused, shoes squeaking on the tiles when Adam tried to make him, so Adam gave up and hugged him from behind instead.

"It's okay," he said. Charlie was shaking, shivering like a wire stretched too tight and plucked. He was going to snap any minute. And it wasn't okay, but...but what was Adam supposed to say?

"Let me see."

Dad. He strode into the kitchen all purpose and wearing his best doctor face, but Charlie shrugged off his hand and turned away. Adam caught a glimpse of those twisted, furious features and bit his lip.

"Charlie..."

"It's fine," Charlie said and Adam threw a look at Dad. He knew what Dad was asking with that face, but he didn't know the answer. He'd never...Charlie had never said his mum had ever hit him. And — and he was still shaking, his hands twitching and Adam didn't know what to *do*.

"Charlie..."

"It's *fine!*"

"Charlie, has that happened before?" Dad asked, his deep voice cutting calmly across both of theirs.

For a moment, Charlie said nothing. Then he opened his mouth and said something totally different. "I need to call someone."

"Who?" Dad asked.

"My..." Charlie started then swallowed and stopped. "I'm... Ads, let go. Let go."

Adam blinked and let go, sliding his hands down Charlie's arms before letting them drop. It felt unnatural to let go and Dad's frown said Adam wasn't the only one struggling to keep up. What was Charlie saying? What did he mean he had to —?

It clicked.

"Do you need to call Dan?"

"Who's Dan?" Dad asked.

"Yeah," Charlie said, ignoring both of them. "I'm…I get…"

He got out of control, Adam realized. When he got too riled up, he got out of control and the way he was just standing and shivering and staring at the washing machine…

And he moved—so fucking fast Adam had no chance of stopping him. He just twisted, hand up, and smashed his fist into the wall above the kettle with such brute force that the plaster cracked and a dull, wet pop sounded. From inside Charlie's hand.

Adam's stomach lurched. Dad jumped, reaching for Charlie's elbow, but Charlie yowled like a cat that had been stepped on and lurched back again, clutching the damaged hand in the other. Flakes of plaster clung to the skin and his index finger was crooked, the knuckle already swelling.

"Mother*fucker*!"

"Oh, my God, Charlie!"

"All right, let me see, let me look."

"Fuck-fuck-fuck-fuck!"

"What'd you—?" But Adam already knew what he'd done that for. Same as the running, the fights, all that impotent rage he'd talked about.

"Oh, good Lord!"

"Kathleen, we'll have to run him down to the A&E," Dad called over his shoulder and Charlie was—Charlie was *crying*, his face flushed red and streaked in tears. Adam's stomach clenched and there was an intense, hard *hurt* in the middle of his chest, like…like his heart was having a seizure or something.

"Don't," he begged, wrapping both arms around Charlie's waist, trying to comfort but trying to let Dad get at the broken hand, too. "Don't. It's okay, I promise."

"I'm so—"

"Don't," Adam said sharply, before the word 'stupid'

could come out. He could almost *see* it on the tip of Charlie's tongue.

"This has to go to the hospital," Dad said firmly, crossing to the sink and wetting a tea towel. "You've probably broken a couple of knuckles, going by the swelling. I'll put in a couple of calls, see if we can't jump you ahead to a quick X-ray somewhere. Is there someone other than your mum we could call?"

"No," Charlie croaked.

"What about Dan?" Adam pushed.

"He won't come out. I just...I just need to talk to him," Charlie mumbled. He was still crying, cradling his broken hand in the other, and Adam slid both hands carefully around his shoulders. When Charlie sagged into him, burying that red face in Adam's shoulder, Adam's chest started hurting all over again.

"It's okay."

"Fucking hurts."

"You *did* punch the wall," Adam said and Charlie's laugh was dangerously thin.

"Come on, both of you." Mum's face was tight and her voice a little too sharp, but her eyebrows were furrowed in the middle and she gave Adam a worried look before jutting her chin out and straightening her stance. "Hospital, now, before that gets any worse. Mark, don't worry about his mother. I'll stay with them."

"Wrap that around it," Dad instructed and when Charlie didn't move, started winding the wet tea towel around Charlie's hand. The tears had stopped, but Charlie looked so...so...

"You're staying here tonight," Adam blurted out.

Charlie blinked.

"Car, both of you!"

"I'll need my medication," Charlie mumbled. "To show them. I can't have some painkillers and stuff. Where's my bag? I dropped my bag outside."

"We can pick up a quick prescription at the hospital if we

explain the situation," Mum said. "Now car. That swelling is getting worse."

Adam tuned her out, slipping an arm around Charlie's waist. They were still in uniform and it was still sunny outside, and…and not an hour ago, everything had been fine and they'd been planning on playing on Nat's old consoles.

"I'm so gonna kick your arse on the PlayStation," he said weakly and Charlie's laugh was…a little shaky, but real.

"Yeah," he agreed.

"Hey," Adam whispered as he guided Charlie to the front door, following his mother and under his father's watchful gaze. "It's okay."

"It's fucking mental."

"The situation's kinda mental, yeah, but not you, okay?"

Charlie grimaced, but said nothing until he'd been helped into the back seat of the car, then grasped Adam's sleeve and leaned in close. "Thanks," he breathed as Mum reversed off the drive.

Adam squeezed his good wrist and decided to hold the questions for later.

* * * *

Adam left the adults talking in the corridor. The doctor and Mum were 'discussing' — arguing — and he left them to it, slipping through into the bay behind A&E and through the blue curtains that led to Charlie's temporary sitting position.

He was perched on the edge of the bed, left hand in a small cast, thumb and index finger sticking out awkwardly.

"You okay?" Adam asked, pulling himself up to sit beside him.

"Yeah," Charlie said and blew upward into his hair. "Sorry for going crazy on you."

"It's okay," Adam said, walking a hand around Charlie's hips until he could — if he actually *touched* Charlie — be said

225

to have his arm around him. "What's the damage?"

"A dent in your plastering."

"To your hand."

"I broke my pinkie," Charlie said. "And there's a crack in my wrist. But everything else is okay, just really bruised and swollen."

"Good," Adam said then grimaced. "Well, you know, not *good*, but…"

"Yeah," Charlie mumbled. He kept staring at their feet, hanging off the side of the bed together, and Adam hesitated before knocking ankles.

"Do you and your mum row a lot?"

"Yeah."

Adam squinted. "Is that your only word?"

Charlie snorted and grinned. The knot in Adam's stomach relaxed at the sight of it. "No. Arsehole." Much better.

"Do you, though?"

Charlie shrugged. "I guess so. I'm…"

Adam opened his mouth and Charlie appeared to check the word on his tongue.

"Volatile," he said finally.

"I'm impressed."

"Shut up. S'what Dan says. I'm volatile."

"D'you know what it means?" Adam teased, and Charlie pulled a face.

"Not really. Means I'm mental, I guess."

"It means 'let sleeping Charlies lie'—not that you're mental," Adam chided and bumped shoulders. "Your mum seemed a bit…"

"Bigoted?"

"Quick to judge?"

"She thinks I'm stupid."

"Um," Adam said awkwardly.

"She thinks whatever I do is some self-harm shit because of Dad. S'all I am to her, a big ball of anger and crazy. She even thinks the trans thing is part of my crazy and that's not crazy at all. She can fuck off with that shit."

"Umm…"

"And she thinks you're another part of it, that it's about your HIV and not *you*. And she doesn't get it. I've been doing really well this year," Charlie said bitterly. "I've been…I've been trying to bring myself into line a bit, you know? I figured you'd run a mile if you knew how totally fucked up I got back then so I was trying to just be a bit more normal, right? So maybe you'd like me back, and she…she doesn't get that, that you've helped."

"Minus the blip when you kissed me."

"Minus the blip when I kissed you," Charlie agreed and Adam found his good hand between them on the bed and squeezed it.

"I get it, though," he murmured. "I mean…I get why your mum's scared. It's okay to be scared about this. I was…I'm *still* scared about this. About you maybe getting it from me, about…about everything, really, but—"

"We don't talk much, me and Mum," Charlie interrupted. "It always ends up in yelling and screaming and—"

"Slapping?"

Charlie paused.

Adam bit his lip. "Has she…does she hit you often?"

Charlie shrugged.

"Charlie…"

"She hurts, too," he said. "Since Dad. She finds me difficult—I mean, who wouldn't—and she's got the girls and the farm, and…it's stressful."

"That's not an excuse," Adam whispered.

"S'a reason."

"There's no reason. It's—"

"She's my mum, Ads. What's she gonna do? She's hardly Uncle Keith or nothing. She can't hurt me."

Adam bit his lip, sensing somehow that that wasn't the point.

"Things get shitty when people die," Charlie said eventually, then suddenly swayed and bumped Adam's shoulder with his own. "Tell your mum I'm sorry about denting her wall."

"Tell her yourself."

"You nuts? I'll be grounded for months when Mum gets here."

"She's not," Adam said and grimaced. "Um. I mean, that's what Mum's arguing out there for. She says you're coming back to ours and she and Dad are trying to get a prescription for your pills so you can just stay over tonight."

Charlie blinked. "You what?"

Adam huffed. "C'mon, Charlie, you've met my mum. Like she's gonna just ring yours to come and get you after that row."

"We've got exams tomorrow."

"You can just come in with me in the morning," Adam said and held Charlie's good hand tight enough to bruise. "Just stay over, yeah? I'll feel better if you do."

Charlie huffed. "Dirty pool."

"Yeah, well." The *crack* when Mrs. Fielding had slapped him was echoing in Adam's head and the way Charlie had just frozen up and paused before going…going batshit. It had been scary. And it had driven home what Charlie had said—and Phoebe and Ollie and everyone, really. Charlie wasn't, you know, one hundred percent stable.

And Adam didn't want to let go of him right now. Not with a reddened cheek and one hand in a cast.

"It'll be a sleepover," he said eventually. "Just you and me. Yeah?"

Charlie laughed and Adam relaxed. He was learning—slowly, but he was—that Charlie's laugh was the little window thing to his moods. When he laughed like that, he was okay. So Adam sniggered along and folded their fingers together, examining the weirdness of Charlie's deformed hand and wondering if it wasn't bad to feel attracted to him even in here.

"Okay," Charlie said eventually and Adam rubbed a thumb over his wrist. "You might as well dig your mum out of it."

"Out of what?"

"There's a blister pack in my schoolbag," Charlie said. "I told you, I always carry at least a day's dose in case Ollie calls an emergency sleepover."

Adam stared then decided to channel Ollie. He drew back his fist and punched Charlie right in the shoulder.

"Ow!"

"You deserved it," he said, sliding off the bed to go and tell Mum.

But Charlie was smiling, when he looked back at the edge of the curtain, and despite the mark and the cast, he looked okay again.

Which meant, really, that everything was kind of fine. Kind of.

# Chapter Twenty-One

Adam hadn't mean to ask — and certainly not just blurt it out like he did — but...

"Does Charlie's mum hit him?"

Phoebe's head snapped up from her phone. Ollie, however, shrugged.

They were sitting on the wall behind the bike shed, waiting for the geography exam to let out and recovering — Phoebe's words, not Adam's — from their own history papers. And Adam had written his entire essay on the League of Nations and its successes in the 1920s with the sound of the slap echoing in the back of his head.

And Ollie just shrugged.

"She's kinda crazy sometimes," she said.

"She hits him?" Phoebe demanded. "What — Adam, what happened, what'd he say?"

"He didn't say anything," Adam said. "We went over to mine after school yesterday and his mum was rowing with my mum on the doorstep then she blew up at Charlie and slapped him."

"Why?" Ollie asked. Her tone was mild.

"What?"

"Why'd she blow up at him?"

Adam ground his teeth. "Me."

Ollie frowned. "Well, she's not the most open-minded of people, but..."

"No." Adam lowered his voice. "My...illness."

Ollie winced. "Yeah, well."

Adam winced. "She does, then?"

"S'not the first time. But she's not abusive or something."

"That *is* abuse!" Phoebe protested hotly.

"No, it's not," Ollie snorted. "When she does, he hits her back, you know. He's not a pussy. They usually trade a smack each and storm off. She's just as easily pissed off as he is. It's a bad combination. I think they have the same illness, me."

"Has it always been like that?" Adam whispered. "Even before his dad…?"

"Yeah," Ollie said. "I mean, you know, his dad broke it up most of the time. But Charlie's never liked his mum. They're too similar. Old Man Fielding was cool. He just wanted to be out with the dogs all the time. He used to take us out in the old farm Jeep and the dogs'd run behind. He was all right. She's always been a bit of a cow."

"It's still abuse!"

Adam tuned them out as they started arguing about it. He picked at the knees of his trousers and turned it over in his head. To an extent—it sounded *awful,* but it was true— he didn't care if it fit the bill for abuse. It wasn't about the physical stuff, anyway, because he'd wrestled with Charlie and he knew he wasn't exactly delicate.

It was the mental stuff. The head case stuff. Surely, it wasn't good for Charlie's brain stuff, having a mum like that? Was she even causing it, when he'd have his bad episodes? It sounded like she'd caused the bus, and Adam *knew* that he himself was responsible for the way Charlie had blown his lid after that aborted kiss and all the awkward avoidance in the halls.

Was Mrs. Fielding just dragging up all of Charlie's issues instead of letting him…you know, get over them?

A bell rang in the depths of the school and Adam pushed the thought away for a while. He'd have to ask Dad if she could do that. And if she could, what then? Keep Charlie away from Stoker Farm more? Invite him over more? Adam would like it, and his parents wouldn't mind, but he couldn't just keep Charlie out of his house forever, right? And Mrs. Fielding had *hated* him. What if she…?

"Charlie!" Ollie hollered.

A figure broke away from the crowd surging out of the main hall and jogged over. He was smiling until Phoebe slid right off the wall to hug him.

"Erm," he said as she clung. "Feebs? Everything okay?"

Her fair hair was nearly white against his dark blazer and it shivered when she spoke. "If you ever need...someone to talk to or somewhere to go, you can always come to me."

"Er," Charlie said. "Um, thanks, Feebs."

"I mean it."

"What's—?"

Ollie shook her head sharply and Adam bit his lip.

"Oh...*kay*," Charlie said and patted Phoebe on the back. "Um, thanks, Phoebe."

"You've always got someone to turn to," she repeated earnestly then let go and squeezed his shoulders in her hands. "Always."

"Right," he said.

"We should probably go," Ollie drawled. "Ads said something about a house with no parents."

Adam shrugged. They'd be back later, but Mum had nagged him about remembering his keys that morning. They were going to see Danni and the twins this afternoon. "Mum said she'd refill the crisp cupboard this morning," he said. "I figured we could just hang out in the garden or something."

"Okay," Charlie said, switching his phone back on. "That exam blew. I might say fuck my gut and pile on a few pounds for that."

Ollie slid off the wall to attack him—or hug him, Adam had never worked out what that clusterfuck of a greeting actually was—and Adam watched contentedly for a couple of minutes. Charlie seemed okay. He'd stayed over last night and he'd seemed totally fine this morning. His hand looked odd in the cast, and the girls had fussed over it when they'd arrived for the morning exam session, but he'd just laughed it off and said he'd been helping redecorate the kitchen.

He was okay. And Adam intended to keep him that way, if his mum wasn't going to be any help. Ollie was maybe a little bit right. Mrs. Fielding *was* a cow.

"You could do with a few extra pounds," he said instead and Charlie raised his eyebrows.

"That a hint?"

"Yes," Adam said and slid down. "C'mon. We have to bus it back."

Charlie was okay, but Phoebe wasn't, throwing worried glances Charlie's way and suddenly paying attention to his cast again, asking what he'd 'really' done to it. "Told you," Charlie said and Adam had to elbow her to shut up and stop Charlie getting suspicious. Adam wasn't totally sure he'd have been allowed to spill that secret.

But it'd be good to have Phoebe on board, maybe. Charlie had only had Ollie for ages — maybe two extra people would make all the difference? He didn't talk much to the other kids at school — or they didn't talk to him, whichever way round it was.

Charlie's phone went off halfway home and, because he was a prick and didn't believe in not answering his phone on public transport, he answered it. And the way he instantly said, "You what? No, m'going round Ollie's," had Adam paying attention.

And the girls too, from the way they turned round in their seats to watch.

"Haven't seen him." Charlie's voice was dropping, in both pitch and temperature, and Adam slid his fingers into the crook of his elbow in lieu of his left hand. "Dunno. Depends what me and Ollie fancy doing after lunch."

Ollie rolled her eyes. Phoebe's were wide and anxious.

"Told you, I haven't seen him." Adam clenched his jaw. "Oh, really? Too bad."

The phone squawked and Charlie pulled a face.

"I said too bad," he repeated. "Thought you'd like it. Keeps me out of your hair and you've got more time for

Erica."

"What?" Phoebe whispered and Ollie shook her head. Adam gripped that caught elbow tighter. The hairs on the back of his neck were standing on end.

"Fine, Jesus, whatever. I won't go near it," Charlie said and abruptly hung up. He switched the phone off, too, dropping it into his backpack and huffing.

"Your mum?" Ollie asked, casual as could be. She'd seen it all before, Adam realized. She hadn't been surprised at his question on the wall and she hadn't batted an eyelid at the cast and she was cool and calm about the phone call… because she'd seen this all before. She'd been around the Fieldings since they were tiny. She *knew* them.

And the realization that it really was a forever thing hurt.

"Mum," Charlie agreed.

"What'd she say?" Ollie asked.

"Can't go to Adam's."

"What?" Adam blurted out.

"I'm still coming," Charlie said, "but Mum says I can't. I'm not to see you, either. And we're breaking up. She says."

Ollie snorted and grinned. "So, I'm playing cover if your mum rings up my mum asking if you're here?"

"Gotcha."

"Cheers, Ols."

"Wait, what?" Adam blinked.

"Whenever Mrs. Fielding says Charlie can't go somewhere, he goes and I pretend he's with me," Ollie said and shrugged. "Even my mum lies for him."

"Only since your mum and my mum had that row outside A&E."

"*What?*" Adam demanded.

"I fell off the shed roof," Charlie said, "and my mum went ballistic at Ollie's mum, who went ballistic right back and ever since Mrs. MacFarlane thinks my mum's a meddling old bat and needs to butt out."

"My mum's *always* right," Ollie said smugly and Charlie laughed.

"So...what? We lie to your mum?" Adam asked uncertainly.

"Well, yeah," Charlie said and squinted at him. "I'm not avoiding you 'cause my mum says so. I haven't listened to the witch in years and m'not gonna start now."

"Your mum's horrible," Phoebe interjected.

Charlie frowned.

"She *hit* you. Mums shouldn't hit!"

"Feebs, who—?"

"I told them," Adam interrupted and flushed. "I had to know if yesterday was...was usual, you know? It was scary and you flipped your shit and punched the kitchen wall, and—"

"You did *what?*" Phoebe demanded.

"Told you I redecorated," Charlie said, still scowling. "Cheers, Ads."

"I had to know," Adam repeated stubbornly.

"Yeah, well."

"Charlie, that's *awful*," Phoebe said earnestly.

"She's not that bad."

"Charlie—"

"Feebs, drop it." There was an edge in his voice and Phoebe quietened, still looking upset. "It's not. Don't poke your nose into what you don't know. Things haven't been easy since Dad died."

Phoebe opened her mouth—and Adam knew she was about to protest that it wasn't an excuse, because he agreed with her—but Ollie shook her head and Phoebe shut up instead. Adam squeezed Charlie's elbow and gingerly rested his head on Charlie's shoulder. When he wasn't shrugged off, he relaxed.

"She'll forget all about it in a month or two. She always does," Charlie said. "Until then, we just keep it quiet for a bit. And I'll be smarter about where I leave leaflets."

"Leaflets?"

"Adam's dad gave us a bunch of safe sex leaflets and stuff. I left one in my room with the right passage circled,"

Charlie said and grimaced. "Bet Erica found it, little sneak. Mum's not been in my room in ages."

"You okay, though?" Adam asked.

"Ads, don't start walking on eggshells, yeah? I'm not bloody fragile."

Except he kind of was, in a way. "Yeah, but…buses," Adam said lamely.

Charlie snorted — then started sniggering, nose wrinkled and freckles creasing along his skin as he laughed. It was infectious, a warm laugh wriggling its way up Adam's stomach and chest, too, then Ollie scoffed and turned back around, muttering, "Boy stuff, probably," to Phoebe in a disgusted tone.

He didn't let go of Charlie's elbow, but he let go of the subject. It could lie for a while, right? 'Cause Charlie was okay and…Adam was learning to cherish the *okay*, and watch for those moments of *fucking brilliant*.

* * * *

"Mum."

Dusk was settling over the back garden and Dad had let them light a little campfire and stack up all the wood ready for the dump he'd hacked off the hedge. It was more smoke than fire, but they'd dragged out the sofa cushions and relaxing against them out in the garden and watching firelight dance in Charlie's hair was giving Adam ideas.

Clean ones. Mostly.

"Need something, darling? Oh, tell Ollie that her mother called and will be dropping by to collect her at nine."

"Okay," Adam said, shutting the back door behind him. "Um, actually, it's about me and Charlie."

"Oh?" Mum was baking, her apron floury and her hair trying and failing to escape from its bun. She'd lost a case, then. She always baked if she lost a case.

"His mum's banned him from seeing me."

"So who is that in our back garden?"

236

Adam cracked a faint smile. "Yeah, well, he's not listening to her."

"Good," Mum muttered. "Frightful woman. Can see where he gets his temper from. She shouted at me for almost ten minutes before explaining who she actually was. I was ready to call the police to get rid of her."

Adam grimaced. "She's horrible."

"You won't find me arguing, dear," Mum said mildly. "But it is what it is. Not everyone who has children ought to."

Adam swallowed. "Some of us get luckier."

Mum chuckled fondly and smoothed down his hair. He tolerated it for a couple of seconds before shrugging her hand off. "And some parents get lucky, too," she said then laughed. "Imagine if you had Charlie's temper! You're going to be easily six feet tall when you stop growing, sweetheart, and I dread to think I'd have to try and control you in a snit!"

Adam wrinkled his nose. He was going to be taller than Dad? That was a weird thought.

"You and Charlie both know," Mum said quietly, "that he's always welcome here if things get a little too intense at home."

"I hate it," Adam whispered.

"So do I, but there's nothing to be done. I heard you two at the hospital, you know. You won't persuade him to report her for it. The best we can do is keep an eye on the situation best we can. And the worst of it is that he's nearly sixteen, and a boy. Take it from me, sweetheart, the authorities aren't inclined to take physical abuse of teenage boys very seriously."

Adam grimaced. "Don't say it like that. It makes him sound like...like a victim."

"He *is* a victim," Mum said. "But I think he needs help with his head more than he does with his mother."

"Yeah."

"And you can do that," Mum said, stroking his hair

again. "You're a good influence on him, darling. And I think between you and the girls, you can maybe start to turn some of Charlie's silly little ideas around."

"Like what?"

"Like the ones where he puts himself down so much?"

Adam started and she chuckled.

"I hear more than you give me credit for, darling," Mum said, returning to her baking and cracking a couple of eggs into the mix. "He's a little fractured around the edges, but he's always seemed calm and happy enough when he's here. And you're certainly happier for him. So as long as you continue to be good for each other, you have my full support."

"And Dad's?"

"Well, your father likes to think you're still ten years old and far too young for all this boyfriend nonsense," Mum chuckled. "But he was the same with the twins, so I think he'll be ready to handle it when you're, oh, twenty-five or so."

"Eurgh, Mum, that's *old*!"

"Less of the old, young man," Mum scolded, swatting at him with a spoon. "And what are you lurking in here for?"

"I meant to ask a favor."

"Hmm?"

"If...if Mrs. Fielding rings up asking for Charlie, can you lie?"

"That depends on the lie, sweetheart."

"Just say you haven't seen him since she showed up," Adam pleaded. "Charlie's not going to listen—and I don't think I'd let him, anyway—but...I don't want her to get mad and hit him again."

Mum's face softened.

"Will you?"

"I'm sure I can come up with a nice middle ground," she said. "I won't lie outright, darling, because if he genuinely does wander off from all of you, then he'll need to be found—but if we know he's safe somewhere, I'm willing to bend the truth a little bit. After all, if you're both not here, how am I supposed to control whether you're together or not?"

Adam felt a rush of gratitude—for the specific agreement, and for Mum being Mum in general—and hugged her, despite the floury apron. She hugged him back with her elbows, holding her egg-and-flour hands away from his back, and smiled when he let go.

"I am always proud of you, Adam," she said, "but the last few months, you've really come into yourself."

"Mum, you're being embarrassing."

"I'm your mother. It's my job," she said briskly. "Now, go and get Phoebe. Lord knows you know how her father fusses if she's five minutes late home."

Adam rolled his eyes and let himself back into the garden, where Charlie was sprawled on his front in the grass and the girls curled up on a cushion each, giggling as he told some outlandish story.

"Feebs, your dad'll freak out that you've been kidnapped soon."

Amongst the groaning and Ollie's dramatic decision to kidnap Phoebe 'for reals!' Adam flopped down beside Charlie and wriggled close enough to hug him by the tiny fire. Charlie grinned and squeezed his wrist, leaning back into Adam's arm heavily. "All right?"

"Uh-huh."

"I'm going to the bathroom," Ollie announced. "Is your mum making cake?"

"Yeah. Tell her you're peckish and she'll feed you."

Both girls disappeared into the house and Charlie twisted his face to press a cool kiss to Adam's cheek. "Y'okay?"

"Me? Yeah."

"You've been quiet all day."

Adam shrugged. "Still getting over yesterday, I think."

"Hey. S'okay."

"It's not," Adam said.

"It's not been okay since Dad died, but there's nothing we

can do about that," Charlie said pragmatically. "I'm getting better. Dan's helping and Ollie's always been there and you help, too. And Ollie's mum and dad keep saying once I'm sixteen and I can move out, I can have their spare room."

"Good," Adam said. "You should take them up on it."

"Yeah, maybe."

"Promise you'll come to me if you need to. No…buses."

"No buses," Charlie agreed and one hand squeezed Adam's knee in the gloom. "Got better things to jump in front of now."

"Like?"

"You."

Adam snorted. "Sap."

"You started it, with that face of yours today."

Adam laughed and pulled Charlie's hair lightly.

"Ow!"

"You deserved that."

"Hey," Charlie said. "You and me, right? We're getting there. You with your shame-and-guilt complex for whatever reason and God forbid you ever get a paper cut in front of me 'cause I think you'll just go into orbit with the freak-out force."

"Oh, shut up."

"And me with my crazy," Charlie said. "I'm coping, Ads. I'm getting there. And I have every intention of getting it over, too."

Adam didn't know if he could — if it was any more possible for Charlie to heal than for Adam to be cured — but…it was a nice thought. It was a nice intention.

He pressed his lips to the shoulder of Charlie's T-shirt and inhaled the smell of woodsmoke and skin. Of someone who had taken the time to look past the HIV and see Adam himself.

Of someone Adam was finding out was more and more complicated the more he got to know.

"No buses," he said.

Ollie charged back out of the house and flopped into the

middle of their hug with a war-cry and the moment was lost. But the spell—the one that made Adam's stomach clench when Charlie rolled his eyes and his breath catch when Charlie smiled—wasn't broken.

# Chapter Twenty-Two

It was five past ten on Saturday morning, July the twenty-ninth, and Adam was firstly far too hot and secondly, far too keyed up for sitting on walls outside leisure centers. Seriously. How long did a game of squash freaking take?

*Ready yet???*

Phoebe.

*Nope, will text when we leave,* Adam replied and slid the phone back into his pocket as he heard the double doors clang, loud in the still, humid heat.

"There you are!" he called and Charlie shielded his eyes from the sun with a frown.

"Oh," he said. "What're—?"

"Happy birthday." Adam beamed and held out his hands. "C'mere."

Charlie came, meandering across the narrow car park and stretching up on his toes for the kiss Adam offered him. He was getting really freckly from the blazing summer and Adam caught his face between both hands and kissed the newest outburst on the bridge of his nose.

"Lay off," Charlie said.

"Nope," Adam retorted. "How'd it go?"

But he already knew. Ten until eleven every Saturday morning—Charlie's counseling session. The ongoing squash tournament with his counselor. It was still a weird approach, in Adam's opinion, but Charlie seemed to like it, and…well. Anything to stop him going, you know. One flew over the cuckoo's nest, under the local bus and all that. And sometimes Charlie would storm out early—once he'd even come out in tears—and some days he'd sit in the lobby with Dan just talking for ages, and some days—

Some days—most days, now—he came wandering out on time, relaxed and cheerful…and Adam kissed him again. Positive reinforcement and stuff.

"Was good," Charlie said. "I won."

"You always win."

"Not my fault if Dan sucks."

Adam laughed. "Maybe that's part of the counseling ploy."

"Nah, he beat me like once, and he was like mega excited."

Adam grinned, taking both Charlie's hands in his and squeezing them. Even his fingers were freckly now. "But it went okay?"

"Yeah. Talked about me moving in with the McFarlanes next week. Dan thinks it's a good idea, but he reckons my illness might act up a bit with the big change."

"Well, that's what he's there for. And me and Ollie and Feebs."

"Yeah. Talked about you a bit, actually."

"Me?"

"Yup."

"What about me?"

"Ads, c'mon. Patient confidentiality, man."

"You suck," Adam whined, shoving him in the shoulder then jumping down to hug him properly. "Happy birthday."

"You said that."

"I'm saying it again, shut up."

"Meh-meh-meh, shut up," Charlie mimicked and Adam pinched him. "Ow!"

"You deserved that."

"Did not!"

"Yeah you did."

"I di—"

"See you next week, Charlie!"

Charlie twisted to wave at his counselor—a tall man in his late twenties with a jaw that could have, like, exploded someone's ovaries or something. Adam gawked.

"You didn't say Dan was hot!"

Charlie blinked, twisted to look again, and screwed up his face. "What, Dan? He's got a chin like the guy off *American Dad!*"

"He does not. He's well fit."

"Getting a little jealous over here."

Adam snorted. "Liar. C'mon. We're stealing you for your birthday."

"Who's we?"

"Who do you think?"

"Am I working out why Ollie told me I was gonna get totaled today?"

"Yep," Adam said, towing Charlie by the wrist towards the bus stops. "You'll love it, promise. Trust me."

"How about no?"

"Trust me!"

"All aboard the train to Nope City!"

"Oh, fuck you," Adam said then laughed as Charlie produced an amazingly ridiculous pair of sunglasses from his sports bag and dropped them into place.

"Yo, man, what'chu laughin' at?"

"You, you tit!" Adam said. "Where'd you get them?"

"Present from Dan."

"Is he meant to give you birthday presents?"

"Eh, they're just Boots knock-offs. Saw 'em in Stroud the other week when we went to the cinema. Anyway, been seeing Dan for like nearly three years now. He's probably allowed." Charlie propped them on his head and sank onto the bus stop seat in the shade beside Adam. "What's my birthday plan then?"

"You'll find out in a bit."

"Who you texting?"

"Feebs."

"Setting plans in motion?"

"Yep."

"Can I see?"

"I can tell your session went well. You're like a big kid," Adam accused, jerking the phone away from the hand that strayed out to steal it. "Lay off!"

"God, you suck."

"You *wish*."

"I do," Charlie beamed and Adam laughed.

"Mad."

"Hey!"

"You are, but you're the right kind of mad," Adam conceded and bumped Charlie's shoulder with his. "My mad, I guess."

Charlie grinned. He looked so...so *light* that Adam softened and leaned over. The kiss was soft and chaste, sweet and...something else. Affirming, maybe. Or already certain.

*Safe*, Adam decided, and pressed his nose to Charlie's cheek before pulling away.

"You all right?" Charlie asked quietly.

"Yeah," Adam said and at the top of the road the bus peeled around the corner and into view. "C'mon. I am officially declaring this a kidnapping."

\* \* \* \*

The bus stop was right outside the post office and Adam frog-marched Charlie from it to the house, ignoring all Charlie's increasingly mad questions, until they got within ten feet of the garden gate and Charlie yelled, "Mrs. Wood! I'm being kidnapped!"

Mum looked around from hanging up the washing and chortled. "Well, you look fine to me, dear!"

Dad had almost packed the car, but the girls hadn't arrived yet, so Adam shoved Charlie through the gate and sat on it so he couldn't escape again.

"But I'm being *abducted*!" Charlie whined. "I was snatched

from the leisure center, gone in the blink of an eye! What'll they do to me?"

"Demand a ransom?" Adam suggested.

"Oh, that depends on the ransom, boys," Mum said, unfurling a towel over the line. "If it's not too high, I'm sure Mark and I could rustle something up."

"Ooh, extra tray of brownies?" Adam asked.

"We're all out," she said sympathetically.

"Well, that's my ransom," Adam said, folding his arms and grinning when Charlie made a melodramatic noise and sank to the grass.

"No! You barbarian! How could you? I'll never see my loved ones again!"

"Sorry," Adam shrugged and sniggered when Charlie dramatically seized his legs. "That's my ransom. No brownies, no freedom."

"I'm not worth a tray of brownies?"

"Sorry, dear," Mrs. Wood said. "I'm fresh out of chocolate. It all went into your supplies."

"Mum!"

Charlie apparently missed it, though, still clutching Adam's legs. He sighed and rested his cheek on Adam's thigh. "So that's it," he proclaimed dramatically. "Have your way, you monster. I'm not even worth a tray of brownies to be saved from this miserable existence of servitude."

"Very wordy," Adam praised, toying with Charlie's hair. Huh. "What kind of servitude?"

"Sexual. Obviously."

"Oh, good," Adam said agreeably over his mother's alarmingly high-pitched giggle. "It's okay. I might give you brownies occasionally. Between services."

"You filthy git," Charlie said, looking up and grinning. "Seriously, though, why have I been kidnapped just to sit on your front lawn?"

"You chose to sit there."

"Not the point, Ads."

"Totally the—"

"Adam! Charlie! *Charlie*, happy birthday!"

Phoebe pushed at the gate. Ollie had no such qualms and vaulted right over the hedge to land on Charlie in a full-body hug. "Happy birthday, you fucknut!" she yelled and Adam laughed, sliding off the gate to let Phoebe in.

"Kidnapped him from his session," he said.

"Good," Phoebe said, patting her bag. "I've got all the goods. Ollie! Ollie, let him breathe!"

"Get down here!" Ollie said instead and Adam laughed as Phoebe shrugged and jumped on Charlie in a hug, too, burying him in girl. Adam supposed he really *ought* to rescue Charlie from all the girl, being his boyfriend and all, but…meh. *Give it five minutes maybe.*

Charlie had — *they* had — come a long way lately. They'd stalled a bit during the exams — mainly because apparently Ollie had freaked out like a pro after tests, not before like normal people, and kept Charlie busy on best-friend duties and Mrs. Fielding still hadn't let up on hating Adam for his disease, and…

And yet, they were still here. And it was Charlie's sixteenth birthday and Adam felt so light he had to hang on to the gate to stop floating away. He had a boyfriend and they'd been experimenting — Charlie was right about ribbed condoms — and next year they'd be back in the same maths class, only sitting together instead of Adam staring at the back of Charlie's head and imagining what it would be like.

Okay, so maybe he'd still imagine. He'd just be way better at it now.

That was five minutes. "Hey!" Adam protested. "Stop smothering my boyfriend in your X chromosomes."

"Sexist dick!"

Charlie's arm emerged from the huddle. "Help me!" he implored, but when Adam grabbed his hand, he was hauled down into the messy bundle and attacked by the girls too, with Ollie cackling in his ear as she got him in a wrist-lock.

"I cannot *believe* you fell for that!" she crowed and Charlie beamed wickedly from his vantage point, flat on the grass and quite literally under Phoebe's thumb.

"All this girl, I think I'm going straight!" he declared cheerfully and Phoebe detached herself with a protest. Charlie moved like lightning — like always — and had Adam pinned down on the lawn within seconds, still grinning like a nutter, and Adam's heart swelled up and popped in his chest like a balloon, even as he fought back and declared Charlie a conniving, corrupted git. Which he totally was.

He was just...the one Adam was in love with, too.

"You all suck!" Phoebe declared then clapped her hands. "Adam! Adam, your dad's ready! Let's go, let's go, let's go! Get him in the car!"

"What?" Charlie asked, even as Ollie hauled him up.

"You heard the lady!"

"I told you," Adam said. "You're being kidnapped." Charlie's ruffled air — and hair — was enticing, and fuck the neighbors and Dad's awkward cough. Adam seized Charlie by the back of the neck and kissed him hard, tasting summer and sixteen and something impossible. "Kidnapped and assaulted."

"Sexually?"

"Only by me."

"S'the way I like it." Charlie grinned then he was being bundled into the car and Ollie was dropping the secret about the planned camping trip and —

Adam had never, not ever, felt this happy.

* * * *

"I've never felt this happy, you know."

Two in the morning, or thereabouts, and it was Sunday now. The empty lager cans they had smuggled along in Phoebe's bag lay in a haphazard circle in the grass. The girls were asleep in the tent Dad had set up for them and Adam was lying by the warm remnants of their campfire, wrapped in his fleece against the chilly, cloudless night. But it was Charlie keeping him warm, a heavy weight against Adam's ribs, back to Adam's chest, and utterly relaxed.

Staring at the stars, Adam said it again.

"Heard you the first time."

"S'true though."

"Good," Charlie said, squeezing Adam's knee. "For the record? I haven't in a long time, either."

Adam watched the stars flickering and gleaming, pinpricks in a night so black he could feel the darkness like a weight in the air, and exhaled slowly. "Never thought I'd get this."

"What? Happiness?"

"A boyfriend."

"Oh, just any boyfriend. Cheers."

"Shut your face," Adam said and smiled when Charlie shifted and turned over to fold his arms on Adam's chest. "I can feel you glaring at me."

"I'm appreciating the beauty of your face in the dark."

Adam snorted.

"Don't go ruining it with sound effects."

He snickered and found Charlie's hair to pull it. The fire gave him the barest outline of a shadow, but he could imagine the evil expression on Charlie's face anyway.

"Want to know a secret?" Adam whispered.

"What?"

"The universe doesn't revolve around my HIV."

"*Duhhh.*"

"I always thought it did," Adam breathed. "Then you came along and fucked it all up and...HIV's nothing compared to you."

"Er. Thanks? I think?"

Adam stroked both hands through that fluffy hair, feeling the coarse wispiness of it like he'd never touched it before. "It's your fault," he whispered. "You wouldn't take my crappy excuses for an answer and you wouldn't take HIV for an excuse."

"Because it's not."

"You let me not be scared of it anymore."

"Good," Charlie whispered. "You want to know a secret, too?"

"What?"

"I'm scared of your HIV sometimes. I imagine what'll happen if I got it and you know what? I'm not worried about the getting it. I'm scared of what you'd do if I did. You'd never touch me again, or ever even come near me, and I know it'd all be over if I caught it. Because you wouldn't forgive yourself."

Adam swallowed. "Yeah," he breathed.

"But I reckon if I talked you round once, I can try again," Charlie said. "So no. The universe doesn't revolve around HIV, or Dad, or my crazy."

"Mental health."

"My mental health," Charlie amended. "It's just...you-and-me stuff."

"You-and-me stuff," Adam echoed and cool lips found the very corner of his mouth.

"Yeah. S'just you-and-me stuff, not universe stuff. Long as we remember that, we'll be okay."

Adam slid both hands down Charlie's spine to rest them in the small of his back. His clothes felt cool against Adam's skin, but between them, where their stomachs pressed together, he could feel Charlie's warmth and a gentle pulse. Him-and-Charlie stuff. Like the fact they hadn't gone all the way yet and Adam still thought maybe they never would or should, but...him-and-Charlie stuff, too. How Charlie had breached the sex divide by going down on him last month in Adam's room.

Him-and-Charlie stuff.

"Want another secret?" Adam breathed.

The universe—the sky and the stars, the breeze through the grass, Charlie's pills and Adam's blood—it could all do one. The ultimate him-and-Charlie thing...

"What?"

"I love you."

…was that.

Charlie kissed him, soft and sweet, that little lip-clasp, mute-gasp kiss he did, the barely there touch and all-over-here-emotion one that could make a room implode. The one Adam never saw coming and the one he loved the most.

"V'you too," Charlie whispered.

There was something else in Adam's blood and he could feel it in Charlie's skin and mouth and pulse, too. Not HIV, not illness, not insanity, not even desire.

*Love.*

It was totally girly, really sappy and he wasn't saying it again until Charlie's seventeenth birthday because *c'mon,* but…

It was love.

# More books from Finch Books

*Angela always knew there was something different about herself. When she realizes she's really Adam, his whole life changes in ways he never expected.*

SUSAN TRAUGH

Can she find brilliance stumbling
through the dark?

The Edge of
Brilliance

*Volatile and unstable, Amy stands at the precipice. Will*
*she fall into the chaos and despair of insanity or ascend*
*into brilliance and redemption?*

*Like the colorful strokes of her brush, love changes the canvas of their lives.*

the *possibility* of you and me

She's lost...and only he can find her

LILLIE TODD

*Her whole world has been flipped upside down. She's lost...and only he can find her.*

# About the Author

**Matthew J. Metzger**

Matthew J. Metzger is an asexual, transgender British author juggling books, an office job and a love of travel with the human need for sleep once in a while. He writes both adult and young adult books focusing on LGBT+ characters and their relationships, particularly those from the less salubrious areas in which he was dragged up over the years.

On the very rare occasions that Matt isn't writing, he can usually be found at the gym, halfway up a mountain or collecting new tattoos. (And yes, he does have book ink...)

Matthew J. Metzger loves to hear from readers. You can find contact information, website details and an author profile page at https://www.finch-books.com/